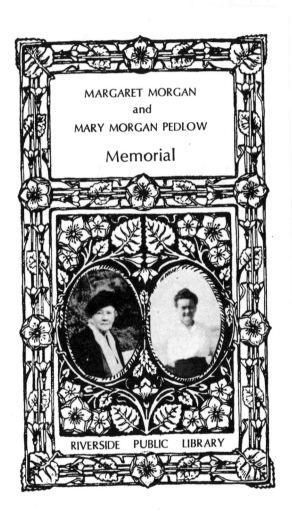

MARGARET MORGAN
and
MARY MORGAN PEDLOW

Memorial

RIVERSIDE PUBLIC LIBRARY

The Happy Island

DAWN POWELL

STEERFORTH PRESS
SOUTH ROYALTON, VERMONT

Copyright © 1999, 1998, © 1938 by The Estate of Dawn Powell

First Published in 1938 by Farrar & Rinehart.

Introduction Copyright © 1998 by Tim Page

For information about permission to
reproduce selections from this book, write to:
Steerforth Press L.C., P.O. Box 70,
South Royalton, Vermont 05068.

Library of Congress Cataloging-in-Publication Data

Powell, Dawn.
The happy island / by Dawn Powell.
p.   cm.
ISBN 1–883642–7–5 (alk. paper)
I. Title.
PS3531.0936H36   1998
813'.52—dc21   98–25225
                                              CIP

Manufactured in the United States of America

SECOND PRINTING

$\mathcal{D}$AWN POWELL'S *The Happy Island* (1938) is among the first books written after Roman antiquity that is peopled with gay and bisexual characters but is neither a hate tract, a psychological study, an apologia, a plea for tolerance, nor an under-the-counter titillation.

This was Powell's first novel written after the breakthrough *Turn, Magic Wheel* (1936) had established — or, rather, *should* have established — her as one of America's finest satirists. In *The Happy Island,* she set out to examine the sham and posturing in the world of "cafe society," rather as she had neatly skewered the literary scene in *Turn, Magic Wheel.*

"Fairy" was Powell's customary term for a gay man and she used it with affection, as in this diary entry from May 23, 1935:

Fairies as an oasis in midst of country villages; alone you find them—sure of some intelligent conversation and wit. Little cosmopolitan posts on the prairie, a little lamp. Here is conversation, here is imagination for the weary traveler, worn down by Babbittry.

The following year, she began to sketch a novel based on the "fairy" circle around *The New Yorker's* first theater critic, John Mosher, and his friend, the nightclub entertainer Dwight Fiske. Powell often modeled her characters on real people but rarely provided such a direct key as she did in her diary entry for March 2, 1936:

John Mosher, unattractive to women, silent in the home, finds balm in getting the pale silent young man in borrowed evening clothes away from Dwight. He has him in his home where he encourages him to go on with his cooking, gets him Escoffier, Brillaet-Savant, Sabatini, Moneta, brings him home little gadgets, egg slicers, canapés, entertains, proud of his pompano in fig leaves, his *duck a la presse*. John talks, educating him culturally; Dopey listens, says salad too wet . . . John encourages Dopey to write cook book a la Brillat-Savant but week after week Dopey gets gloomier. Presently sees manuscript. "Cooking is the art of making something to eat. Everybody likes to eat. People mostly put too much water on in cooking vegetables." John's heart sank. "You ought to get out more."

She finished the book (originally called "The Joyous Isle," after an English translation of a piano piece by Debussy, "L'isle Joyeuse") on May 31, 1938. It was published that fall by Farrar & Rinehart as *The Happy Island*.

Powell's "heroes"—the solemn and somewhat dour playwright Jefferson Abbott and the flighty nightclub singer Prudence Bly, who hail from the same town in Ohio—are supplemented with many and disparate secondary figures that are pure New York: a washed-up alcoholic pianist and his estranged wife, a radio crooner with a ridiculous sub-Charlie McCarthy prop dummy, libidinous young marrieds, old roues, Broadway agents, Armenian chefs, autocratic dowagers, thin-skinned gossip columnists who take public revenge after every imagined slight, and a pet dog named Sofa.

And, as reviewer William Soskin put it in the New York *Herald-Tribune,* all of them "are involved in such a series of promiscuities, adulteries, double-crossings, neo-perversions and Krafft-Ebbing exercises as would make the towns of Sodom and Gomorrah seem like mere suburbs of li'l old New York."

In recent years, *The Happy Island* has won some distinguished admirers—most notably Gore Vidal, who, in his extraordinary essay "Dawn Powell: The American Writer," compared its closing lines favorably to Thackeray. But it sold poorly at the time and it is the last of Powell's mature New York novels to be reissued since interest in her work was revived.

And with some reason, for this is Powell at her most caustic. *The Happy Island* is a provocative, decidedly "hardboiled" novel, and far from the most immediately appealing of her works. Powell herself never regarded it as one of her important books (although she was never so embarrassed by it as she was by her first novel *Whither* [1925], which she did her best to disavow, or the later *A Cage For Lovers*).

The English author and editor, Michael Sadleir, had been responsible for Powell's first British publication—*Turn, Magic Wheel*—and his enthusiasm ensured that *The Happy Island* would be published there as well. During contract negotiations, however, Sadleir became anxious that Great Britain's strict libel laws might leave his firm open to a suit from one of the book's real-life models. Powell hastened to alleviate Sadleir's fears in a letter dated September 23, 1938:

There are no portraits in *The Happy Island*. Aside from fear of libel suits, I find no profit or pleasure in straight portraiture. There are frequently snatches of this or that person cautiously pinned to other persons' bodies and love-life, and it is true I have changed one real man into a woman but as he has done this himself so often I cannot see that he should object and have furthermore combined him with two other people . . .

One young man called on me, very upset, and said he recognized himself in my book and wondered if everyone did, as there were some rather sacred thoughts exposed. As he has been far from my thoughts I was embarrassed, then realized that here was the pallid pansy whose whole career had accidentally fit into the Bert Willy pattern. I was horrified. But it turned out the figure he recognized as himself was, of course, the splendid hairy-chested young playwright from the West. But I had a bad twenty minutes of apologizing frantically in the dark.

Blunt-spoken, tough-minded, unflinchingly direct, *The Happy Island* was controversial in 1938 and, unlike most once-daring books from an earlier era, it promises to be controversial today.

Tim Page
New York City
June 7, 1998

The characters in this book are all imaginary.

. . . West Forty-fourth Street . . .

𝒯HE BUS WAS LATE getting into New York. The young man who had boarded it so exuberantly in Ohio the evening before slouched indifferently in his seat, hat pulled down over face, scuffed pigskin bag clasped between his knees. The older man across the aisle with the ingratiating fixed smile and natty green fedora, brushed his suit carefully with a small whisk broom. He shook out a threadbare fawn-colored topcoat which had been rolled into a pillow during the trip and arranged it over his left arm to conceal the frayed lining. He sent an occasional reproachful glance toward the young man, but his bright remark to each passenger who stumbled over his suitcase on the way out was cheerfully toned to indicate no hard feelings.

"Sorry! . . . Oh, *so* sorry! . . . Watch out, madam . . . oh, *so* sorry!"

The young man presently straightened out his long legs, ran his hand through his thick black hair, jammed the hat back on his head, and stood up.

"Well, here we are!" offered the older man genially. "Not a bad trip, all things considered."

"Every bone in my body is broken, that's all," said the other and stretched long gangling arms out in a great yawn. Either he had not stopped growing, or his clothes were hand-me-downs, for the gesture showed by how many inches the cuffs missed the wrists. His beard, too, was clearly the kind that snarled for attention every four hours, and the young man rubbed his cheek, frowning, as if this wonder of nature had never ceased to annoy him.

"Tell me do we smell like the bus, or does the bus smell like us?" he asked.

"Suffering seems to have softened you," said the man in the fedora. "That's the first polite remark out of you the whole trip."

"Ah, I never talk," was the brief answer.

He stooped to look out the window into the great sunless cavern into which other busses were now running, snorting and sniffing like swine called to the trough by the mega-phoned summons to Miami, Cleveland, Chicago, Seattle, Denver, Boston, St. Louis. Names of far places rolled and bowled through the cave, and from the waiting room bundles with human escorts emerged and crawled into their proper coaches.

"New York, eh!" exclaimed the young man. "What a dump!"

"The gateways to a city have nothing whatever to do with the citadel itself," pronounced the older man. "Just as the first im-pression of a woman is not the real girl. I've been around, I know. Don't think that because I got on at Oil City I don't know the world, my boy! Shanghai—Hawaii—South Africa. My name is Van Deusen."

"So you said," answered the young man and continued to peer out the window, as if this keyhole view of the city must be permanently recorded. The last of the other passengers had removed her bags and babies to the curb. Mr. Van Deusen drew on chamois gloves, which, with the tilted hat and deftly revealed blue pocket handkerchief, transformed the disheveled bus traveler into a dangerous man-about-town for all to see.

"I am a pianist," said Van Deusen. "You, I see, are not a salesman. The way you wear your hat, as if it had nothing to do with your head whatever, makes me think you are a newspaper man. Personally I count them as my best friends."

"Is that a fact?" the young man answered evasively.

"I knew Vincent Sheean and George Seldes and, of course, Walter Duranty. Before that—Huneker."

"What do you say we get out?" and here the young man gathered together his bag and book—it was one of the more pontifical Huxley novels, Van Deusen noted—and started out.

"Are you here for a visit or just to make your fortune?" unabashed Van Deusen pressed after him, for one of his vanities was that he was a good mixer, a point that had to be proved in spite of hell and high water. "Perhaps I could help you. I've come here a dozen times to make my fortune. Sometimes I come by plane and leave by bus, it's the other way round this time. Have you friends here?"

The young man set his bag down on the curb and pulled an address book out of his coat pocket. He was a lean, wiry fellow, not at all handsome, the arrogant, ugly type that sometimes gets the women even more, Van reflected.

"Look," the young man indicated a page in this notebook, "is that north or south of here?"

Squinting his eyes Van Deusen read off an address on West Fifty-eighth Street.

"Why, I know D. O. Lloyd! A relation?"

"Not exactly," answered the youth. "We had a mutual aunt and we met last spring at her funeral. He asked me to stay with him when I got here."

"So you're staying with old Dol?" exclaimed Van Deusen, stroking his mustache. "Well, what do you know about that? Old Dol! One of the best. I'm not in his good graces right now—a financial misunderstanding. We artists are careless folks, you know."

He hurried after the other through the gloomy tunnel to Forty-fourth.

"You could do me a favor by mentioning that you saw me. Put him in the mood so I can look him up. You might say I'm planning to give a concert here. Mention my name—Van Deusen. Perhaps I can do you a favor sometime. Do you know anyone else?"

The young man accepted one of Van's cigarettes and lit it.

"A girl I knew came here once," he admitted. "I'll look her up and maybe learn the ropes from her, unless things have gotten too tough for her here."

"She from the home town?"

"Yeah. Silver City."

"Silver City?" pondered Van.

"Prudence Bly's her name."

This brought a light to Van's eye.

"Not Prudence Bly, the nightclub singer? Not *our* Prudence Bly! Why, young man, if she's your friend, you're absolutely made. I'll see her this afternoon. What's your name?"

"Jeff Abbott," said the young man and picked up his bag, hooking his right arm firmly over it since the handle was gone, "but it can't be the same girl."

"Of course, it must be," cried Van, delighted. "The odd name—why, there's not a doubt of it! Wish we'd talked this over sooner. It's a small world after all, eh?"

"Can't be the same," said the young man, waving a hand in utter indifference to the smallness of the world. He strode off and had put a row of taxis between them before Van Deusen could collect himself. Van Deusen looked after him, pondering on the surly hostility of these new young men come to conquer the city. You would deduce from their pose they expected to conquer it by slugging it into a stupor. He was petulantly pleased to see the young man was not too clever to have dropped a telegram when he replaced his address book, and this Van examined with interest, for it might be just the wedge needed to revive his connection with Dol Lloyd. It was addressed to Jefferson Abbott, Silver City, Ohio, and was signed by one of Manhattan's rising young producers.

CASTING COMPLETE THIRD ACT NEEDS REWRITING COME
IMMEDIATELY.

B. HYMAN

Van Deusen carefully folded the telegram and placed it in his billfold, then tenderly reassuring himself of the solitary five-dollar bill therein, hailed a passing taxi.

"Hotel Ansonia," he said after a moment's consideration.

There was always some musical old lady staying at the Ansonia, willing to vouch for him, some former opera coach or pupil, someone who had known Van Deusen in his brief heyday. He adjusted his cigarette in its amber holder and looked out the window with interest. New York looked much the same, arriving by bus or train or plane. There was something a touch premature, however, about being catapulted from a Main Street right into Times Square with no Grand Central preparation. The trains made a more dramatic introduction, he decided; it was shut-your-eyes-and-open-your-hand, darkness, then presto—the gaudy Babylon of the underground railroad terminal, New York's bargain basement, the roots of the city, and then the flower.

Come to think of it Times Square had changed—more fritter,

more cluttered up. Pineapple juice instead of orange juice. Hotels cut up into even more slices than before, so their actual space would hardly permit their full signs—"Astor"—or "Claridge." Side streets dug up a little differently. Broadway and Seventh Avenue buses. Streetcars as clumsily out of place as horse trolleys. A new ten-cent store. Cigar stores swallowed up in cut-rate drugs. Pipe displays lost in rubber goods, Hollywood Make-up, and Mama Dolls. Still, the same old town, even if its equator had floated a little north.

Crossing Forty-seventh Street, Van leaned forward, startled. He had caught a glimpse of his young friend of the bus padding up Seventh Avenue, bag without handle still clasped under his arm. Hoofing it all the way up to Fifty-eighth Street, believe it or not. Van stared incredulously. Young men must be hardier these days, he decided, and sank back in his seat.

. . . Fifty-eighth Street . . .

*J*EAN HAS JUST TOLD ME," said Prudence Bly in the telephone booth, "Stevie, I can't believe it. She says you've been in love with her for three years. Darling, that's what I've been listening to all day! She says all the time you were with me in Paris you wrote her a letter every day at Cannes, and . . . hello, hello, operator, you're cutting me off! . . . Steve, can't you say something? Tell me a lie, a nice one, or else come over here to the Savoy and keep us from confessing too much. . . . Do come, Steve.

I want you to see her in this soft mood, so soft she's melting away like a popsicle. . . . You know popsicles. . . . No, Steve, I do *not* mean Good Humours; these are on a stick. P-o-p . . . Steve, I am definitely *not* being hysterical! . . . I'm calm and wise and mellow. Why else would she pick my chest to weep on? . . . And Steve, she tells me you tried to make her leave Harvey! . . . She did, too, say so! . . . Well, I didn't think you'd ask *him* to fly with you, too, still it would have been *nicer!* . . .

"No, of course, I didn't tell her anything about you and me. She's seen so much about us in the columns she knows it must be a lie. She thinks I'm just like a sister to you now. . . . What? . . . All right, if this seems such a nasty situation, and you think it's as vulgar as all that, come on over and stop us. We've talked all day and we'll be sniveling into our cups all night. If you don't want me to hear anymore of the grisly details, you'd better rush in. . . .

"Steve, do me a favor. . . . Tell me something pleasant. . . . No, not anything about me, sweet, I know everything nice about me, just tell me something about her. Tell me she has varicose veins. Please. Or make it a beard. Oh please, just a teeny beard on her chin! . . . I'm not nervous and I'm *not* silly. I only telephoned to tell you how fine your two girlfriends are getting on. Just like men, don't you know? Best fellow win out and all that. . . . We've had a dandy little lunch here, a few manhattans with our fish the way the French do and a little whisky and splash with our coffee the way the English do and a few old-fashioneds the way everybody does and next we're going down to the New Yorker and have a boo-snooker. Darling, do you remember the day we tried out all the funny drinks in all the funny places? Wait, I have to put in another nickel. . . .

"Steve, do say something tender and strong. Say I made you a lovely onion soup the other night with only a rusty can-opener. . . . Thanks. . . . Honestly, I could kill you. . . . I wish you'd stop saying 'Please' and 'Please, Prudence' and 'Please, darling.' You ought to have more to say than that, after all you're a college man. . . . Jean says you dropped her like a cold potato. Potato is her own figure. She said you were very cruel to her. I'm glad to hear that, anyway. . . . I'm *not* shouting. . . . Anyway I've got a right to shout for two nickels. . . .

"Oh, we'll be here for days. We've been here since noon. Jean's catching a little nap now, she's resting on the table, up to her knees in potato chips. . . . I ran out when she started on the intimate details of that Majorca rendezvous. . . . Of course, she told me all about it, how you ran over to meet her there, leaving me holding the Alps. You told me you were just going over to visit the Chopins and hear some catchy tunes. . . . And I cried like a fool till you got back. I should have cried harder! . . .

"I may run out myself any minute. The hell with my contract, I'll go to Sweden. Sit under the smorgasbord bush and drink aquavite with the laughing Swedes. . . . What? . . . I should what? . . . Wait, till I find another nickel. Now I've dropped it. . . . All right, all right, I'll go back to the table, sure I will, and shove my big shoulder under her little red nose. . . . I'm *not* maudlin, darling, I'm only mad as hell!"

. . . the loving cup . . .

$\mathcal{M}$RS. JEAN NELSON propped her elbows on the table and with considerable care placed her head in her two hands as if it was a very fine melon. She found that, adjusted thus, she could swivel her head in all directions, pushing it a soupçon to the left to watch the glittering bar, which had in the course of the afternoon become a misty mirage of bottles and light, or to the right to watch the door for Prudence's return. A few couples were dancing in the indifferent shall-we-promenade style that was still in favor, but these moving figures were not as real to Jean as the proud white steeds on the murals whose riders, lovely ladies and fair men, leaned from their mounts with third dimensional ease to release falcons into the blue. The falcons swirled about Jean's head charmingly, and if she had been stronger, she would have attempted to catch them. Here she had sat all afternoon, while outside the late September sun had shone on Central

Park, on happy children roller skating in the Mall, on fat ponies resigned to fat little riders, on caged elephants and flamingoes and snorting sea lions, on punctiliously habited riders from the riding school galloping over and under little rustic bridges. It shone on swinging, sliding, scooting, crying boys and girls, on a green flowered earth, a benign smiling old Madam Nature with political protection, relieved to see such innocence masking her sometimes sinister operations. September in New York was being its most charming, reproaching the summer deserters for their absence, reminding them that here after all was everything: sun and roses, orchids and adventure. Wonderful to be back, faces said in the street, looking through the September lens into a new season of fabulous rewards.

In the café September meant that one corner by the south windows still had momentary flashes of daylight inferior to and conflicting with the chandeliers' brilliance. There were new faces, too, in the café in September, people's babies of last year now debutantes or collegiates, last year's earnest workers now turned playboy by success, smiling or somber husbands alone, freed by Reno, that Abraham Lincoln of cities, and always and everywhere the afternoon women. Afternoon women with their young men or afternoon women merely talking about young men or other afternoon women. Afternoon women telling other women's secrets to conceal their own.

Jean looked at her watch again, but whatever hour it recorded meant nothing to her. She felt peaceful and dreamily relaxed as someone should who has spilled the beans in all directions and has nothing more on her mind. The sight of Prudence, returning at last, trimly tailored, violets still fresh, smart crazy hat set jauntily over one eye, made her feel competent and sober, as if this was the way she, too, must appear. It could not be true, with Prudence before her as her evidence, that her own hair was tumbling all about, her hat under the table, her face as pink and wet as a puppy's nose.

We are two very able women, she thought with dim pride. We certainly can drink like gentlemen.

"Prudence," she quavered as the other sat down. "You aren't cross with me for what I told you? I mean about Steve and me. I know there used to be talk about you two, but he said there was nothing to it."

"Oh, he did, did he?"

"You aren't jealous of me, are you, Prudence?"

"Jealous? *Jealous?* Good God, Jean, you must think this is the Middle Ages!" exclaimed Prudence and popped the floating maraschino from her old-fashioned into her mouth. "You're a beautiful girl, why shouldn't Steve fall for you? After all, we're modern women, let's not be silly."

"I'm not beautiful at all. I'm simply terrible looking," protested Jean. "My thighs are too thick. Look."

"Try my Sigrid," Prudence advised. "She whacked two inches off my tummy and during the bock beer season, too. She's at the Park Central. I'll take you up tomorrow."

Jean powdered her nose. It was a fine large Roman nose and the midget puff from her quarter-size vanity seemed singularly inadequate.

"Prudence, you're wonderful," she said. "I couldn't be the way you are. I'd be terribly mad and jealous in your shoes but then I'm just plain female, and you're so modern and so clever. You are, Prudence, really, you're wonderful."

"Oh, come now," Prudence said with a graceful laugh. "You drink up your lunch there and see if you don't feel better."

Jean's nose wrinkled up ominously.

You never cry, do you, Prudence?" she sighed. "I guess I'm just spineless."

"Now, Jean. Don't say that."

"It's true. I'm weak," she insisted, tears welling again in her lovely blue eyes, "I haven't the least resistance. I've always been

that way. My own mother used to tell me so. 'Jeanie,' she'd say—
I had a little green winter outfit, green broadcloth with bands of
ermine and an ermine pompon on the bonnet; she sent to Paris
for every stitch she put on me, particularly after Papa ran off
with the telephone operator in Hyannis so we had to show a lot
of swank just to make people forget, you know how summer
Colonies are. And Mama never would use the telephone again!
Literally! She even sent telegrams to people in the next house
rather than touch the telephone. And then sending to Paris for
my clothes, wasn't she foolish?"

Paris or Sears Roebuck, reflected Prudence, who cared?

"Mother was a Robbins, one of the Cape Cod Robbins," said
Jean. "I don't suppose they cared about that sort of thing in your
family. Darling, what *is* your family anyway?"

"Just a floating father and a grandmother. A grandmother,"
said Prudence, "who wears a wig and veils. For all I know she
might be a man."

Jean began dabbing at her eyes again, pleasure in splendid
blood vanishing.

"I'm so weak," she sobbed, "utterly, utterly weak! I know you
think I'm just saying that, but it's true, absolutely. Steve always
said I was just plain, fundamental woman, and that's what I
am—just helpless female."

Now, thought Prudence, while the orchestra played *Siboney,*
she's going to boast of all the things the matter with her and be
proud of them and cry over her femaleness. Why do I lunch with
women, anyway? Take Jean. Just because we've both fought all
the other women in town is no sign we're friends. We always end
up sniveling over men and life and we always tell something that
makes us afraid of each other for weeks to come. Women take
too much out of you, they drink too much and too earnestly.
They drink the way they used to do china painting and crewel-
work and wood burning.

"It's seven o'clock," said Prudence, as a few black ties began to appear at the bar; and James Pinckney, who wore dress like a pallbearer, and whose evening social manner was exuberantly lugubrious, bowed to her—from the waist!—across the room. "Let's get out"

"You're sick of me," accused Jean.

"I expect Van Deusen tonight," said Prudence. "I'm fixing up a recital for him."

"You're so good to everyone," sighed Jean. "You really are."

Nothing could have enraged Prudence more or been more untrue.

"Come on, Jean," she exploded. "Let's scram. Anyway I start work tomorrow night at the club. I can't keep on."

"No," persisted Jean in a strangled whisper. "You're mad because Steve likes me. And you're sick of the sight of me."

"Now, honey," implored Prudence, swizzling the dregs of her drink busily. To tell the truth, she *was* sick of her, sick of looking at that perfect profile, that fine broad white brow, the evenly arched eyebrows, the clear, beautifully spaced eyes. She recalled how often she'd praised that serene profile to Steve when they met her for the first time on the Bremen. Well, apparently she sold him the idea. She should have been warned by his too casual disparagements. She was sick of la belle Jean's face right now, even though there was no getting round the fact that it was a noble one, with a stark-hewn heroic beauty. Still, it was no pleasure to the eye as a plainer face can sometimes be. One look was enough. Ah, there, Beauty, ok Beauty, farewell, Beauty. For there was nothing unknown here, no other quality suggested beyond the patent virtues of contour and hue, no hint of magic, no twinkle of malice. Here was Beauty Clear, and it was not enough. The treacherous eye must hunt furtively for a mole, a dimple, or even a fascinating wart, something to spice the whole, contrast with its major perfections. Under tears this noble face collapsed, the simple weak little creature behind it emerged, the sweet small nature peered lonesomely out of its beautiful stained glass window, cathedral home for wee mousie.

"We might call up Steve," said Jean.

Prudence drew back shocked, as if she had not just returned from that very enterprise.

"Not me."

"Should I? *Should* I, Prudence?"

"If you like," Prudence shrugged.

"You."

"Call up Steve Estabrook? I wouldn't dream of it."

"Well," said Jean, pleased. She stood up, and a dish fell off the table, her glass tipped over and rolled lazily from left to right, her chair fell; but Prudence sat there so stiff and haughty, perhaps a touch *too* proper, that Jean was reassured of her own propriety.

"Why is everyone staring at me?" she asked.

"The Barrymore profile, honey," consoled Prudence. "You can't get away with a face like that in this town without people staring."

"Silly! I'm not *that* handsome," giggled Jean, lifting her chin nevertheless to show the fine throat line. "9326 Plaza."

"Rhinelander," corrected Prudence. "If you can't get Steve, call Neal Fellows."

"That's right, it's Thursday, isn't it, so he'll be on the loose."

Prudence looked meditatively after Jean as she wove her way earnestly through tables and knees. The girl did look like a goddess, but the trouble was she walked like one, too, as if her legs had been too long wound in a flag. She operated them, drunk or sober, from the knees with a resulting wooden waddle that was far from an invitation to the dance. Prudence felt a sudden imperative need to talk about her friend, to bury every word the girl had spoken under a mountain of fun. Bury her, yes, and Steve, too, Steve, holding her in his arms by night and in the morning smiling over his letter from Cannes!—I'll bet he didn't write her every day, I would have noticed something!

She hurried over to James Pinckney, who was imbibing without visible glee the simple vermouth with which he always inaugurated the evening's drinking. She suddenly wanted to fly out of the whole mess.

"Come on up to my house, James," she urged, for no one had ever called him Jimmy. "Now."

"My darling Prudence," said James reproachfully, "you know perfectly well—or you *should* know—that tonight is the Museum dinner."

"Yes, and I know that no one but you will be there till ten," Prudence answered and at James's wounded look she seized his arm coaxingly. "You've got to save me. I'm jittery and jealous and I need the masculine angle."

Flattered only slightly, he took the exact change for his drink from his pocket, for he lived very cautiously, laid it on the bar, and allowed Prudence to hasten him from the room.

"I've got a lovely new watercolor, a Marin," said Prudence, "and a Sealyham, also a broken heart."

"I hate managerial women," said James, clapping his hat upon his scant gray locks gloomily. "They have no womanly pride."

"Do you like Jean Nelson?"

"Certainly not. She looks like a ship's figurehead or something on an old coin."

"A buffalo," said Prudence.

Keeping a tight hold on his arm, they were well on their way across Sixtieth toward Prudence's place, when Jean returned to the deserted table and sat down, too blurred to register disappointment at first, scattering potato chips and peanuts about her like confetti at Mardi Gras with each clumsy move; but presently she felt lonely and began to cry, this time so wholeheartedly that the waiter turned her over with some firmness to the attendant in the ladies' room.

"I've hurt Prudence's feelings!" wailed Jean in the matron's arms. "She's such an old peach, and now I've hurt her. Oh, what makes me such a horrid nasty person? I'm terrible."

"There, there, dear, you're not terrible at all."

Jean stamped her foot angrily.

"Of course I'm terrible," she cried. "Don't be an ass!"

. . . not for publication . . .

$\mathcal{A}$T SEVEN O'CLOCK Silver City's second hostage to New York was desperately praying for Mr. Lloyd's cocktail guests to leave so he could eat, while its first and leading representative was embarking on a tale of lover's woe to James Pinckney in a futile effort to reorganize her cosmos. Silver City had for at least twelve years been no part of this cosmos, which at this moment seemed to revolve exclusively around Steve Estabrook; and although Prudence Bly was a well-known figure in the Manhattan press, her extensive publicity had never mentioned the provincial past. Such a sturdy, essentially pioneer past would never have done her reputation for international sophistication any good. Who wanted to hear of a Toast of the Town achieving that eminence by hard work, penny-pinching, and rather dowdy misery? So far as New York was concerned Prudence had been passed on to them by the crowned heads of

Europe, the gilded dictators of the Riviera, London, Paris, Vienna. For her present purpose, which was to maintain a night-club eminence as long as possible, such a background was far more useful than a backwoods one. Nobody in Silver City ever dreamed that this was its own Prudence nor would anyone have cared. She may have made the English aristocracy but she never made the Silver City Woman's Club!

Mrs. Queenie Bly, Prudence's grandmother, still kept a house in Silver City. This painted, red-wigged old eccentric probably had done a phenomenally bad job of bringing up her only son's only daughter, but Prudence never held it against her. The old lady owned the Queen Flour Mills and had an enormously ugly old mansion, an electric brougham that finally gave way to an incredibly venerable Rolls Royce with a chauffeur. No one ever was sure whether she was tremendously rich but tight or poor but extravagant. Certainly Prudence as a child had received no evidence of wealth, for she never had clothes nor spending money. Once her father, an admitted ne'er-do-well, on a rare visit home, promised her a little blue Swiss watch if she would stop biting her nails for three hours. Prudence, aged nine, sat in the hall not biting her nails for three hours, and then he never gave her the watch at all. The incident conditioned her to a lack of faith in humanity and provided her with a rather wry philosophy.

At twelve Prudence was sent away to a small ratty girls' school where she learned to say "Oh, too heavenly! . . . But, my dear, how perfectly *leprous!* . . . My *word!* . . . Oh, not *really!* . . . How too sick-making! . . . She enriched this culture with a vocabulary learned from the mill hands, since she spent many happy vacations playing in the grain bins, nibbling shorts and cracked wheat and field corn and napping among the flour bags all marked in great red letters: QUEEN CROWN FLOWER.

Mrs. Queenie Bly, when she was not gliding about town in the brougham, heavily veiled as for the Pyramid Tour, goggled, and painted like a totem pole, was touring the country with her surly young Swedish chauffeur in the Gibson-girl Rolls. There were rumors in the county that she and the chauffeur quarreled hideously over expenses on these trips. She wanted to buy one dinner with two plates, as if he were a Pekinese, and, more alarming still, to take only one room in the hotels where they stayed. After all, she explained, she always slept with her clothes on so there was nothing indecent in it, and besides on the continent, where she had always been a favorite, it was the custom. She was always forced to run down roads to bring Emil back and compromise with him after these terrifying false steps.

Prudence was left to shift for herself in the old manor when she was on vacation during her grandmother's tours. All alone night after night she lay in bed trembling, wild with fears, while the wind blew the shutters, banged doors, made the rats in the walls scamper and squeal. Daytimes she painted herself up in the unguents from her grandmother's dressing table (which was practically a laboratory in itself), and hung around the mill, basking in the dusty milky smell and the gossip of the men, ruining her clothes. She had no feeling for her grandmother, who, when all was said and done, was like nothing on earth in the human line and was definitely crazy in the world-traveler fashion. Even her grandmother's anecdotes did not hold her fancy, they only made everyone sneer at the whole family. Prudence sneered back, but she held it against Queenie.

Every year Mrs. Queenie Bly's anecdotes became more wonderful. By the time she was sixty-five, the date Prudence saw her last, she had been a belle at Windsor, had danced six times with Edward and later, to hear her tell it, had the pleasure of the Czar Nicholas's favor. She was on the Titanic when it sank though she did not think of this till twenty years after the calamity, and she had racy cosmopolitan relations with maharajahs and Ethiopian royalty. In any adventure where a gentlewoman's presence would have been palpably impossible she sent her late husband. She lashed his tired ghost through wars and brothels and opium dens and Bourbon boudoirs and on her sixtieth birthday she promoted him, dead then thirty years, to the Foreign Legion where he did all the things she had ever seen in movies especially *Morocco.*

Prudence was always glad her grandmother had been neither kind nor affectionate. The tender cloying love that protected and imprisoned other children was divinely absent from her life; and after she grew up, she rejoiced that she had no one to thank but herself for whatever she wrested from life. How did anyone ever strike out from those other fond homes, how break through the suffocation of loving parental domination, that hidden law that forbids a child to go further than its parents' limited aspirations? At sixteen Prudence, on her way back to Miss McNally's School from Easter vacation, got off at Pittsburgh, found a job waiting table in a railroad restaurant, went with a sailor one night to a street fair in McKees Rocks where she sang a song she had made up herself called *Queen Helen and the Gypsy* while the sailor played an accordion. The sailor had to go back to the *S.S. Pennsylvania,* but not before he had *taught* her to play the accordion; and thus equipped Prudence entered New York. Petite, jaunty, blond, and hard as nails to the casual eye, she began by singing in a Greenwich Village speakeasy, on MacDougall Street. This was to be, so she had thought, just a stepping-stone to a career of world travel and adventure. In June she sent a wire to Silver City.

DEAR GRANDMA I'VE GRADUATED

She gave a General Delivery address as an afterthought to receive a possible cash graduation present. Nothing came but postcards of Old Faithful, a Drive Through Yellowstone National Park, Painted Desert, Yosemite Valley, Orange Grove, Agua Caliente, and a cramped penciled inscription on the back, "Beautiful! Your grandma." "A paradise on earth. Your grandma." "Lovely country!

Grandma." So Prudence gathered that the old lady was scourging the western highways with her Rolls and Emil. Sometimes a Christmas gift would come to the General Delivery. The gift was never money but a camphorated moth-eaten lace cap, a large book of Omar Khayyam, flyleaf torn out, a few mussy French handkerchiefs, a dressing sack of pink albatross trimmed in marabou, indeed anything that had lain around the attic long enough definitely to establish its uselessness.

This, then, was Prudence's sole contact with the town that had bred her and three previous generations of Blys. Queenie expected nothing of Prudence. Prudence expected nothing of Queenie. It was a perfect arrangement; and even in those early days when she received only her room upstairs and dinners in the restaurant where she entertained, Prudence felt no bitterness toward her grandmother. "He who expects nothing is never disappointed." So however shabby those first months were before the uptown customers discovered her, at least Prudence never was disappointed. Her luck came overnight, overnight she erased Silver City and overnight invented a new personality into which she stepped and like her grandmother kept this dress on day and night.

Even among best friends it is safer to keep a few things under lock and key, no one is really trustworthy. In Prudence's group families, old love affairs, disadvantageous connections of all sorts were locked from view. Either the gay front did or did not justify one. Secrets that discredited others were fairly told but none that damaged oneself. Prudence, learning this first lesson in success, kept back Silver City but told all about her best friend two-timing her with her lover. As she told it, she and James Pinckney were both aware that she was making a frightful faux pas; confession of any defeat was too often the beginning of the big breakdown. Mr. Pinckney shook his head sorrowfully at being a party to this unfortunate lapse. He could hardly wait to get to his dinner and start the amusing story on its way.

. . . Central Park West . . .

$\mathcal{A}$LL VERY WELL to have a Liberty Night, and
ten thousand couples in New York felt very original about it; but
how and why did this weekly fiesta fall in almost every case on
Thursday? Thursday, for over a decade—ever since everyone had
been analyzed at least—was Husband's-Night-With-the-Boys or
Girls, Wife's-Night-Out-With-Gay-but-Trusted-Old-Suitor. It
was, to begin with, Bachelor Night but, as might be expected,
soon became Wives' Holiday. Whatever its title, the night of
freedom was definitely a gesture away from domestic tradition, a
proud toss of the head in all directions. All over the city, as soon as
the cocktail whistle blew, the freed husbands wandered, wearing
their freedom like a dead uncle's overcoat, standing on corners
wondering what grisly form their fun would take, staring at
posters before burlesque houses, knowing it was the same show as
last Thursday, the same Georgia Peaches, the same Southern

Rose, sometimes wondering morbidly what the little wife did with these Thursday nights he had fought to have, for pride in liberty collapsed on going home to an empty house—who the deuce said she was to have a fling, too?—fun in smug secret was lost in frantic curiosity over what the little woman was up to. The rule, as he himself had firmly laid it down, was that no questions were to be asked, no answers given. Fair enough, and sauce for the goose, too, no doubt; but, damn it, the whole thing was spoiled by her equal independence. Maddening to have a secret no one asked about and, moreover, to have secrets kept from one in return. But then women have a gift for spoiling everything.

On these Thursdays when men and women step out of their ruts and visit other ruts, samples of other lives are snipped off, studied during the week and sometimes the entire pattern adopted. It is a night for changelings, and the very night Prudence Ely kidnapped James Pinckney was the night two married couples on opposite sides of Gotham mixed their celebrations and so became drawn into the witches' brew of Prudence Ely and Jean Nelson.

One of these couples was Mr. and Mrs. Fellows. No man in New York made more of his Thursday freedom than Neal Fellows, as if every other night wasn't his own as well. Not only did he train Anna, his wife, but his successive sweethearts as well into regarding this as exclusively a masculine outing, not for ladies, for he was a man who must have one-man women and plenty of them. The other couple was Mr. and Mrs. Eugene Brent, of Central Park West, who took Bachelor Night fifty-fifty. This chanced to be the Thursday Mrs. Brent summoned courage to call up Mr. Neal Fellows, playwright, on seeing his picture in the paper and remind him of an April in Bermuda six years ago, a breathless April ending in Mrs. Brent gasping that Mr. Fellows did not seem to realize she was a married woman, really! Every time she saw his polished plays afterward Mrs. Brent blushed to think how backward she must have seemed to the great man! That slap in the face! She could have died of shame and intended ever since to show how much more sophisticated she had become. So at five o'clock she called Neal at his University Place studio—the residence was nicely distant on East Fifty-third. At the same hour Mrs. Neal Fellows, who had been a big girl on the campus at Holyoke or Smith, got together with her old crowd the Cosies, and honestly the Cosies had more fun, just girls together, than anyone can imagine! This left Mr. Brent out on a limb, but, as Max Baer once said, somebody always has to get hurt in these affairs, and anyway it had been Mr. Brent's idea to have Thursday off in the first place. Sometimes he went to the club and played poker. Sometimes he went to a rowdy night club with visiting firemen and danced happily with the chorus girls. But lately he had not liked the poker crowd, visitors were scarce, so Brent idly walked up and down Central Park West, slashing at trees and hedges with his notched cane, sitting over a beer in a dreary brauhaus under the El near Sixty-sixth Street, browsing among detective novels at a circulating library, discovering that the new Agatha Christies were really just reprints, and looking at his watch every five minutes to see how soon his fun would be over, and he might go back to the house and lounge in peace in his birthday pajamas with beer and a box of cheese twigs.

Every Thursday Mr. Brent found himself getting home a little earlier, and this was bad. If he didn't use the holiday to the hilt, it might be taken from him, and then he'd be an ordinary tied husband. Tonight Brent was gloomy for his series of Thursday night beers had put quite a pot on him; even his secretary had remarked on it, to say nothing of his tailor. He would not have another beer, he decided, nor, glancing again at his watch, would he trot home at any ten-fifteen like any tamed husband on leash. He thought of a certain house on West Sixty-fifth with the girls dressed up like nurses that a fellow at the office had told him about, considered its possibilities with a sense of infinite weariness, remembering how dreary those houses were that sounded so devilish in story. He felt outraged to think pleasure could become so tiresome. He was only thirty-four, as healthy as the next one, if a little on the slight side so far as hair and shoulders were concerned.

He had lingered over a beefsteak sandwich and several glasses of a light Holland beer, for which he had a weakness, at a grill on Amsterdam at Eighty-fourth where the dark oak wainscoting, racehorse portraits and stablelike booths gave the illusion of a masculine retreat. Now it was only ten, and he was determined not to go home with only this small picnic to boast of. Aimlessly he wandered over to Columbus Avenue and walked a few dark blocks, gloomily soothed by the roar of the El. In shop windows cats prowled over stacked groceries or slept peacefully on banks of oranges, a golden-wigged head swiveled endlessly exhibiting a marcel and grisly crack in the cheek, a bubbling blue light enhanced a display of Ex-Lax and Tweed cologne; the shops slipped off the block one by one like colored balls on an abacus string.

Brent stood still, without realizing it, wondering all of a sudden what Nora was doing. He hoped to God she was as lost and restless with her free night as he was, but the chances were she was having a fine time. Women always had a fine time alone, even if they were only doing their nails or plucking their eyebrows. It was the man who was the trapped one, unable to sleep if she was out, fidgeting around the apartment in summer when she was at the beach (and very pretty Nora was too in her bathing suit). Nor was this lack of integration due to his being the more infatuated of the two, because he wasn't. It was because it had taken so much out of him to get used to double harness, and now he had lost the knack of single joy. It made him angry at Nora. He stood in front of a radio store thinking of Nora's irritating power over him while the orchestral music of a radio swirled over his head and around him, amplified, ducking its plumed chords now and then under the El's rumble.

"Death and Transfiguration," said a voice at his elbow.

Brent jumped.

"Imagine meeting it on Columbus Avenue," continued the stranger, "having it follow you around on a walk like a well-trained mutt. I swear it tagged me from the Seventh floor of the Ansonia all the way up here. I thought I'd lost it on Eighty-third Street, but, no, it had run ahead to jump out and surprise me up here."

Brent realized now that his thoughtful pose before this store was construed as that of a man under the spell of music, and he was relieved that he appeared thus to strangers instead of as a man contemplating wife murder. Embarrassed, he held out his lighter for the stranger's cigarette. They both stood waiting for the finale as if nothing less would release them from the spot.

The stranger, Brent saw, was a thin, ruddy-faced fellow of about forty-five with bushy gray eyebrows over intensely eager blue eyes. A meager spray of stiff gray bristles made a mustache that was fondly oiled and clipped; his prominent Adam's apple nestled nervously in a soft blue collar over loosely tied cravat and his lavishly jaunty air made Brent suspicious of him, but here at least was something happening in which Nora had no part, it was a man's adventure, it was something to postpone the beer and cheese twigs another hour. He contemplated asking the stranger to have a drink but decided to wait further developments.

Applause and static marked the last triumphant chords, a signal for the shop owner to turn out his lights and shut shop.

"A pity," said the stranger.

"I could listen to it all over," said Brent for conversation's sake, and they walked slowly northward.

"Why not?" queried the stranger. "See here. I have a friend who has a marvelous machine, a Capehart, all the best recordings. We could run over there and have a feast of music."

"We—ell," Brent began backing down before music.

"I mean if you had a few minutes to kill. Of course, if your wife or family are waiting for you—"

"Oh, no, not that," Brent hastily said.

"Say we pop in a cab and run over there. It's this side of Carnegie. He'll be delighted. Always open house, that sort of thing."

"Why not?" agreed Brent.

"My name's Van Deusen," said the other, putting out a hand. "I'm a pianist. Been touring the provinces the last two years. And Europe."

"Is that so? I'm Eugene Brent. Butternut Biscuits."

They shook hands. Mr. Van Deusen's hand was thin and bony and quivery. On the little finger of the right hand there was a large extremely fishy-looking diamond. He kept his eyes intently on Brent's face as he talked as if to register an almost aggressive honesty once and for all. I can look every man squarely in the eye was the obvious implication, right smacko in the eye, nothing to be ashamed of in *my* life. At least he hadn't worn his gold watch, Brent comforted himself, suspicious of such a blatant show of probity, and he could refuse to be drawn into any card games.

"You will come? Great!" cried Van Deusen. "Taxi! Old Dol will be delighted at a surprise like this. West Fifty-eighth Street, driver, turn off Broadway."

He settled back in the cab, crossed his legs and beamed at Brent. Brent beamed back. This was the Thursday night of his fancy, the casual adventure, the chance acquaintance.

"I think I can promise you a real treat," said Van Deusen.

. . . five cent alibi . . .

RHINELANDER 9326? . . . Mr. Estabrook please . . . Neal Fellows speaking. . . . Steve? . . . Steve, old man, you put me up last night. . . . I say, you put me up last night in case you should ever be asked. Let's see—we had dinner at—oh, say the Harvard Club, that lets out women, doesn't it, and they do have a dining room, don't they? . . . Yes, we had a nice dinner there. . . . Thanks, Steve. How's Prudence. Seen her lately? . . . Good. Don't mention this to her, she might spill it around Anna, you know the girls. . . . Yes, let's see—as a matter of fact you're putting me up tonight, too. . . . No, of course, I won't come in really. . . . But let's get together sometime soon. Lunch or something. . . . Thanks, old fellow."

"Yes, this is James Pinckney speaking. . . . What? Who? . . . Oh, hello, there. . . . Yes, I was in bed, but it's quite all right; hadn't been in long. Are you in the neighborhood, Harvey? . . . Too bad. We never seem to see each other anymore. . . . What? . . . I'm to say you spent the night with me? And last weekend, too? . . . Oh, now, see here, Harvey. You never call me up, never see me at all; why, I haven't seen you since that Beaux Arts Bail, the time Mrs. Brocken fell downstairs. . . . But I'm *supposed* to see you constantly. . . . It's not amusing at all, Harvey. . . . This happens far too often. I'm the alibi for every married man and woman in New York City—the single ones, too, as far as that goes. I don't see why *I* should always be the goat. I wouldn't mind, only look at all the wives and hus- bands who won't speak to me, won't invite me to dinner anymore, think I'm a dangerous influence. . . . Honestly, Harvey! Me, of all people. . . . Never tight in my life and always trying to discourage people's love life. . . . No, Harvey, you were *not* here last night. We did *not* go to any automobile show, and you did *not* have to bring me home and put me to bed! The idea! I don't care, this business has gone much too far. Harvey, now, I mean it, seriously, now Harvey . . . I tell you, you cannot; I won't allow it—hello, hello— hello—operator—oh, damn."

"What? . . . Who? . . Yes, this is Mr. Pinckney. Who is this? . . . Yes, I am asleep. . What? . . . Who? . . . Anna Which? . . . Oh, Anna Fellows. Anna, I'm sorry, it's long after midnight, I'm in bed and I'll call you tomorrow. . . . What? Did you say is Neal here with me? . . . Damn it all, yes. . . . Yes, I said. . . . Of course, he's here. He's in bed with a beautiful blond. . . . Two blondes. . . . Yes, you heard me, Anna. . . . Yes, I said. . . . Yes, yes, yes!"

. . . L'Ile Joyeuse . . .

$\mathcal{V}$AN PLAYED DEBUSSY, and everyone put his
hands over his eyes, leaned on his hands as if in prayer or merely
lay back wherever he was and sighed long music-loving sighs.
Sometimes a crude tenant in the apartment below would rap
smartly on the ceiling. Sometimes an uncultivated voice would
boom through the court, "Say, over there! Have a heart!" Once a
milk bottle crashed against the window sill. You could tell a new-
comer at Dol's by his uneasiness over these interruptions. The old
crowd, the bunch, continued to sit in a rapture often bordering
on stupefaction; the host quietly slipped about seeing to everyone's highball and particularly his own. He would be a distinguished figure anywhere, this spare gaunt man with clipped
blond beard, sleek, gray-blond hair, fine, thoughtful brow and long
nervous white hands with the ruby signet ring, the plaid English
dressing gown with folded white cravat. Yes, he belonged in one of

those plays, thought Brent at first. In a way—and he hated these dependent thoughts—he wished Nora could be here, for she could get something out of it; all he could feel was a fierce regret that he'd ever met this Van fellow and how in God's name could he get out of the place now he was in it.

The apartment, in the dignified shadow of the Plaza Hotel, was stuffy with rugs, tapestries, upholstery. It seemed caged with iron railings, and there were dozens of steps going up or down for no reason at all to other levels. Chinese sculpture and majolica vases peeped down from high shelves, and dyptichs, tryptichs, or ikons were in every corner. There was an enormous electrical gramophone in an alcove hung with gold brocade, and the walls were pocked with etchings. You could tell Dol was a man who'd been around the world, spoke seven languages, knew everybody, just to look at his apartment.

Men came and went, Brent observed with increasing bewilderment. Some seemed to have their own keys. Some were in dinner coats, some in tweeds, all of them youngish, and none of them glad to see Van. Brent blunderingly inquired of one of them what business was their host in, what was the reason for this easy hospitality. But the answer explained nothing. That was just Dol's way: highballs, easy chairs, music—that was Dol.

"Oh, it's you again?" was all Dol said when Van had effusively grasped his hand and introduced his old pal Gene Brent.

"I daresay you know all these people," Dol said, waving them into the room.

"I brought Brent to hear some music," said Van breathlessly. "It seemed a good chance to look you up, too. I just got in today. Traveled with young Abbott. Did he get here?"

"He did," said Dol noncommittally.

"A nice lad," said Van. "I'd hoped to see him tonight." It had been plain as the nose on his face that Dol did not care whether he ever saw Van again or not. Brent felt wretchedly uncomfortable and observed his friend's desperate efforts at affability with a fixed smile. He was not impressed with the other men, either.

"Paint?" one asked Brent. He shook his head.

"Write?" asked the second, passing him a beaten silver cigarette box that would have crippled him for life if it fell on his foot.

"No," said Brent, "I sell," and he hastily wolfed his highball.

His increasing gloom was not relieved by hearing Van speaking in a low undertone to one of the men.

"I'm sorry I didn't get that ten to you," Van was murmuring. "I had Mrs. Cutler drop me at the Players' especially to give it to you, but Hampden hailed me, and it slipped my mind. You know Hampden."

Brent heard him saying something on the same order to someone else later on. Always some great name had stood between Van and the payment of his debts.

"I'm having a recital, people," announced Van presently with a radiant smile. His voice had grown perceptibly more affected under Scotch as some voices do.

"Not *really* this time!" exclaimed Dol.

It seemed to Brent that with Van's announcement everyone breathed more freely as if "at least he's got *something* lined up, he's not at loose ends expecting somebody to do something for him."

"Prudence has helped me, of course," said Van suavely, sensing the tide turning toward him at last. "Prudence has been perfectly wonderful. Really. I don't care what anyone says she's been perfectly marvelous to me."

There was only one Prudence of any significance in New York, Brent reflected, Prudence Bly, the nightclub girl.

"Prudence simply said, 'Van, it's outrageous your dropping out of the world, this way, you must have a recital.' It was as easy as that." Van took the opportunity of being momentarily tolerated to pour himself a fresh hooker of Scotch. "And, Dol, I'm playing your Debussy."

"Not *L'ile Joyeuse?*" Dol asked and now all hatchets were buried. That was the moment Van chose to leap to the piano. He played eagerly, intently, and always looked up at Dol or one of the other men as if "this, this is *your* favorite, you clever connoisseur!" so that even though he was certainly no Josef Hofmann, his manner was so assured, and his confidence in his audience so flattering, that in no time at all everyone had forgiven him for existing, and there were whispers of "Lovely! Perfectly lovely!"

Brent adjusted himself in his antique uncomfortable chair, fastened his eyes on Van's feet beneath the piano bench and was mildly interested to detect that the left sock was wrong-side out.

"Prudence wanted me to play the *Ondine,* but I don't know," he said, this time deferring to the blond pasty-faced young man who had slipped in and who was a Mr. Willy; but this beardless lad out of the entire assembly refused to even speak. He seemed a bare sixteen at first, but a closer glance showed him to be merely a perennial juvenile, a blank childish face with only the sly alert eyes to betray experience. He sucked sourly on a pipe and returned Van's gaze with a belligerent babyish scowl. Van tried to pacify him by running lightly through the opening bars, his vivid blue eyes fixed on Willy, smiling coaxingly at him as if "of course, you know every note of this—of course, you do!" Mr. Willy persisted in ignoring the tribute to his intelligence and rather noisily shook the ice about in his glass until the host poured something in it.

Brent wondered how he could get out of the place. It was nearly two o'clock, and he had suspected for some time that his legs might not be altogether dependable. He had had a brief repartee with Dol, discovering that the gentleman's name was Darwin O. Lloyd, and the initials had given him the nickname.

"You knew Van here or in Paris, Mr. Brent?" so ran the repartee.

"Er—no—that is, I've never been to Paris," said Brent.

"Well, Paris is dull now. I prefer London really."

"Never been to London."

"Then you knew Prudence before she went to London?"

"Don't know Prudence. Didn't say I did."

Brent felt a wave of fury at his curious position and nothing less than passionate hatred for everyone present, particularly Van. All stared at him as if he had entered under false pretenses, insisting that he knew the password; and here he was, basking in the club privileges, the club secrets, the club music, and not even knowing Prudence Bly. It occurred to him that while he might be unable to make a graceful exit right now, at least he could make a dash for the johnny, and this he did, tumbling up the railed balcony into the first door he could find. He banged the door shut behind him before he realized that this was not the bathroom at all but a small bedroom occupied by a young man who cursed roundly as Brent entered. The young man was seated in bed, in pajamas, a typewriter on his lap, papers scattered about him, and a green eyeshade over his eyes. He looked out from under this at Brent unfavorably.

"Well," said Brent, now accustomed to rebuff. "Hello."

"I'm working," said the young man.

"I see," said Brent and knew he should leave but could not move for the life of him.

The young man threw off the eyeshade and shoved the typewriter off his knees with a groan.

"How the hell can I get this act in shape with that racket going on?"

"I don't know," admitted Brent. "Haven't I seen you before?"

"Picture in the paper," explained the man.

"Prizefighter?" guessed Brent.

"Nah—playwright. Jefferson Abbott. What they doing out there?"

"Drinking to music," said Brent.

The young man snorted.

"Plastered, all of them. They were talking vintage wines out there all day. Connoisseurs they call themselves. Soaks, I call them. How am I going to get out of here, I'd like to know?"

Brent didn't know.

"This would drive me nuts in twenty-four hours," said the writer.

He suddenly leaped out of bed, a tall muscular fellow, with too scanty pajamas. His wavy black hair needed a cut, and his face needed a shave. His muscularity was not that of the beach Adonis but of the knotty farmer sort.

"Where do those guys come from, anyway?" he begged to know. "I expected to find New Yorkers different but not another race of mankind. Sure, I listened to 'em for a while, but it's not my language, not even my country they're talking about. Don't they speak anything but Stravinsky and Hollywood? Didn't anything ever happen to them but the opera and *Esquire?* Where did they get that way? Where the hell do they come from?"

"Iowa," ventured Brent. "Iowa, Fall River, Terre Haute, places like that. I don't know their language, myself. I'm a New Yorker. We're rather simple here."

He looked around the room uneasily.

"The can's in there, if that's what you're after," said the youth. He looked at Brent curiously. "If they are really from everywhere in the world but this town, what makes them wipe themselves out? Why? What do they put in themselves to make up for the first twenty years?"

"Search me," said Brent. "Alcohol, it looks like."

"Ah, that's not it," said the young man. "Look, you wouldn't know of a cheap hotel, would you—some place I could keep clear of this sort of thing?"

Brent scratched his head.

"You might try downtown in the Thirties and Twenties, on the East Side. There are small hotels and rooming houses there."

The young man made a note on a piece of paper. Brent opened the bathroom door, but when he came out, he took the opposite door by mistake and found himself in a larger bed-sitting room, probably the host's, that opened directly onto the living room. No one looked up delighted at his return, and he would willingly have turned back to his late acquaintance if he had dared. He stumbled down to the studio couch and fell into its soft depths, resigned. He could see that Van had worn out his brief popularity, for young Mr. Willy was openly sneering at his shoes and kept repeating Van's "Chawming! Puffickly chawming!" after everything that Van said.

In spite of this growing coolness Van would not relinquish the piano but revenged himself subtly on his audience by running over Viennese waltzes very badly and with the lack of swing that characterizes even the best concert pianists, though somehow they do pride themselves on being able to dash through popular music as well as the experts who play nothing but that.

"You'd better stick to Chopin," jeered Mr. Willy. "That's all you're good for."

Even Debussy's liquid runs were now stymied by Van's drunken fingers, but he would not give up. Brent did not mind music, he told himself, even good music, but the trouble was it made exit so difficult. He wished he dared walk out now, but to leave before the music was over betrayed such a shabby cultural background. At any rate, he consoled himself, it wasn't any worse than somebody reading poetry out loud with expression, that was something. Both made him feel a little soiled. He felt now that he dared not leave without distinguishing himself in some way. He had been pleasantly ignored all evening and could have slipped out as unobtrusively as he had entered. But he was so conscious of having been sponsored by the wrong person and of having done nothing to erase this unfavorable introduction that he felt compelled to stay until he had made a mark, however faint, on the company.

He might tell about his cruise to the Virgin Islands, only there was so much to tell before he got to the point, which was that he passed the Vanderbilt yacht and he was invariably stopped before he reached this climax. He might run off an anecdote about Cole Porter whom he met once on a liner, but, again, that was all there was to the story. "I beg your pardon," he had said to Porter, though he had forgotten just why and he had forgotten Porter's laughing rejoinder. He was furious with himself for not being able to twist these little encounters with the great into something personally creditable, the way other men did. Any one of the men around him tonight would be able on even less material to launch out, "Cole and I were crossing from London last year and a curious thing happened. Beaverbrook and Marlene had just joined the rest of the party in the bar, and we were waiting below for Noel and Bea. Suddenly—" Bitterly pondering his inadequate gifts, Brent saw Van approach Dol.

"Bye the bye, old man," said Van, "how about putting me up? I seem to be rawther at loose ends. I expected to stay at the Ansonia, but my friends there weren't in town so—"

"Ha-ha!" sneered Mr. Willy. "What friends?"

Van smiled benignly.

"—so I sent my bag on to Prudence, but, of course, it wouldn't do for me to stay there. Any old pillow, old man—just a few hours is all it will be. You know me."

"You mean a few years!" jeered Willy.

Dol shook the ice in his glass.

"Sorry, Van, I have a guest."

"But I know him!" Van exclaimed eagerly. "Young Abbott's an old traveling companion. I don't mind bunking with him."

"Can't manage it, Van," said Dol. "Sorry."

"He'd be here all winter!" said Willy. "That guy!"

"That's all right, Dol, forget it," Van flourished his hand in a forgiving gesture. "I'll just tuck in with old Brent. I'll be ok."

Brent heard this without being sure he had heard aright. He saw Van getting into his coat rather haughtily, considering that he was tangled up in torn lining. A picture of Nora Brent's horrified face—for she was a born New Yorker—on being faced with any unexpected guest rose to Brent's mind. He followed Van in a daze. Dol gave him his stick and hat. Van bowed his good-byes very formally with an attempt at a sardonic smile.

"Tell Jeff he dropped this," said Van and produced from his pocketbook—now, alas, minus its five dollar bill—the telegram. "It may be important. Tell him I'll be getting in touch with him."

"I will," said Dol, with a courtly nod.

Brent kept shaking Dol's hand, waiting for a last-minute inspiration.

"Good-bye, Mr. Brett," said Dol.

Tight as a tick, thought Brent, surprised at the glazed eyes.

"Brent's the name," said Brent. "And I met Cole Porter once."

. . . Prudence by Day . . .

PRUDENCE AWOKE in the swing on the terrace.

When she groped for the clock, usually on her night table, and encountered only chains and hammock fringe she groaned, for this inevitably meant a hangover, sleeping in the swing was a sure sign. She was always topping a few hours' dissipation with some simple unaffected gesture such as sleeping under the stars. She opened her eyes now to the bright autumn sun and a prim row of geraniums along the brick wall. A plane whirred overhead, scuttled in and out of creamy clouds like a rat in a dairy. Prudence's eyes followed this busy flight as Robert Bruce must have watched his spider but without deriving a similar moral.

As no one had dared disturb her, the ashes, glasses, and siphons of last night's refreshments were all over the straw rugs, wicker chairs, and tables. She had a grieved conviction that she had missed dinner, too. Who had been her guest? What friend could she blame for this headache, whom should her flexible affections now turn against with righteous resentment? Ah, yes, it was Pinckney. And why did she have this gone feeling of having lost a valuable jewel, a private treasure? Because, idiot that she was, she had bleated all over James the fascinating story of her three-timing triangle: Jean, Steve Estabrook, and herself. Jean's astonishing confession still cut to the heart. Jean and Steve! A whole summer right under her clever nose? It infuriated her that with all her worldly training she had been as dumb about that situation as any fatuous suburban wife. Even James must have sneered a little at her naïveté.

"Why do you tell *me* all this rot?" James had shouted plaintively. "You know I've got a bicycle, you know perfectly well I run from door to door with everything I hear, you know I'll tell the whole thing at dinner if there's a pause in the conversation. Why do you tell me anything? Why does everyone tell me things and make me cross my heart? God knows I don't invite secrets. I've tried to shunt people off, but, no, they must tell all, they must give names and addresses, but why, why to *me?*"

"Because you don't want to hear, darling," Prudence explained. "Nothing invites a confession like a dead pan. People feel in you a challenge, Jamesie boy, your pained indifference whips out every shocking detail—one *must* make you interested, one simply must."

And now, thought Prudence angrily, James could tell all over the town that Prudence Bly had as hard a time holding her man as anybody else and had been beautifully two-timed by her best friend—oh, laugh, everyone, jeer, ha-ha, as the lady herself has so often laughed at your amorous fumbles. He could tell how he had been wheedled into calling up Steve Estabrook at this and that club or café, how he had complained, "But, Prudence, it's so silly. If Steve wants to see you, he'll call up, no use sending out warrants for him."

It had all been Van's fault, Prudence suddenly remembered. It was all because Van had never showed up as he promised. She had rather feared he wouldn't, because that always happened when you counted on Van—especially when you were doing something handsome for him, such as arranging a recital. She'd wangled the money, the manager, the press agent—everything but the date and selection of hall but she should have known he would slip up on his part. Everyone always believed in Van if he hadn't seen him for a long time and was always surprised when he failed just as he always did. He was part of everyone's past. He was in Paris when you were in Paris, he was in London, in Moscow, in Alaska, at the Kentucky Derby, Washington, Santa Fe—he was everyplace everyone went. He was in the Dome, the Adlon, Shepheard's, Stewart's Cafeteria, the Rainbow Room, he was everywhere, he appeared to everyone in their highest and lowest moments, people liked or disliked him in proportion to the nature of the reminiscences he evoked.

Prudence liked him because he had been an eyewitness to Steve Estabrook's devotion to her. Van could definitely swear, in any group, that Steve was crazy about Prudence; he'd seen the situation in Paris and Havana; they had seemed to like the same things, have the same thoughts—yes; and Steve had sent whole roomfuls of flowers every day. Van had seen them. Nice, casual, utterly standardless Van, symbol of Miss Bly's happiness. Only now he was getting her in a jam, as he invariably did his most loyal friends, by not coming through on this recital after she'd lined up the backing. Above all he'd betrayed her by not showing up last night, so she must pass the time putting her head in Mr. Pinckney's big mouth! Where was James having lunch today, what people would know her humiliation by two this afternoon?

She flung off the bear rug she had used for a blanket and sat up. The clatter of dishes on the adjoining terrace, separated from hers by a vine-covered iron grille, suggested that her neighbors were having breakfast outdoors.

"Nellie!" shrieked Prudence. "Where's my wheaties? Hey, Nellie."

From north and south walls came indulgent laughter. The entire neighborhood felt better. Our Miss Bly was up and screaming, jolly Miss Bly was bawling out her manager over the telephone, delightful Miss Bly was calling up all her friends and giving them hell—in a word it was another day at The River Hotel.

Nellie, large, black, good on cooking, bad on cleaning, weak on perfumes and odd jewels but straight as a die on small change left around, full of negro folklore learned out of *The Green Pastures* and more natural lore learned from waiting on a series of gay ladies, stepped out of the French windows with a tray of coffee and toast and the delicious *suisesse* that opened the pretty eyes.

"Nice day for your opening, Miss Bly," she said.

Prudence groaned. Her neck ached, her hand was asleep, and the swing trappings had left sinister marks on her arm. It was no morning to face one's future candidly, and certainly the beginning of a twenty-week contract at the newest supper club was a future as Prudence saw it. Nellie slid the tray on the glass coffee table, ineffectually swiped some ashes with her apron, picked up one ginger ale cap out of a dozen, and allowed in the process the morning papers to slip out from under her arm. Prudence picked them up, saw they were folded to the dramatic or gossip pages—wherever her name had struck the devoted eye of the hallboy.

In the ten years of her fame the printed word about her had come to be the woman, and even her private thoughts had now a publicity angle. Sometimes in her bath, Prudence would have a brief ghastly thought that this little body under scented suds had no more to do with herself than a window doll's, two Prudences separated under water; and for the life of her she could not find the time or place where the little girl from Ohio, the ambitious, industrious little village girl, merged into the *Evening Journal's* Prudence Bly, the *Town and Country* Bly. These were queer moments between personalities, moments such as the hermit crab must have scuttling from one stolen shell to the next one. In these nightmare seconds Prudence wondered if one could permanently become the third person singular, lose oneself, be nothing but one's name in a society column, one's photograph in *Vogue*. There were brief bad periods, times that she wondered if even her long passion for Steve was real, if it were only whipped by the printed word about their romance, lashed by other published news of his outings with other women. Supposing they were removed from their fame, set together on a raft—but Prudence's public-trained mind at once changed "raft" to "yacht," and there were ten other guests as audience.

As James Pinckney had once said to a small gathering of backbiters, Prudence Bly was not a person so much as a conspiracy. She was guarded by those who knew her as jealously as the sucker list of a benevolent organization. In her hotel, doormen, bellboys, chambermaids—all felt part of the conspiracy of Prudence-Against-the-World; they read the papers for news of her and like her own close friends followed her progress as if she were a baseball tournament. In her they dimly felt they had a valuable machine gun, a weapon against society, their private egos were avenged by her destructive wit, they crowed over her ability to mow down large and small potatoes with a barbed word, for among the fallen was sure to be a rival or, better still, a friend. She inspired a respectful terror rather than affection. To dismiss her as not-so-clever-as-someone-else was an open admission of having failed to register with her. It signified she had pinked you or, worse yet, ignored you. Hence very few had the courage to admit dislike of our Miss Bly. Most people hastened to praise her, for to praise her was to boast of being high in her favor. Women often truly liked her, for she was as brutal as they longed to be; and no one was more brutal with these very admirers than Prudence. If, however, they showed an equal knack at verbal uppercuts Prudence hastened to turn mellow and even cloyingly kind.

That was the difficulty with her saber tongue. It was an instrument only of attack, could never be counted on as a defense, even when its ruthless operations made the wielder a proper victim for counter-thrusts. Prudence slew with a neat epithet, crippled with a too true word, then, seeing her devastation about her and her enemies growing, grew frightened of revenges, backed desperately, and eventually found the white flag of Sentimentality as her salvation. For every ruinous *mot* she had a tear for motherhood; with a stroke she annihilated an artist, but wait!—hear her sobs over old organ-grinders, starving streetwalkers. Her unexpected bursts of rampant tenderness left her waiting enemies bereft, impotent; no one could strike at a woman weeping over *Hearts and Flowers,* only a cad would crack down a lady heartbroken over a dead turtle in the fountain. So, guarded by the quick handkerchief, armored with tears for old waltzes, as secure as a pious man of the cloth among hoodlums, Prudence blithely cut her witty path with sword and flame. How like her to leap from her car, leaving her friends still writhing from her neat thrusts, and snatch up the poor dead pussy from the gutter, hold it all the rest of the journey tenderly on her lap, thus immunizing her from well-merited vengeance!

A conspiracy, said James Pinckney, and Prudence herself realized her curious position and was depressed by people's firm refusal to permit her ordinary human weaknesses. A look of disbelief on their faces when she talked—as she rarely did—of a childhood in a mill town made her swing back into the role invented for her, a role that lost all glamour reduced to its mere synopsis: Small-Town-Girl-Makes-Good-in-Metrop. A conspiracy, a tack on the sofa seat, cracker crumbs in your bed—all these were

Mr. Pinckney's descriptions of his chum Miss Bly; and Miss Bly sweetly reciprocated by giving him a name he alone out of the whole town never knew, though he might have surmised something of it from the suppressed titters whenever he spoke of his native state, for, yes, he was Pinckney the Oklahoma to more people than he ever dreamed.

The friends of Prudence and the friends of Prudence's friends were born, so far as each other knew, with a canapé in one hand and a dry martini in the other. Their roots, except for the documented Europeans, flung back to covered wagons, mining camps, village poolrooms, lonely farms on the prairie; but these parts were snapped off like admission coupons at the gates of the great city. Where had they met? On transatlantic steamers, in a star's dressing room, at a duty dinner—for each other the past began there, the previous years were mere nourishment to the plant, the twisted underground roots were forgotten by the gay blossom. So Pinckney once lived in an Oklahoma oil town, shabby offspring of a telegraph operator? So Prudence grew up in Ohio flour bins? So Dol Lloyd came from generations of rich eccentrics in an Iowa town? So Van Deusen came from a broken-down Boston family? So what? These roots were buried, a whole dimension lost, until the day the flower itself faded and dropped, forgotten, into its cast-off cradle.

. . . oh, happy day! . . .

$\mathcal{H}$APPY OPENING, CONGRATULATIONS and dozens
of other kind thoughts were expressed in telegrams and flowers
all over the apartment when Prudence went inside. Sometimes
she wept a little over this fond evidence of her continued popularity but this morning she found it extremely silly. She said as
much to the bath maid and the somewhat gloomy vacuum-
cleaning man and to Nellie, who was at the most absorbing of
her futile duties, namely, washing the goldfish.

"Imagine people sending this sort of thing year in and year
out," exclaimed Prudence, examining a box of brown orchids.
"Back where I come from they send potato salad. Nellie, did you
order food for tonight? I may bring a crowd up after we close."

"Really," said Prudence, fussing through the mail on her desk,
"you'd never think I opened and shut at least three times a year.
You'd think this was my tender debut."

"Miss Prudence, what exactly do you do at this restaurant?" asked the bath maid, a big Irish girl, who willingly acknowledged Nellie's racial superiority. "I don't hear you practicing dancing and I don't see no violin."

"I'm a strong woman," said Prudence and tore up some bills. "I roll my great big eyes and put my finger in my mouth and sing M-I-s-s-I-s-s-I-p-p-I."

"Is that all?"

Nellie tee-heed appreciatively at the girl's surprise. "Well, I throw kisses," added Prudence, "about four in all. Then I jump out at all the bald-headed men and pull their ties out."

The telephone rang. Nellie laboriously got to her feet and answered it; Miss Jeanie.

"I'm out," said Prudence. "I'm dead. I'm abroad. I'm in conference. I'm in my bath. I'm the wrong number."

"But she's downstairs," said Nellie. "She's on her way up."

"Oh, my God," groaned Prudence. "Why can't women leave me alone?"

She switched on the gramophone and flung herself down on the sofa, listening with deep absorption and not by any means for the first time to a record of her own voice chanting her celebrated number, *Queen Bessie and the Last Page.*

"'*She didn't say a wor-rd—*'" sang Nellie along with the record.

"'*Oh, she didn't say a word—*'" boomed out the vacuum-cleaning man in an extraordinarily resounding baritone for such a small man.

The doorknob rattled inquiringly, waited for no answer; and Jean burst in, gorgeous in a silver fox cape and a veritable festoon of gardenias. The concert of baritone, Nellie, and Miss Bly's metallic canned voice did not pause; and Jean, accustomed as was everyone else to a proper reverence for Prudence's art, stopped short in her tracks, tiptoed to a chair, and sat down, waiting with bowed head for the finale; it was in a whisper and so familiar was the hotel staff with every nuance of Prudence's numbers that the cleaner switched off his buzzing machine and he and Nellie dropped their own voices to the merest gasps, Prudence tocked off the pauses with her finger going back and forth like a metronome, the bath maid's mouth moved following Nellie's: *"'the last—the very last—alas—oh, definitely the last, the very last page.'"*

"Lovely!" said Jean automatically with these final words and leaped to enfold Prudence in her arms.

"Darling!" cried Prudence happily. "How divine of you to come in. Look!" She pointed to a huge pot of lilies on the piano. "Steve."

"How sweet of him!" said Jean with a long face. "Lilies are so funeralish, aren't they? I was going to ask if you'd mind if I came with him tonight. I know you hate me for telling you everything yesterday—oh, yes, I know you'll never forgive me, but I do adore him so and I'll never get over it; it's no use. I'm insane about him and you were marvelous about understanding. So if I came tonight with him—"

"But, of course, foolish," said Prudence. "I won't have a minute for the old dear. But where's hubby?"

"We fought all night," said Jean dramatically. "He said you were a bad influence on me, and I told him I cared more about making something of my own life than I did for him, and he said next I'd be leaving him for you just like The Captive, and I said I wished I could do just that."

Prudence squeezed her hand.

"I only wish you could," she said.

It was the wrong thing to soothe the beautiful caller for tears welled again in her eyes, and she whispered, "I do love you better than anyone, Prudence, even better than Steve."

"Hangover, Miss Jean?" asked Nellie politely, waddling out of the bathroom bearing her rejuvenated aquarium. "How about one of them *suisesses?*"

"Thanks," said Jean, "I'll have a stinger instead. That's what Steve and I always took for hangovers in Majorca, Prudence. Darling, can I stay with you today? Through wave-set, manicure, and everything? I have something terribly important to talk over."

"Don't leave me for a single second," said Prudence. "I'm so proud of you for talking back to your husband. What else did you say, pet?"

Jean got up and strode in dramatic silence about the overcrowded but jolly room. She picked up the huge silver-framed picture of Steve on the piano and stared at it intently, then put it down and walked on. At the terrace door she stared out over the river, arms folded, profile rampant.

"I told him about Steve," she said hoarsely. "Everything. Every solitary thing. I knew that's what you'd want me to do and I did it! The truth!"

Prudence choked back a scream. Rather desperately she reached for a cigarette.

"You must have been stinko," she murmured. "Kinda tough on Steve, considering it's been over so long."

"Oh, of course one wouldn't confess if the affair was still on," admitted Jean. "But I did tell Harvey I still cared, and he said, 'Then go to him. Go to your lover, then,' that's what he said."

"He—he said *what?*"

"'I will not live with another man's ghost between us,' he said," repeated Jean. "'I love you far, far too much,' he said and right away called the superintendent to send up my trunks from the cellar."

"Good God, Jean!"

"Yes, he said I must go straight to Steve," continued Jean and permitted a wan radiance in the smile she turned on Prudence. "He called up Steve and said he was giving me up. He was terribly upset but he said, 'She loves you, Steve, so you can damn well take her.' And Prudence—I'm going."

"Good God!" was all Prudence could say.

"It's the decent thing," said Jean happily. "I always try to do the decent thing in my weak, female way. And of course, Steve is a free man. You're through with him, you said."

"Oh, yes," said Prudence and reflected that she might make a fool of herself when she told the truth, as she had to James Pinckney, but at least she lied beautifully when she lied. Or was Jean clever? That was a worry-maker. Yes, she must be clever to play dumb enough to get what she wanted.

"I'll go to Steve's tonight," said Jean. "After your opening. It will be so absolutely fitting, won't it? Steve and I used to hold hands while you sang before. It's something in your voice, darling, something made us feel terribly romantic."

"Thanks," gasped Prudence. "Oh, thank you, dear."

"So tonight we'll be together listening to you again, and then afterward I go to him to stay," mused Jean, now leaning on the piano before Steve's picture. "It's all very clear to me. He'll have to take me."

"Why?" Prudence gently asked. "I mean—*why?*"

"Because he's afraid of Harvey," explained Jean softly. "Harvey's firm is the chief sponsor for his radio hour."

Awful, Prudence thought, oh, awful, oh, help, oh, Stevie, poor lamb, what a fix for you and even worse for Baby. The gramophone had hurried through an Eve Symington disc, and her own voice poured through the room again with the accordion accompaniment. *"The Mocha Lady and the Java Man."*

"'Hi-dee-dee-oh-oh-oh,'" Nellie's echo came from the terrace where she was sweeping. *"Hi-yi-yi, said the Mocha gal.'"*

"'Hi-yi-yi,'" hummed the cleaning man, dragging his machine from the bedroom across the room and out into the hall. *"'Oh-ho-dee-deedle.'"*

"The queer thing is that my chart says today is a great emotional upheaval in my life," said Jean.

"You've been to Dolores already?"

"But, of course," said Jean. "Everything she's told me is true. I never make a move without her. A new life, she said, beginning with this birthday. Today's my birthday, you know. I'm twenty-six."

"You bet you are, honey," soothed Prudence. Poor, poor little Stevie, framed by a radio program and an astrologer's chart! If she could only think! Her black Sealyham, named Sofa because he seemed to have broken-down springs, was playfully chewing up Jean's furs on the piano bench.

"Nice doggie," said Prudence.

. . . studio seven

$\mathcal{H}$ELLO, EVERYBODY, here's your old pal Stevie Estabrook and his Sweet Potatoes from way down south on Forty-ninth Street. Folks, we're bringing this program today from the largest imaginary nightclub in the world, the old Yellow Moon Inn. The Old Yellow Moon Inn, folks, *siterated* on a pile of old featherbed clouds a mile or two above Radio City and just a couple of doors from the Great Dipper. Folks, if you're ever traveling in the old stratosphere just you drop in the Yellow Moon Inn and have the best imaginary dinner you ever set your two teeth—ha-ha—in and as my personal guest, if you please.

"And while we're planning the party, how about talking things over with old Otto the chef, see what he's got in the icebox. This is the third year of Otto's cooking at the Yellow Moon Inn, largest and, don't forget, finest imaginary nightclub in or off the world.

So he knows plenty, eh, Otto? Otto's a Swiss . . . oh, what's that, Otto? . . . Says he's only half Swiss, the other half St. Bernard. Here's Otto. You tell 'em, cook."

"Turn him off, please," urged Prudence in the chair at Raoul's, Inc., watching through the mirror the expert hands contrive a fascinating swirl of taffy hair above her left ear.

The manicurist, about to seat herself at Prudence's side, obligingly switched the radio dial to the Mother's Hour. Jean looked wistfully at the radio, as if the owner of the vanished voice would pop out of the box, his lips quivering at Prudence's harsh words.

"He isn't always that bad," Jean said. "People *are* crazy about him. He must have something."

"Nerve," said Prudence briskly. "And I daresay people realize it takes brains to sound like such an ass."

"Prudence!" protested Jean, just exactly as if she was little Mrs. Estabrook already, Prudence thought.

"It's too bad you don't have a radio personality, too," Jean observed thoughtfully after a while. "But then so many people haven't, Harvey says."

Three ladies from New Jersey, guests of Our Mrs. Campbell of the Radio Mother's Hour, stood watching Mr. Estabrook through the glass window as he conducted his Sweet Potatoes through *The Goona-Goona;* they beamed with fond admiration even though he scowled most ferociously at them. They exchanged an understanding smile when his forelock fell down on his right eye and they seemed only able to get on with their personally conducted tour when Otto the chef went into the commercial giving his recipes for dishes neatly combining the products of five sponsors. Mr. Estabrook sat gloomily with a beautifully manicured hand over his eyes during this interlude and then, catching the engineer's signal to stretch it out, filled in the extra forty seconds by endeavoring to repeat Otto's last words into the mike.

"So you have to use nothing but Crandall's Flour for these wonderful cakes, Otto?"

"I never use anything but Crandall's Cake and Biscuit Banana Flour," firmly corrected Otto; and the Crandall program manager listening in Office B, made a memorandum that this was Mr. Estabrook's third defection in today's program; and damned if they'd pay a thousand a week to have their flour misnamed along with four inferior and unrelated products; better pay more and get Rudy Vallee or Eddie Cantor.

Unconscious of the malign influences working all about him—Dolores could have told him all this or something like it if he had only listened to Jean's advice on an astrologer—conscious indeed of only his immediate dilemma, Steve Estabrook got up from the piano—for he was a pianist conductor—as the second hand of the great minute clock on the wall passed the dot. He nodded toward the clock.

"On the nose," he said.

The gentleman in shirt sleeves on the other side of the glass partition smiled sourly.

"On the nose today, ok," he said, "but seven seconds overtime yesterday."

Mr. Estabrook blazed.

"Seven seconds! And why not, for Christ's sake, when I'm carrying five commercials!"

"Watch it," was the imperturbable reply.

Steve Estabrook, heavy, ruddy, more the bull-necked football hero than the musical idol, certainly far more the husky farmer lad than the Broadway type, adjusted his blue linen shirt, wound his handsome solid silver wrist watch, and strode across the hall to the reception room. The suave blond receptionist stroked her slender bosom and coughed.

"Oh, Mr. Estabrook, a message from your apartment to call up there at once," she informed him. "Very important, they said.

And the Club Vedado called up to know if you had any preference about tables for tonight, otherwise Miss Bly was giving you your usual corner by the balcony stairs."

"I don't give a damn," said Mr. Estabrook, moodily lighting a cigarette. "And if my house calls up again, tell them I didn't get the message, that I've left and will not be at home, either. You don't know where I am."

"And a man called up to ask if you would introduce him to Miss Prudence Bly. Said he saw you with her at the prizefight the other night and wanted to meet her personally."

"Help!" begged Mr. Estabrook.

"He'll call back in ten minutes to see where to look for Miss Bly."

"Tell him to look under all the bars on Fifty-second," suggested Steve.

"Oh, Mr. Estabrook!" she laughed delightedly.

"You're looking mighty pretty today, pootchyboo," said Steve, tweaked her ear, and was off in a cloud of smoke.

. . . table for eight . . .

*A*T TWELVE O'CLOCK Mr. D. O. Lloyd's table for eight in the Vedado was occupied by Mr. Lloyd alone, lean, tall, distinguished, his ruby studs discreetly gleaming, his beautiful long fingers playing with a whisky and soda, his beard a badge of some mysterious distinction.

It was a happy day for the Vedado, this opening night, for it marked its first full year's anniversary under one name. A small expensive restaurant, it had been opening and shutting for years under different names and in different national disguises, uncertain whether to be quiet and smart, noisy and intimate, foreign-flavored and cosmopolitan, or just a shambles. The arrival of Prudence Bly as entertainer had solved this problem, for her clientele at once gave it a character. It became discreetly rowdy, a place where things happened; if there were fist fights, they were between earls or cinema stars and made the newspapers and camera weeklies, so that all the best people, seething with photogenic grudges, fought for tables. A string trio of elegant darkies entertained, troubadour style, during dinner seated above an electric fountain in the middle of the room. At ten the fountain disappeared into the floor and became a mirror dance floor, and God knows what the string trio became. Prudence performed at midnight; and while not more than a dozen people ever heard her, her fame rested not on that loyal dozen but on the hundreds who ignored her performance and enjoyed themselves during it in their own rude fashion and thanked her for the coincidence.

Tonight was a special occasion for Dol Lloyd, a definite sacrifice. He preferred his own home or a quiet beerstube but was conscious that this seemed like niggardliness in a man of his means so he drove himself to the midnight glamour spots his young friends talked about. Here, even more than at home, his entertaining was complicated by his inevitable choice of friends. He could not help preferring irresponsible, undependable, and frequently ill-bred men; yet he was always expecting them to behave like gentlemen, always harboring an illogical dissatisfaction with their manners. Despising his own life, he despised all people like himself from a stiff middle-class background, but so insidious is the poison distilled through genteel ancestry that he could never quite free himself of family traditions nor wholeheartedly adopt the bohemian class he adored. His guests tonight were—he was well aware— likely not to appear at all or to come in tweeds or quarrelsomely drunk or both. They were likely to come bringing whatever companions they happened to find, thus ruining his carefully ordered supper. Dol knew he was incurably foolish to expect consideration from the odd characters he elected as friends; but, nevertheless, he could not withstand a flash of anger when he saw Bert Willy his protégé walking toward him in dinner jacket—he had distinctly said white tie and had a right to expect it since he'd purchased the entire outfit for Bert from his own pocket!—and with

Bert was an equally pallid, chinless youth, smaller and younger than Bert, rattling about in Bert's own dress clothes but with the ill-fitting costume piquantly enlivened by ox-blood sport shoes.

"This is Leslie—Leslie Biggs," said Bert, off-handed.

Something about Leslie's anemic dependence made Bert seem more animated, and Bert animated was very heavy-footed indeed. Dol, by formal extreme courtesy, hoped to point out his young companion's wretched taste, but his chill was not effective. Depressed, he saw Van in the doorway, quite the Parisian artist as to dress—ascot plaid jacket, tan trousers, loose tie. Waving happily to Dol, he cut across the floor leading a rather good-looking but somewhat average young couple.

"I brought Gene and Nora Brent, Dol," said Van radiantly. "I knew you'd love them and I absolutely insisted they come along. They're putting me up."

"Look here," said Brent in a choked voice to Dol. "We're a little jingled—hope you don't mind—been swilling mint juleps all evening, but—look—we're here on our own, really. Wouldn't have crashed if we hadn't been tight, and my wife wanted to hear Prudence Bly. Van dragged us into the thing—terrible imposition—"

"Waiter," called Dol, smiling suavely at his guests. "Everything's worked out beautifully. I couldn't have planned a better party. Highballs—"

"Champagne," giggled Bert Willy. "Leslie and I want champagne."

He nudged Nora Brent, a smooth, athletic-looking brown girl with vivid blue eyes, quite a handsome wench in her gleaming white satin and turquoise jewels.

"Leslie wore my dress clothes, so I wore the tux," murmured Bert, almost convulsed with strange merriment. "Dol's sore! But my shoes won't fit him so look! He's got tan ones on, he thinks nobody notices! And I had only one waistcoat so we tied a girl's scarf around him for a cummerbund! Look! It keeps falling down. Look at him! He thinks nobody notices."

"How funny!" said Mrs. Brent in a bright metallic voice.

"Dance?" asked Leslie of her.

Mrs. Brent thought of the tan shoes and blanched. She looked at his putty-colored, sly, child's face with definite dislike; he was even more pasty-looking than Bert Willy. Her violet eyes stole in dread from the brown shoes to the purple Roman striped sash around the waist. Either she must refuse him and then refuse everyone else during the evening—she loved to dance, too!—or suffer with him now and enjoy herself later. Dol, supported by the instant dislike he had taken to Leslie, rescued her by declaring they could not give up their one lady even for the brief period of a dance.

Dol liked to have a young couple along, a happy, good-looking, well-dressed young pair; and except for an occasional mad young spinster he never invited women except with their devoted husbands, for he found they disrupted a party, ruined a musical or contemplative evening, made all social occasions a garish hodgepodge of sex and swing and chatter. Tonight he would have two couples for the Fellows were coming. The Fellows, in spite of Neal's laxity, always put on a rather charming public show of domesticity, enough to balance a group of overcivilized young men. He saw them coming in now, Neal pausing at every table to flatter some lady—how they glowed and twinkled as he passed, like flowers before the bumblebee! Atina, fine-busted, creamy-skinned, flat-hipped, thirty-five, and proud of all these things, proud of Neal's promiscuity, proud of her long double A Size 7 feet, of her Budget Shop black crepe meteor, of her Mexican beaten silver bracelets and earrings, proud indeed of everything that touched her life. A nice thing about Anna on a party was that she drank very little, did not at all mind being featured as "the wife of Neal Fellows" but gloried in it, talking about the theater and all of Neal's private business to ambitious tyros in that field whom Neal had snubbed; moreover

she was bound to look after all the bores, finding pomp and exhibi-
tionistic pedantry very instructive and flattering. She liked to "get
something" from people, she enjoyed being instructed, she liked to
take something home to think about, the more technical and complicated the better, and she earnestly peppered her conversation
with these little culled educational gems. Needless to say she was
proud of being intellectual and sometimes smiled at the bleak little
faces of Neal's honeys, confident that she could always hold a man
by sheer force of mentality if nothing else. Her college bunch still
rallied round her as their leader and with the "girls" behind her she
had nothing to worry about.

"Here are Neal and Anna!" said Dol with a rapid glance at his
table—if his other guests did come, they could be squashed in
somewhere. Of the three uninvited guests he only minded Leslie,
not only for his lack of charm but because of his tacit testimony to
Bert's invincible stupidity.

"Neal writes all those plays," explained Van affably.

"Not *all* of them," corrected Neal. "Just those by Maxwell
Anderson."

He sat by Nora Brent, and it struck Dol as a little odd that for
once Neal made no effort to engage the handsome stranger nor,
for that matter, did she appear overwhelmed by his name and
presence. This struck Mr. Brent too, and he stared hard at Neal.

"Didn't you meet Mr. Fellows before, Nora?" he asked. "I
thought you said you met him in Bermuda. Right after his first
big hit, I believe."

"Oh," said Nora, bringing herself to look at Neal. "Oh, yes.
Oh, yes, of course."

The ever adaptable Neal took his cue from this.

"Naturally *I* remembered," he said heartily, "but I was hurt
that Mrs. Brent didn't."

Anna beamed, Mrs. Brent toyed with a charm bracelet, and the
orchestra members dispersed to make way for the star of the

evening. Lights dimmed, dancers hastened to their tables, there was a round of applause, and Prudence came in, striding rather arrogantly for such a small person, her sleek blue Vionnet molding her slim childish body, tiny jeweled accordion hanging on a heavy gold chain from her neck like a lavaliere.

"Ah!" exclaimed Mr. Brent and added, "Excuse me."

At twenty-eight Prudence was ten times more attractive than she had ever been at eighteen. The good jaw had been too grimly set during those early ambitious years, the fair hair severely clipped, the gray eyes cool and honest rather than seductive. Her present creamy luster was infinitely more agreeable than the earlier scrubbed, healthy stern look. But then no man present was able to compare the two Prudences, for there was only the Prudence of tonight.

In an audible whisper Van explained characters and tables to Nora Brent, who smiled fixedly into space and wished he would shut up.

As if I wasn't here to get all this with my own eyes and ears, she thought, annoyed.

"That old gentleman at ringside with the young group is Marshall Bearding; he's just married his son's divorced wife; that's Stephen Estabrook just coming in with—oh, yes, Jean Nelson. Jean's one of those girls who're around town a couple of years, look well, dress well, go everyplace and live down their commonplace background; I believe she came from a little town in the East. Jean managed to marry quite a bit of money on her second try but every fall she gets rather romantic about whoever is the man of the hour; one year after his first success it was Neal—"

"Oh," said Nora and did some figuring in her mind. "—then it was, I forget who, but it must be someone rather arty always and uncouth and, of course, poor so she can feel Lady Bountifulish; then in the spring, naturally she wants to go abroad or cruising, so she cries it all out with both husband and protégé and gives up the young man in a way that makes him always her slave; she goes everywhere with Harvey for a few weeks, looks pale and brave and weak, then autumn comes again and with it a young English poet, perhaps."

"How nice," said Mrs. Brent. "Now we really must listen to Miss Bly, Mr. Van Deusen."

"Call me Van," said Van. "After all I am your house guest!"

Nora Brent's lips arranged a smile as she speculated just how long the man really intended to stay in their apartment. Wild plans for creeping away from him tonight with Gene and barricading the doors against the genial guest occurred to her.

"Isn't Prudence amazing?" Van mused audibly. "Very slight gifts to offer but so absolutely insolent, you know, she doesn't care what anyone thinks, so of course they have to go on thinking she's wonderful. No one ever expected her to last this long. Those little songs of hers, now. This one, for instance—"

"I'd like to hear it," said Nora firmly, "every word of it."

"It's really too suggestive," said Anna. "Frankly I like Prudence but I do not like her songs. There are certain things that are simply *not* funny."

"Now, child," admonished Neal tolerantly.

Nora Brent flushed and leaned toward her husband. If Neal Fellows was going to be her lover, she simply could not endure him calling his wife pet names right before her. "Child," indeed!

"A light, please, darling," she requested breathlessly of Gene.

Dol murmured that it was good indeed to know there were still women of Anna's moral fiber in this naughty world, and Neal looked away from his wife's downcast smug smile at other gay tables, obsessed with his usual conviction that wherever Anna was—be it café or desert island—was Home; and Home was merely a jumping-off place, a telephone number.

"Hope Prudence will join us," he murmured.

"Prudence *is* fun, I mean as a person," said Anna.

"I've asked her to join us," said Dol. "I planned a very special sort of surprise. I was going to confront her with my young friend Jeff Abbott just in from Ohio. He hadn't the faintest notion of what a personage the little girl he used to play with had become."

"Can't he read the papers?" asked Neal.

"They read the front pages out there," exclaimed Dol. "Where we turn to the column, the theater, or market, the Middle West takes this quaint interest in what the president is up to, and whether there's a war. So Jeff was astonished that I had heard of his old playmate in this big city. I got him here to the door, he took one look around, said it looked too awful, and, if she could stand this sort of place now, he didn't want to see her. Ran right out."

Prudence was bowing to applause, in which Dol's party hastily and guiltily joined. All tables, with a common regard for café manners, waited courteously for the opening notes of a new song before they resumed their conversations. It might be smart to be seen where Miss Bly sang but the cachet did not depend on listening to her.

"Imagine anyone walking into a really top spot like this on his first night in New York and not liking it!" said Dol. "It isn't normal! I can't understand Jeff."

His tired eyes were already belying his words. The shrill insistence on fun oppressed him even more mightily than usual, though he smiled stiffly and tried to keep the exhaustion out of his voice. He had always felt the way Jeff did, but Jeff shouldn't. No one should. Stodginess was the foe here, and stuffed-shirt-mind. He must be more elastic, he reflected, taking a lesson from Jeff's uncompromising prejudice, more convivial but again he felt exhausted, recalling a career of unflagging sociability, endless forays into the world to disguise his unpardonable love of solitude. He classified as either cheaply genteel, neurotic, or meager-spirited those persons such as he who disliked cosmopolitan night life; he preferred his present discomfort to being identified with those groups. Jeff should be warned against his older friend's faults; if he was to be a great playwright, he must open up to the City, to people, noise, light, the garish flags of progress and vice. Moreover, added to Jeff's genteel reaction this evening was his teetotaling. Dol despised the soggy drunkenness of Van and Bert Willy, but more than that he despised teetotaling. To a person who had bungled lavishly the best years of his life, it was irritating to see a young man husbanding his ego, his health, his talent, his sleep, his digestion, his morals.

He's gone back to my apartment now for a good night's sleep, he thought jealously. He's going to feel fine and fresh and young in the morning and probably talk about how good he feels.

When he had offered the young man his hospitality—it had been three months ago when he flew to Pittsburgh to an aunt's funeral—he had looked forward to seeing New York through young eager eyes; but young Abbott's self-absorption to the utter exclusion of Gotham glamour had made the gesture foolish. The young man thought only in terms of his work, where he could get it done best and quickest; and though he had selected the drama as his chosen field, he seemed to feel none of its magic, actresses were merely ladies who did or did not give his lines their proper meaning, backstage was just the workshop, no more thrilling than a carpenter's shop. This was the way it should be for a serious worker, reflected Dol, but the truth was such sterling youths did not deserve the beautiful temptations they refused; those golden apples should be thrown to charming sinners who could appreciate them.

Dol looked at his watch secretly. He felt here, as he had in his school playgrounds, that his hatred of noise and games was a defect in himself, a deviation from the normal that had better be unconfessed. Jeffrey's attitude annoyed him by reminding him of his own. He wondered why he preferred Bert Willy's spineless surrender. He had befriended and supported Bert for two years and to what purpose? Bert made game of his benefactor, snickered of his weaknesses, mocked him by his choice of companions, and by his sly possessive sneer before Dol's older, finer friends. Now, with a muffled giggle, Bert had left the table to join James Pinckney and the elderly maiden lady, a piece of dramatic effrontery that Pinckney, with his taste for the gruesome, the outrageous, secretly enjoyed; but the maiden lady chose the occasion to retreat haughtily to the powder room where she remained long enough to powder everything and everybody within a puff's throw.

Dol took all this in, even while he complimented Anna on her gown, even while his hands vigorously applauded Prudence's last encore, and his voice joined in the little flattering coos that followed her exit.

"Isn't she in top form tonight! . . . and that divine dress! . . . of course there's no one like her! No one!"

Dol saw her appraise his table, very briefly, slyly, register the Brents and Anna Fellows against it. He saw her—though he realized that after this drink his sight and brain work were going to blur—wave with great casualness to Steve Estabrook's table where Jean Nelson, buried in dewy white violets and a wistful white chiffon whose demureness was belied by its lack of foundation, looked radiantly up at Steve with the same sweet joy Anna bestowed on Neal, the fed, happy look of "Ladies, do your worst, he adores me!"

The Cuban orchestra appeared and played a rhumba. Nora was tight enough to get on the floor for this with Leslie Biggs. Neal, not too pleased and showing it, tried a dignified married version of this number with Anna. Mr. Brent looked red and bored, and his stiff shirt bosom popped out of his vest. Van's eyes were all over the place for even the most half-hearted signal from a smarter, gayer party.

"That young fellow visiting you," Mr. Brent shouted to Dol above the din. "Funny his being from the same town as the entertainer here, eh? Seemed like a sort of old-fashioned chap. So he went right home after a look-see here?"

"Yes," said Dol, surrendering quite unexpectedly to his phobia, "and I must hop back to the apartment and get him. Have a good time till I get back."

"Absolutely," said Brent. "We've got to see that happy reunion."

Dol, restraining his fierce sense of escape, walked deliberately to the door. Now, he thought, now—and flew to a taxicab.

Prudence ran lightly after him, brushing aside a grim blond in almost bridal white satin who stared after her.

"Me, too," she said and got in the cab with him.

"I can't stand it," she said. "I really can't. I can't tell you about it now but, if I had a gun, I'd shoot them. Only I don't want to shoot. I'd rather get even."

"You are wonderful, Prudence," he murmured, patting her hand. "You are, indeed."

Yes, he was tight now and he thought what a splendid word it was—"tight"—the moment when your words and deeds swell up to fit your sagging personality, leaving not a chink for reason to probe, not a crease where dignity can hide; now you are tight, neat, exactly as big as you are small and as small as you are big; now the lens of the mind magnifies to include only the immediate object, this cigarette, this match flame, this forefinger.

"Prudence, my dear," he heard himself say carefully, "I have a surprise for you."

"I need it," said Prudence as they drove downtown. "Dol, believe me, I need it."

$\mathcal{T}$HE LADY in near-bridal-white whom Prudence had so brusquely pushed aside, retired to the powder room and drew pencil and pad from her rhinestone bag. She was Mademoiselle Merrylegs, the new society reporter for the largest and worst paper in New York and, after setting down the following tidbit, she went out to a much noisier bar and got quite blotto with half a dozen impossible people.

Although tables were reserved by Gotham's leading socialites as well as stage and screen luminaries, few of these actually put in an appearance at Prudence Bly's opening. It may be that the clever young artist has run through her popularity. If so, everyone agrees it is due to her too enthusiastic clique or shall we say *claque?* These young men and young ladies about town, none quite top drawer, follow their idol everywhere, quote every utterance and in general make themselves and their patrons obnoxious to real cosmopolitans who have seen a hundred Blys come and go in the last decade. It was rumored that most of the fashionable names announced as having reservations for her opening had no desire to risk the inadequate service of the Vedado even to hear Miss Bly exploit her modest gifts and hoydenish personality. Many of these cautious aristocrats were to be seen enjoying pleasanter and more established spots such as . . .

. . . boy meets girl. . .

$\mathcal{D}$OL'S FACE WAS quite gray when they reached his door. Prudence looked at him uneasily. Some day he would drop dead, and a bevy of pasty-faced lads would mourn him and, mourning, betray him. There had been periods of heart ailment, perhaps even now he was in pain, stumbling with pallid lips and waxen eyes into his living room.

"You're sure you feel all right, Dol?" she asked involuntarily.

"Perfectly," Dol articulated through rigid lips.

He reached his favorite wing chair and sat down carefully, hating, she knew, for her to see him less than himself. She should not have noticed anything out of the ordinary, of course, these defaults into a common denominator of pain or oblivion should be private and unmarked. Dol's eyes begged her to respect this rule. Everyone knew about the bad heart and everyone knew he should not drink, but no one could help save him.

"Don't tell me the surprise you promised me is that there's no liquor in the house," she babbled, then as he made an effort to rise she said, "Let me make it myself. I'm going to rob your Coca-cola cellar and fix a Cuba Libre. They kill me, but that's just what I want."

She ran to the kitchen, eager to get away from the disturbing picture of a gentle, kindly man turning into stone; for it seemed exactly that, a lesson to the frivolous, a check to gaiety. Not that she felt gay. She felt beaten and baffled. If she could cry on some shoulder instead of having tears boil inside her, searing, corroding every thought and impulse before she even bore them! With increasing surprise she explored almost hourly now the memorized fact of Jean-and-Steve, and it seemed to her the fact lay in the center of her thinking like a china egg in a nest, unwarmed by the heat all about it. There it was, and that was all there was to it. She had thought it could be melted away by a dozen amusing stories about it, by rage, by logic, by talking with Dol *around* it. But now Dol was past helping anyone, even himself, though the moment of terror he had given her had, it is true, frightened the fact into momentary shadow.

The kitchen, as in most of these so-called mansionette-style of dropped-living-room apartments, was up the steps off the entry hall; but before she reached it, Prudence could hear the sound of a typewriter within and hesitated, surprised. Who was staying with Dol now? What wretched little beggar was taking advantage of the too well-known hospitality? She pushed open the kitchen door and peered in.

Jefferson Abbott was seated at the white kitchen table, typing, his papers scattered about mingling with peanut shells and pencils. He was in a b.v.d. top and trousers, his bare feet hooked on the rungs of the kitchen stool, a green eyeshade over his eyes, so that on second glance she was not so sure it was he. Even before she recognized him for Jeff Abbott, she had the queer flash of self-identification, as if this man were a part of her, as if her name were on him. There was an odd expansion within her as of light suddenly let into a locked cellar, waking an old ghost. Silver City!

"Will you look at the eyebrows on the woman?" said Jeff, staring coolly at her. He got up and kissed her. "And the ermine. You've certainly streamlined yourself, haven't you, kid?"

Prudence found herself laughing hysterically. The relief of forgetting Dol in the other room and the odd sense of being completed by encounter with this long-lost self made the laughter pour out from deep inside her, as if a well, long-covered, had bubbled over again. For a while she had no feeling but sheer wonder at this slow-spreading content, remembering that this was exactly what it was like twelve years ago when she was sixteen and crazy about him and happy just being around him that summer. But there was a second feeling, a warning flash, that this was no way to control the world, this surrender to frank content was not for her, there was no safety or power in it. She drew away from him and looked him over.

"You might have streamlined your own ears," she said.

They looked each other over curiously.

"I liked you better ugly," he said. "Sit down, and I'll make some coffee. Go ahead and ask me about the home town. Your old lady is still the town talk, the mills open and shut and lay off and rehire. The daily paper folded, but I got a job on the *County Courier*. Any other questions?"

Prudence shivered.

"I have no questions, thanks just the same. I don't care if I ever hear of the place again."

"Afraid of it?"

"Don't be silly."

Afraid—yes, maybe that was it. You were afraid of your own roots. Just being with this echo of Silver City made her feel defenseless, then weakly defiant, as the town itself always had.

There it was: first you had the free sensation of being with someone who knew all about you, no need to dissemble, no need to rise above yourself; then you had the after-feeling of being betrayed, stripped of honors and parade plumes, reduced to the family pigeonhole. Yes, she was afraid of it.

"If you're ashamed of being a nightclub singer, you needn't worry," said Jeff. "Nobody knows about it back home—I didn't believe it myself till this minute."

"Ashamed?" Prudence flared up.

"Well, you certainly couldn't be proud of yourself," Jeff said frankly. "If you had waited on table like you did that time at the Beaver Hotel, you might have some cause to be proud. But hanging around that honky-tonk—I don't see how you stand it. You've changed, of course. I see it now. Too bad. You were a nice kid once."

"When?" Prudence scornfully demanded. "You know perfectly well I was never a nice kid. I'll bet Silver City still talks about the time you and I got caught necking behind the freight house."

"That's right," admitted Jeff, grinning. "I'll never forget you running down the tracks bawling."

"Why not?" Prudence bitterly recalled. "Your gang yelled at us, and you said 'Why, hello, fellas' and walked off with them leaving me all alone. You never even said anything when they called me 'Tracks' after that. I was cured of love, then, all right."

Jeff placidly blew a smoke ring.

"I was just trying you out," he said. "You were a snooty kid, and I was mighty surprised to find you were so easy."

"I suppose that was why you dropped me after that," Prudence said. "You behaved beautifully, you know."

"A fellow doesn't like a girl that lets him take her behind the freight house," he informed her. "A fellow likes a girl who boxes his ears. I was very disappointed in you, Prudence, pleased but disappointed."

Suddenly she flung her drink in his face and felt tears filling her eyes.

He wiped his face without saying a word.

"So you're the surprise Dol had for me," she cried. "A nightmare from home. Listen, I still wake up screaming, dreaming I have to go back there."

Jeff took her by the shoulders.

"What's changed you, anyway?" he asked. "What are you so darned mad about?"

"I don't know," she muttered. "Let me get out of here."

He pushed her gently down on the chair.

"Wait, I'll take you home," he said.

She sat there hating him for stirring up her dead life. He tied his shoes. In the silence they heard Dol's heavy snoring and it sounded like shutters rattling on an old forgotten house.

. . . Do Not Disturb . . .

$\mathcal{I}$ HAVEN'T THOUGHT about Steve for an hour,
exulted Prudence. That was one advantage in a thorough quarrel,
it did anesthetize you to other worries; and so Prudence did not
feel ungrateful to Jefferson Abbott. Now that he was gorging
himself on the dainty buffet Nellie had laid out, Prudence had
time to reflect that he wasn't as ugly as he seemed at first and he
was new. If Jean saw him, she'd go for him because he was new
and crude and rude, and his play might conceivably be a hit under
Hyman's reputation as producer. Indeed in one week this boy
might be the talk of New York, and, much as you hated to, you'd
simply have to recognize him. Inevitably his success appeal would
be construed as sex appeal, and he'd make a fool of himself. Oh,
inevitably! True, the run of fiction writers did not blow up under
the accolade as fast as actors or singers did, but playwrights did.
They had more chance to lose their head than novelists, since

ladies went for anybody connected with exhibitionism, and a play was flashier than a novel. Moreover a touch of theater tainted the mind like a bad fish corrupts an icebox, the gaudy twist that made them turn to dramatic form confessed the secret unstable tawdriness of their character. Women, society, politics—any of these could purchase their tinseled egos. Granted talent, motives for theatrical writing were highly materialistic, how else explain the after-the-first-hit progress of a playwright, the eager social climbing, the quick splendid marriage, the rapid overthrow of old friends? Traveling light, single, unknown, unconnected, Jefferson Abbott would have nothing to lose in his race, Prudence thought, just as she herself at the outset had had nothing to lose. It was: "Look Out, New York, Here I Come," just as it had been with her. At eighteen, though, she had been better armored for the encounter than this man was at twenty-eight. She felt suddenly sorry for him. My God, she thought, I'm getting maternal.

It was four o'clock in the morning. So this was the gala little supper for her opening, just a few of the gayest, very dearest friends, no real invitations, just last minute impulses! She couldn't imagine how it happened that the nice little celebration had turned out to be only one man eating up the caviar, complaining bitterly that there were no onion sandwiches!

The telephone had rung for a while, but Prudence did not answer it. Let Jean call! Let Steve wonder, let him fumble through his problems by himself, the double crosser! Let them figure out between them what had happened to her, let them call James Pinckney, let them pump Van, let them all be informed she was seen entering her hotel at a late hour with a strange man, a new lover, let them all go to hell. As soon as she had made this decision, she was against it, and dialed Steve's private number. No answer. She dialed his hotel number. Mr. Estabrook had been in some time but was not to be disturbed till eleven A.M. Prudence caught her breath. That was that.

She looked at her guest, now calmly reading magazines, one leg thrown over the end of the sofa. Inconceivable that this stranger, rude, surly, conceited provincial that he was, had wiped out two vital hours of her life, hours she should have been fighting Jean Nelson for Steve with all her wits. Now they were "not to be disturbed." Steve must have given in. Or had he? And why in heaven's name had she deliberately cut herself off from finding out what happened? She'd cut her nose off to spite her face so many times in her life that it was a wonder she didn't look like Bessie in *Tobacco Road*. Now she'd go crazy till morning, wondering what happened, reminded every minute by this lanky guest of the impermanence of success, the bitterness of triumph.

"Have you any money?" she asked and was instantly sorry for now of course he'd want a loan.

"I saved a little, writing on the town paper, enough to stay a while. This play'll make a lot, then I'll go live on an old farm I got my eye on outside Silver City."

"A farm?" Prudence laughed. "Is that all you want?"

"All I want is to write what I want to write in the place I want to be," said Jefferson. "I don't want a tiger rug and a yacht."

Prudence thought how wonderful this is going to sound when he sails away someday with a bouquet of fine names on a yacht. His laurel wreath withering under a tiger rug, very likely, like that Cliquot Club ad. It's really too good, she thought! Only he had to have success to give the story point, and for the sake of the future story she was almost willing to fight for him. He made coffee in her kitchen, sneered at her wine cellar with its different grades of liquor for different guests. Just wait till he came through! She must be there to see it.

"It's a trifle late," she suggested. "Why don't you spend the night in my library?"

"I told you I liked girls who boxed my ears," he said calmly. "I never yet stayed all night with a girl who asked me to."

"I said in the library," said Prudence coldly. "And by the way if I were you I'd cultivate either manners or a sense of humor. I wouldn't ask you to have both."

"I never yet found anything to laugh at in this world," said Jeff. "You never heard of a great man with a sense of humor, did you? Humor's an anesthetic, that's all, laughing gas while your guts are jerked out, your honor sold. I prefer straight thinking."

"Then you ought to have charm at least!" expostulated Prudence.

"I'd rather have BO," said Jefferson. "Charm's just a lot of work to get something that isn't worth anything anyway or charm wouldn't get it."

Prudence thought it was better to let it pass. Now he was walking around the little perfumed room she called her "library," sniffing at the low row of books, the dainty black-plumed pen, the pictures on the walls, the Marie Laurencin, the Segonzac.

"Library, ha! Three hundred books, all best-sellers, the cream of the circulating library. Who do you get to cut your leaves, Miss Bly, and who summarizes the plots for you? No, lady, when I want to stay here all night I'll ask."

Prudence poured herself a Vichy. If she took brandy, she might be genial. She did not want to be genial. No. She would keep her head, remember every word he said for that future revenge. Days when he would be sleeping with all New York. Days when the whole city would reach out warm arms to lead him further into the labyrinth, days when gentle voices would drop sweet advice to the gifted guest, lovely lips would actively declare their longing for him and him alone, and presently he, too, would be devoured by poisonous wisdom, he, too, would lie in wait for new knights, new Amazons to seduce, and the victory banners for the Golden City would fly as high as its rivers ran dark and deep.

"I'll give a party in your honor the day the play opens," said Prudence thoughtfully. "I'll get Bertram Flees to give it with me.

That puts you on the society page right away, and you're made."

"I'll make myself, if you don't mind," said Jefferson. "Since when does the society page have anything to do with the drama?"

Prudence laughed nastily.

"My dear innocent, since when has the drama got anything to do with the drama?" she inquired. "A society page pet can turn out a painting or play and it's automatically a Rembrandt or an Ibsen. The whole system is behind it. So don't be an ass; let me help put you in the proper golden frame."

"It's complete rot," said Jefferson, and it annoyed her that he went on leafing through *Time* as if she was a child teasing for candy.

"You admit you need clothes," she said. "You might get away with that rugged style if you were Montana but my dear boy you're only Ohio. Practically a suburb. The first thing is evening clothes. And you'd better make up your mind right away which side you're on."

"What do you mean?"

"Your morality may be misconstrued, you know. Even Galahad's was."

"What are you getting at?"

"Of course, if you really want success more than anything, go on living with Dol. Most of the boys around town find they get farther that way. But maybe you're still Silver City enough to mind talk."

Jefferson poured the last of the coffee in his own coffee cup, though she had pushed hers toward him.

"Why should I care about talk?" he said. "Dol's a generous, fine person. I don't even believe that stuff about him and even if I did—"

"You'll find out," said Prudence. Now she was quietly furious with this young man who felt so arrogant, so secure, so damnably sure of himself, as if he could stand where others fell, as if he belonged to some Olympian race that was unaffected by human problems. "Do you think everyone is seduced merely by their own lust? You're seduced through pity, through fatigue, through failure, or maybe by sheer conventionality. You, for instance, are so conventional you'll probably end up doing whatever some conventional old rake proposes."

Jefferson got up and picked up his hat. He stood looking down at her very coldly.

"You're a horrid little girl," he said. "You always were. I don't know why or how I got you in my system. The chances are I won't see you again, so good-night, and, I hope, good-bye."

"You think you don't need the things other people need," said Prudence. "You're so fine you don't need publicity or the right people or being seen at the right places. You'll see. Right this minute I could show you that I myself could get a play produced, and it would get better notices than yours just because I play the game and you don't."

"It would be lousy, too," said Jefferson, unmoved.

"All the better proof that it isn't the play that counts," said Prudence, now very angry indeed. The telephone rang.

"Who are these guys that call you up all night?" exploded Jefferson. "My God, what a nasty life you live!"

"There'll come a time, my pet," said Prudence. "You'll re-member me."

She watched his proud march to the door, high bony shoul-ders lifted even higher, coat sleeves and trousers skimping a good inch too short; how could anyone so awkwardly assembled be so damned complacent? Banging the door behind him, too! No one had made her so mad in years, absolutely no one since—yes, since he left her crying behind the freight house in Silver City!

"Pig," breathed Prudence. "I'll show him."

She picked up the shrieking telephone.

. . . terribly, terribly happy . . .

DINKY WAS FOR LUCK. His rosy, sly little face
was the first shock you encountered in Steve's apartment. His
little sailor suit and cap with *S.S. Dakota* on it was the conventional uniform for the boys of his school which was the school for
ventriloquists' dummies. Dinky had been a prop in Steve's ear-
liest appearances on the Mutual Wheel, and every time Steve had
tried to discard him for a classier act, the act had failed, until
Steve grew afraid that without Dinky he was a flop. Without the
Dinky act he was only a beachcomber in front of the Palace.

"Go back to the doll act, Steve," the agent used to say. "It's not
good but it's not bad. They book it, anyway, that's something.
Looks like you can't get anywhere without it."

"It's a jinx," Steve used to say, but he saved his band finally by
sticking the dummy in it with a sax and after a while he gave up
trying to get rid of it; he looked on Dinky in time as the only

stable thing in his life, the only real friend who could get him out of scrapes. He owed his radio job to Dinky and used him once in a while over the air in the saxophone solo act, not for the radio public's sake but for luck's sake. He kept him in a place of honor in his bare modernistic apartment on Beekman Place and had gotten in the habit of holding long private conversations with him. In the main Dinky was a hard-boiled answer to Steve's doubts and, though at first a slave to Steve's whim, presently took on a will of his own that sometimes frightened Steve. He jeered, spoke out of turn, phrased secret thoughts, spared no one, kept up Steve's courage in a racket that required it. Now that he had made a name for himself in radio, people asked why he had the doll around; there wasn't room for two Charlie McCarthys; but Steve was ashamed to explain his superstition about Dinky or his ever-increasing need for someone, if it was only a doll, that he could be on the level with. Women sometimes thought it was a little queer for a man to be so loyal to a doll, it wasn't quite normal, they didn't like it. Steve let them think what they would, played up to their apprehensions sometimes, out of sheer self-protection. He never explained, though once in a while when Dinky was voicing all of Steve's thoughts and not merely the selected ones, many of them thoughts he did not know he had till he heard them spoken, he asked himself if, perhaps, this strange radio life wasn't driving him nuts.

"Well, bud, if you're nuts, I'm nuts too," Dinky whined out before Steve realized it, "and think what a stunt we could put on at Bloomingdale's."

The apartment itself had an unpleasantly mechanistic personality, being post-depression gaga from pantry to sunroom. Steel and glass and onyx gleamed and repelled the eye on every hand, aluminum Venetian shades sliced the walls like knives, monobased, tufted, red and white leather chairs promised nothing to the Edwardian rump; the pseudo-Dali screen and the Miro above the fireplace gave no encouragement to feminine visitors hoping to see their own photographs or a few indications of sentimentality rising above streamlined decorative scheme. No, the room was as soulless as Dinky, an ideal home for robots. Steve's valet was quite as Martian a figure as Dinky, a bleak, bald, rigid little man named Beals, who popped in and out when a bell was pushed, like a mechanical Mephisto. The black bedroom with its white leather bed was an added warning to ladies who hoped to find a chink in the baffling gentleman's armor. No, here was a man who took but was not to be taken. The evidence of the Iron Man was here, but only Jean Nelson ignored it. She loved Iron Men. She thought they were perfect darlings.

"But he's adorable!" cried Jean, sweeping Dinky to her chiffon breast, her white fox cape falling unheeded in her impetuosity.

"Who's the dame?" *sotto-voced* Dinky. "Thought you was resting up, old boy."

"Steve, you didn't! . . . It was exactly as if the words came from his mouth!"

"Just a gift," said Steve. "I'll get us a drink."

What to do until the trunks came, he wondered—she *had* mentioned trunks. In the bedroom Steve called the desk. If any trunks came, send them right back where they came from. He sat for a moment, his hand on the telephone wondering what to do. He'd been in jams before but not like this. A drink and a phone call—was that all that could save the day? He tried to remember how he had extricated himself in other messes. You had to have a pal for this sort of thing, and he hadn't had a pal since he got in the big money. A wise, dandy old boy, the sort who in the old days instructed you how to lure women to your rooms and in these days told you how to get them out. That was the pal he needed. There was Prudence, usually.

"Jean," he called. "Does Prudence know what's happened?"

Prudence might help, even if she was sore.

Jean, still clasping Dinky to her arms, trailed into the bedroom.

"Of course," she murmured. "Prudence was the one to suggest it."

Steve's jaw dropped.

"Oh, she did, did she?"

"She said it was the only clean-cut decent thing to do. Go to him, she said, Steve needs you more than Harvey does."

"Prudence said that, did she?"

Jean took the telephone from Steve's hands.

"What are you thinking about, Steve?"

"Just thinking you looked a little like Gladys Cooper. No, it's someone else, Binnie Barnes. No. My mistake. Dietrich herself. Who are you calling?"

"Harvey," said Jean. "I just want to let him hear my voice. Even if he's given me up he's entitled to something of me."

But for some reason Harvey wasn't home. Not home at three in the morning? Did Steve suppose Harvey had done away with himself after sending his wife to a rival? Steve looked at the telephone with narrow eyes. Something dirty about this. Very dirty. He was the goat in it. The big-hearted husband was laughing his head off—where? The solution was simple. It was Harvey's week squiring the blond receptionist at the Studios. She had a nice little apartment, too. Steve knew the number.

"Try Gramercy 3-1001," he suggested softly. "The Studio Club."

Jean didn't know Harvey had such a club, but she dialed. Yes, Mr. Nelson was there. Or, no, he wasn't. Or, wait a minute. Or, yes.

"I just wanted you to know I was happy, dear," cooed Jean. "I just want you to carry on. Try to forget me."

"That's a mighty nice little club of Harvey's," said Steve.

It was a frame-up, he thought bitterly, a damnable frame-up. His sponsor fobs his wife off on him, and he daren't insult the man by turning her out. Men were very sensitive about how their wives were treated by the boyfriends; and, of course, in this case there was his job at stake. But what in God's name was he to do with the woman? Jean dialed again.

"I must tell Prudence how happy I am," she said. "It's wonderful to have made a decision at last. Of course, I owe it to her as much as to Harvey."

It was Prudence, who had set this thing. After Jean had bleated out that unfortunate bit of news about the surreptitious and fairly casual affair good old Prudence had to have her revenge. Let him eat cake and have it too, she had probably said. Nobody but Prudence would have planned such a diabolical revenge, and Steve ruefully had to admire the little fiend as usual. Go to Steve, he needs you, she had cooed to Jean, knowing well enough what a spot it would put him in, knowing, too, that nobody wanted to encore an affair dead three years ago, let alone go through a scandal for its sake.

"Prudence isn't home," said Jean. "How queer! She was going to have a party, and I knew she would miss us there. So I wanted to tell her we just had to be alone on our first night together."

"Alone with our telephone," said Steve. "Pardon me while I call up James Pinckney and tell him I'm terribly happy. And then it will be your turn to call up. We'll have another telephone put in during the first busy days of the honeymoon."

"I do think I should call Harvey again," reflected Jean. "He sounded so desperate."

"Do that," urged Steve. "Give him a call. It's hardly four o'clock, he hasn't shut his eyes yet."

"Funny I never heard him mention that club," said Jean.

"Oh, no," said Steve. "It's changed every few months, you see. Last summer it was a Plaza number. Myrtle was the custodian, then."

"That's right, call up the old man," said Dinky, "and what's the matt with having him come over for brek?"

"Harvey, dear," Jean choked into the phone. "I just wanted to tell you this is one of the biggest, finest things you've ever done. Steve wants to thank you, too. Here, Steve."

Steve reluctantly faced the mouthpiece thrust at him.

"Thanks," he said briefly.

"We're terribly happy, Harvey," said Jean. "We went to the Voodoo dancers after Prudence and to Hamburger Mary's and now we're here all alone. Steve wants to tell you how happy he is."

"Awfully happy, old man," Steve barked into the phone.

"You sound so tired and miserable, Harvey dear. Take a couple of luminal, why don't you, if you can't sleep. . . . You did? . . . I hope they work. I'll call back in a little while and see if they did."

There were a few ways of getting women out once you got them in, Steve recalled: (a) You said "let's drive down to the Battery in the dawn and see the sunrise," a romantic suggestion that challenged the lady's youth and spirit of whimsey; or (b) you said "let's go to Coney Island and have breakfast at the Half Moon with hot clam broth"; or (c) you said "let's go wake up old So-and-so," a devilishly hilarious suggestion, and, of course, once out of doors on any of these counts you scooted to a Turkish bath, and she was bound to look sufficiently messy to want her own bath and new makeup. But here was a double problem. Prudence had planned this little mix-up and was probably smiling in her sleep to think how well she had avenged herself on her false lover. Well, he would teach her a lesson. She was smart enough to surmise that nobody could stand Jean's lovely sweetness for more than a couple of weeks—look at Harvey!—and thought she was putting something over. The only way to get even was to fool her, urge Jean to stay forever, put on Jean's own act of dewy joy.

Jean, having shown her love for Dinky, now allowed the little monster to fall face down on the floor.

"Lady, have a heart," burbled Dinky, "no fair pushing."

Jean was trying to get Prudence again.

"I'll talk to her," said Stephen. He was rather startled to see that Jean had modestly finished off a stiff highball, the steenth during the evening but then female drinking was on such an Olympian scale nowadays he shouldn't have been surprised, especially since her passion for the telephone was always a sure sign.

"I just wanted to tell you Steve and I are together," he heard Jean say as this time Prudence answered. "Oh, darling, I'm so thrilled. And Dinky! Just like our own little boy."

"A dummy," Steve could hear Prudence say.

"We've been having a wonderful time. We didn't stay at the Vedado, dear, because we wanted to be alone, just quiet, you know. So we went to the Voodoo dancers, just the two of us. . . . Heavenly. Darling, I wish you'd come and see us. I mean right now."

"No!" cried Steve and then passed on the word to Dinky, who merely whistled. Steve snatched the phone. "Don't you dare come here."

Jean looked at him like a wounded doe.

"But I adore Prudence. Prudence, dear, I want to see you, I must. I have loads to tell you. If Steve won't let you come here, I'll come there. Of course, I will, dear. Of course! This very minute. Instantly."

The white fox cape was over the beautiful sloping shoulders again, the nose repowdered, the lips examined.

"Why, Steve, look, my lipstick isn't even messed!"

"The telephone was very careful," explained Steve.

"And let me tell you, you're not going to Prudence's, and let her have the laugh."

Jean stared, moist-eyed, at him.

"Prudence needs me, Steve," she said in a choked voice. "Just because I'm happy I mustn't forget my dearest friend. Prudence is so lonely, she says."

It was unbelievable and outrageous. Steve seized her in his arms. It was no use. Of course she loved him. Hadn't she given up Harvey, everything for him? Now Prudence needed her. Prudence came first. All alone there the very night of her opening. And besides Jean had so many things to tell her.

"You can play with Dinky till I get back," said Jean. "You dear, dear boy."

She floated out in a cloud of violet fragrance. Steve placed Dinky firmly in his chair again.

"Boy, have you been framed by those two hairpins," said Dinky. "What a dish they made out of you! Can you take it, pard? Another dame can get your women away from you? Don't make me sneer."

"It's Prudence's work. Hers and Harvey's. The whole thing from beginning to end," said Steve. The hell with all of them. He was suddenly inspired to dial the Gramercy number and shout into the transmitter, "Harvey, old man, I just wanted to say I'm terribly, terribly happy and thanks just loads."

"There," he sighed and lying back on the white leather bed fell promptly off to sleep, square chin nestling in the wings of his collar, one little paddy round his highball glass, and Dinky toppling over on his tummy.

. . . Manhattan Left-Over . . .

𝒯HE MAN NOBODY remembered ran through the
rain up Sixth Avenue as if he was going somewhere, as if he had an
appointment, very important, Harms, Berlin, Waters, must not be
kept waiting. At street corners red lights stopped him, and this was
bad; for in these pauses he must wonder where he was going, where
and what next? But this was not as bad as the sunny days when a
false benevolence masked the sky, promising rewards for everyone,
Bank Night every day, "step right up on the platform and receive
the money, every player a winnah." The sun shines, the band plays
Dixie, the city cheers, the prize once won can be won again. No, the
storm was much better than the radiant betrayal, for it was an in-
convenience to all alike, rich man, poor man, no preference here, no
racketeering in lightning; Gleason, the crooning songwriter, yesterday's darling, whose name was already forgotten, received exactly
as much thunder and lightning as Irving Berlin or Bing Crosby,

even more, for in his zeal to get his full share of something in this world he had gotten soaked to the skin. Up Sixth Avenue, across Thirty-ninth Street, up Fifth—he dared Fifth Avenue only in this disguise of rain—and at the corner of Fifth and Forty-first, southeast corner right by a fireplug Gleason found a penny.

Luck! A signal from the gypsies that the new day was here, the pennies from heaven were being tossed on Arch Gleason once again, pennies from heaven and nuts to you. Up Fifth Avenue across—

The rain veiled the city, swirled stone and steel in gray. A fire engine rushed out of nowhere and attacked the town, its *"wuhuhuhu"* sang through the wind and thunder, *"wuhuwuhu-hu"*; it left skyscrapers rustling like paper screens, buildings that stood firm under hurricane cringed under dissonance, *"wuhuwuhu,"* where's the fire, the fire—the shrill joyous query threaded through dogs barking, trucks roaring, babies crying, rushed in a cloud of bells up here, down there, then somewhere far off in Chelsea its lust for flame was appeased, the sound died into a clatter of rain hoofs on pavement and roof.

The noon chimes soared in the fog, angel voices floated over the great town, Presbyterian and Episcopal bells sang in metallic close harmony like the Boswell Sisters, they sang of the Redeemer, an elegant white-tie Redeemer from an old Virginia family, Mr. Rockefeller's personal Redeemer, purveyor also to Their Majesties. Dim Gothic doorways, naked without their rich wedding canopies said "Welcome, This church is never closed," welcome to velvet hush, the canonical whisper, the ecclesiastical cough, the damp handclasp, the camphorated air, the chill drafts from fluttering vestments.

Outside, the homeless, in paper-thin suits, collars pulled up, hats yanked down, scuttled along, dodging the great benign open door as if it were a manhole, a trap; freedom for them was only in the rain, the sweet rain for rich and poor alike, truth was only in thunder and swift rip of lightning; here were the angel voices unmasked, here was Truth, the terror that ruled beyond skies, high over cathedral spires; here was the loneliness that nipped through the little men's lives like winter wind—this they knew, and this, for them, was Truth.

The penny from heaven was not to be spent, not to drop in the peanut slot machine in the shop entrance, it was for luck. The man who once entertained thousands, who helped Prudence Bly get her first job, ran across Fifty-third Street, invisible in the rain; when he reached in his pocket for the lucky penny, it was gone, fallen through a hole in the trousers, and it was damned, damned unfair, a lousy cheap trick. Tears of rage came into the man's eyes, a lousy trick; and now as he ran, he grew angrier and angrier, he swelled, he grew, rage blew him bigger and bigger, there was no limit to his fury, it was bottomless, skyless; Olympian he stalked, immense, larger than the tallest building, not an ounce of fear or hunger left in him now, nothing but rage, hate, a giant now, the Enemy, the Enemy of the Town.

As if they recognized him as Foe, the desk clerk at the River Hotel an hour later hesitated to send him up to Miss Bly. As the shabby dripping figure stalked through the lobby, people drew aside to let him pass, they snatched their skirts back, they glanced quickly away as if a look was contamination; here was Failure, the Enemy, merely to brush against him was misfortune.

To Prudence his mere name spoiled her day. Ten years ago that name for a season or two had spelled the same magic as her own did now, but look at him! A wreck, a reminder that this could happen to the mightiest. What had he done that was wrong, what possible warning could he give? He had done the right things, as she herself knew them; he had kissed the proper fingers, insulted the proper people, gone to the right places at the right time, achieved the proper professional mixture of insolence and mocking servility. Ah, yes, he had made the mistake of having TB for a while, long enough to get broke and pathetic, out-of-date. No one, least of all Prudence, wished to be reminded that luck knew no rules, gave no prizes for good behavior.

"I only have a minute, Archie," said Prudence.

If he wanted money, she would give him twenty. Or maybe ten. Better still let him borrow twenty with a quick date for its return, so he would feel too guilty in not paying it back ever to bother her again.

"I've written a new song," said Archie. "No one will buy it. God damn them, why won't they? They used to beg for my stuff."

Prudence reflected.

"I might use it," she said. Of course, she could not use it. But this was pure blackmail. "Would you sell it to me for fifty dollars?"

"Fifty dollars?"

His mouth opened. The least a person could do when poor was to have his teeth fixed. That was only fair to others. It was horrible looking at Archie's toothless mouth. Indecent.

"Bring it up tomorrow," she said. "I can always try out a new song."

"Prudence," he was sobbing in her lap now. "You are so good. Oh God, how good you are."

It was gruesome, a man whimpering in your lap that way. Prudence shuddered. She struggled to her feet, and he kept his face buried in the chair pillows, his shoulders shaking with sobs. Sofa ran out from the bedroom and barked at the strange spectacle. She wanted to give him a hundred, anything to stop this torture—well, twenty anyway, though probably five would do well enough in his present condition. This inner bargaining, she thought, that's just what Jeff says all of us do, so she hastily said, "Here's twenty, and you can ask the desk to give you the rest on your way out."

"Oh God, how good you are," he went on moaning. A horrible little man, horrible. Prudence sat shivering after he left, just thinking about him, that once he had been in her place, but she would never, never be in his! Never.

. . . the basket on the doorstep . . .

$\mathcal{J}$AMES PINCKNEY was having a very odd experience. He was not at all sure how to classify the strange emotions that kept his stomach seething and roaring but approximately he decided they were the dawn of his paternal instinct. Here he was sewing buttons on a lad's trousers and a half-hour before he had darned a sock, not beautifully, of course, he had merely bunched the thing up and whacked at it with a needle and thread; but still his heart had been in the right place. He had stolen a look from time to time to the bedroom door behind which the miracle snored, the little fellow left in a basket on Scrooge Pinckney's door yesterday daybreak. The little man in there had a way of throwing off his covers, horrifying James by careless exhibitions of anatomy. But what touched the gnarled economical heart of Pinckney was that the boy had come to him of his own free will. With all the rich, celebrated eager bachelors to choose from in all New York, the lad had silently turned to ugly, unrenowned Pinckney, had knocked at his door at dawn, asked to be taken in. James was dumfounded, had stood in his door in flannel pajamas, long bony feet in woolen slippers, for he was always cold, a great hot-water-bottle man even in late spring.

"But why don't you go to Mr. Lloyd? You've been living there all these months," James piped up.

"No, sir," said the young man firmly. He was drunk, no doubt of that, still he did know what he was doing. "Dol won't have my friends there, so Dol can't have me. I'm through."

Through with Dol Lloyd! James could not control the sudden elation at winning Dol's protégé away from him, for he had admired Dol for years, hoped to be like him someday. He was always conscious of his own shortcomings, a mother had pointed them out to him so frequently years before, and it seemed to him the greatest compliment of his life to have, without lifting a finger, lured Dol's charge away from him.

"Come in," he said, and Bert Willy entered his life like that, passed out on the bed, and was still there when James returned from the Museum the next evening. Without anything being said, James realized Bert was now as established a figure in his ménage as Sebastian the Persian. Now he was a settled man, he thought, rather proud, rather frightened, and what a responsibility having won someone away from a far superior, infinitely more distinguished man. So James's veins burbled with a curious mixture of joy and fear and pride. Part of the fear lay in his stinginess; he could not help a little gasp when he found himself buying two chops instead of one at the market, a half dozen eggs instead of three white Leghorn signed beauties. In fact he considered now throwing his trade to the A&P; he could creep in there early in the morning, no one would know, only he did enjoy economizing de luxe at the Ambassador Market. "And a kidney, please, for Sebastian," he was wont to command. "A beef kidney. Not that one, no, no, I must have a delicate one.

"James!" said James to himself breathlessly, "This is the turning point!"

He detached himself from his own body briefly, a habit he had, and looked fondly down at himself, hovering above himself like a kind fairy godmother about to change things into other things. He enjoyed these detached tender scrutinies of himself, shook his head now over his paternal palpitations, observed the thinning hair on his scalp, but was touched by the innocent eager eyes under the uncontrollably bushy blond brows. Dear, dear boy, he thought, dear amusing Pinckney!

Living alone all these years, he had really never been lonely for he talked and felt about himself as a very quixotic charming friend, and wherever he went, he watched his own reactions as if he were his own little pet, too precious to be consigned to the baggage car, rather to be tenderly born on the lap. When he took his first trip—the Dalmatian Coast and Antibes—he was not alone; he was taking that charming eccentric Pinckney, and taking him right, too, amused at his naïve astonishments.

James was a faintly funereal wag, he believed in fun that was more grisly than good-natured; he reeked of moth balls and old ladies, expected cancer with a wry smile, welcomed decent calamity with calm, so long as it was something slow and fatal and respectable rather than garish and dramatic. One wouldn't want to be shot, for instance. He had achieved his assistantship, or whatever title his rather vague unimportance was at the Museum, without trouble, wrote reports in a beautiful longhand, and by some fluke, and also his own talk, was considered Pinckney the Littérateur. Like so many other gifted young men, he had slipped somehow into one of Henry James's lesser mantles, assuming with authority the role of dean of letters without ever going to the bother of writing. This slight lapse in preparation for his present dignified reputation in local belles-lettres passed unnoticed, for by this time those of his own generation—those bright precocious meteors in the literary sky of the '20s—had all stopped writing anyway, so really one could not tell which brilliant man once wrote a fine novel and which had merely intended to do so. At any rate serious old ladies who floated in the Museum's wake deferred to James Pinckney on all counts. What did James say about *Winterset?* What did James think of *Good-by, Mr. Chips?* Before he went to a dinner, James prepared his opinions, phrased them neatly, organized his mind in such an ingenious fashion that no matter from what angle it was approached, it could throw off a penetrating comment. Once in a great while, purely for a lark, he would say to himself, "Tonight, let's just follow the stream for the fun of it, let's see where it runs without me to guide it," and it was gratifying to see in what bogs and aimless deserts the conversation would meander without the deft Pinckney guidance.

Now James looked at Bert Willy's long pale hairless leg dangling from the side of the bed and reflected that Bert in his dumb, inarticulate boyish way, had admired this conversational mastery for a long time, had, perhaps, heard Pinckney quoted, found him sharper than Dol's pedantic angle, so that the unaffected appeal to his hospitality was the flattering appeal of a lost boy looking for a proper teacher. Definitely D. O. Lloyd had not been that. James thought, my goodness, this queer unsettled feeling in my stomach (it was something like an unborn burp) must be happiness!

He got up from the sewing rocker that had been his mother's, as indeed most of his simple black walnut pieces had been, except for his darling Biedermeier dresser that he had bought from his own hoardings at Flattau's, and tiptoed over to the kitchenette. He dropped one, two—no, three (with a gasp) slices of Irish bacon into the frying pan, lit the flame once again beneath the no longer bubbling percolator. Through a crack in the half-open door, he watched the effect of these magic rites on the exposed bare leg in the bedroom. As the bacon began to zizz, sending out through the dampish dark rooms its little gastronomic birdcall, the toes of the foot spread out startled, fanwise; the coffeepot cleared its throat and sent out strange little adenoidal hiccups and now the knee flexed, a hand flung itself over the side of the bed. Craftily James clucked for Sebastian the Persian, and the beautiful little walking rug under the bed arched its blue tail so that it brushed the dangling fingers of the sleeping boy, then strolled exquisitely toward the kitchen door. Mr. Willy drew in foot and hand. There was a cough, a hangover groan, then a waking silence. James decided it was the moment.

"Breakfast!" he chirruped sunnily.

"OK" grunted the little stranger and threw the covers off the bed.

. . . woman with a purpose . . .

$\mathcal{J}$EAN'S TRUNKS WERE in Prudence's basement, the spoils of two marriages hung in Prudence's closets.

"And when we're terribly old, dear," said Jean, "we can run over to Vienna together and have horse glands or something grafted on, so we'll always be young."

"You don't think we'd better take a run over right now?" inquired Prudence. "It doesn't seem fair to our friends to pop out with animal spirits thirty years too late."

Jean shook her head lovingly at her friend. She was lying on the chaise lounge, all bathed and cologned and newly curled, ready for her intellectual hour that consisted of talking about life while holding a book.

"You never have a serious thought, do you? That's what I love about you, Prudence."

Prudence, preferring the chaise lounge, was doing her nails a gaudy lobster shade at her dressing table.

"Of course, I have serious thoughts, Jean, but I don't call them that. I call them clichés and try to skip them just like the English teacher said."

"Clichés?"

"Of course. Is life worth while, is there a divine destiny, am I getting the most out of my life, and so on. If that's what you mean by serious thoughts."

Jean laughed indulgently.

"Darling, you *are* funny. No, I mean—well—now in a way it *is* what I mean. For instance, when I'm feeling awfully well, no hangovers, no snuffles, I just naturally have to think seriously. It's my Teutonic ancestry. This morning I thought, here I am, happy at last, living with Prudence, no men's things messing around, but I must do something worth while, I must make something of my life. I'm not content to just be happy and be sort of a parasite. I want to do things."

"What do you want to do, honey?"

Jean raised herself on her arms to accent her earnestness.

"I want to open a little shop," she said firmly, "a little shop off Madison Avenue."

"What kind of a shop?"

"That's just it," mourned Jean, allowing herself to droop back among the cushions again. "That's the whole trouble. I haven't the ghost of a notion. Something attractive and chic, though. Like—hum—oh, those nut and marshmallow bonbons."

"There are some left," said Prudence. "The box is under the table there."

Jean eagerly reached for the box, which had been gnawed and rifled by Sofa, but a few heavenly morsels remained, and these she thoughtfully devoured.

"I think I'll call Harvey and ask him if he'll stake me to a little shop," reflected Jean. "He'll see I'm really serious about it. And, of course, he ought to be grateful that I come to him instead of to Steve for help."

"It hardly seems fair to Steve," said Prudence. "You consult Harvey about everything and only call up Steve four or five times a day. What must Steve think?"

"I'm disgusted with Steve," said Jean. "A man who will talk to a doll all night when you're calling on him! And have the doll answer back the most insulting things! Besides the man knows I care more for my friendship with you than for him. I told him so."

"You did?" crowed Prudence. God keep James Pinckney from me tonight, she prayed, so I don't tell him that wonderful bit! She held no grudge against James for gossiping about herself and Steve; she was only mad at Steve for causing her to lose her poise that way, upsetting her little applecart of feelings, letting jealousy, pride, love roll all over the gutter for everyone to laugh at! All she could do was make him learn his lesson and himself be laughed at.

Last night he had come to the club at closing time for her. When she saw him, Prudence had the familiar delight at sight of his big shoulders, excellent tweeds, thick bullish head, but she remembered Paris three years ago—that little idyl now stained by Jean's shy confession of her simultaneous idyl at Marjorca. Prudence could not tell whether her pride was most stabbed by the infidelity or by this simple evidence that she was as blind a fool as any other woman where her lover was concerned. Anyway the anger she felt was unquestioned, for it swept her first pleasure into fury, the sight of Stephen was then only a signal for new war maneuvers. She would twist the knife, she would make him cry "enough." The only difficulty was that Steve was as tough as she was; the ordinary weapons wouldn't work, and even the special attack could not stab the public-calloused heart, it would only cause a mild squirm or two. So she did not join him at the bar for her nightcap after her final encore as she used to do but waved prettily to him and went directly to her dressing room for her cape. He met her in the lobby.

"Changing back into a pumpkin so soon?" he asked.

"I must, Steve," she said primly. "You see Jeanie is waiting for me.

"I heard she'd moved in with you," said Steve. "Look here, Prudence, what the devil have you got up your sleeve? If you're trying to get even for that little business with Jean three years ago, I could remind you of a couple of episodes that same spring that *I'm* willing to overlook. That Argentinian heel, for instance."

Prudence had forgotten all about that little inconsequential affair, she had deliberately erased it at the time as that was the year she was tasting loyalty and faithfulness to one man and a few hours with the Argentinian didn't count. As a matter of fact, it hadn't been a real infidelity at all for she had been so busy describing her rapturous idyl with Steve that she honestly hadn't noticed what the sympathetic Argentinian was up to. Anyway South Americans didn't count. And it had nothing to do with Steve and Jean Nelson.

"If you overlooked it, then it isn't worth discussing," said Prudence. "But I couldn't overlook Jean."

"I tell you that was nothing," insisted Steve, following her out through the entrance hall. "Just that you would keep that apartment so stuffy I had to run out once in a while for a little air."

"So Jean was a little air!—Darling, let's not fuss about it. The only thing that matters is that Jean *was* saved from you. I'm far too fond of her to let her throw herself away."

At the revolving doors she paused.

"You see, Steve, you don't know what close friends women can be. They're much closer than men wish they were, that's why men are always running down women friendships, trying to break them up and all. I simply can't let Jean throw herself away on you."

"As if you could stop her," jeered Steve, incredulous.

"Couldn't I?" said Prudence and braved the revolving doors, Steve right beside her crowding into her section.

"What do you mean by that?" he demanded.

"Well," answered Prudence, lowering her eyes, "you see you thought I was jealous about you, that time."

"You certainly sounded that way over the telephone."

"It was Jean, don't you see?"

"I'll be damned."

Prudence, quietly smiling, climbed into his car. A little later he was appalled at this insolence; she had used his chauffeur for years with his blessing but after a crack like her last one it took a hell of a nerve to drive off waving a gossamer handkerchief from his own car window.

"You get right back here, John," he shouted, but neither Prudence nor the driver gave any indication of having heard. There was nothing to do but call up Jean and ask her out for a drink, but here again he was stymied.

"I can't let Prudence come home to an empty apartment," Jean said sweetly. "Of *course,* I couldn't come to your house, silly, at this hour."

As if he hadn't wondered how ever to get her *out* of his house the other night! It was all too baffling for a simple man and extremely ungratifying. Steve was astonished to find waves of puritanical indignation welling up his bosom, a what-is-this-age-coming-to-feeling and a conviction that he should have voted Republican swept over him.

Like all victories over the beloved, this one was tasteless and Prudence had been obliged to make up for its emptiness by heckling Jean. But heckling Jean was like heckling a moonbeam, there was no percentage in it whatever. The only pleasure was in flattering the girl so that she spun around in circles of joy—this at least was one or two up on Steve.

"What are you thinking about, beautiful?" Prudence inquired as a faintly troubled frown appeared on Jean's broad brow. "And what *is* that book? Isn't it just a little too big for you?"

"It's somebody's autobiography," said Jean. "It's quite good, but I don't seem to get very far. It makes you stop and think. So I was thinking I had better buy a lot of things today before Harvey gets cross with me and stops my charge accounts. That's what Fred Zimmer did, you know, when I left him. Men can be fiends when they want to be. That's why it's so divine living with you, Prudence. I certainly am through with men."

"If you could just see this Jefferson Abbott," sighed Prudence. "He is exactly your type—tall, rough, clean-cut, tweedy, deep baritone voice that makes you shiver it's so divinely brutal, a playwright, besides."

Jean's nostrils quivered like a bloodhound's getting the scent.

"But he's yours, Prudence. I'd love him, of course. But he's yours, and you know how I am about things like that. Then it's so romantic for you, having been childhood sweethearts that way."

Prudence held out her nails, dipped in witches' blood, for admiration. She clopped off in furry mules into the living room, turned on the gramophone. Her own repertoire in twelve records began filling the air. Jean, with all sorts of big thoughts on the tip of her tongue, wondered fretfully how long she would have to live with Prudence before she would dare speak out loud during these canned recitals. It had taken her, she recalled rather hopelessly, over a year of marriage to dare interrupt Harvey's crossword puzzles. There was nothing to do but turn the pages of her book, which it turned out was about a dancer really. She detested all forms of ballet and all of its exponents. Having loyally carried the book with her for months, including one Panama cruise and one Palm Beach fortnight, Jean felt properly outraged at finally discovering its secret subject and threw it across the room, observing savagely that even Sofa wouldn't dare touch it.

So she called up Harvey, who was wound up in ticker tape somewhere below the city's belt, and she told him to be sure to keep up his Hornybrook stomach exercises, the ones Arnold Bennett practiced, he mustn't let himself sag just because she was out of his life. She didn't mention the little shop just then, partly because it was not the right moment and partly because she'd forgotten all about it.

. . . man with a future . . .

$\mathcal{V}$AN DEUSEN, chamois gloves in hand, walked springily down Seventh Avenue, regretting that he left his cane in some bar, since the day, the mood, the man, all screamed for a cane. He had been shopping for halls. He had, in a lofty manner, requested "someone in authority" to permit him to look over Steinway Hall, he had followed a not too impressed young woman into the concert hall, had poked at chairs, hummed and hawed, unbuttoned his gloves and flapped them together, twisted his mustache, cocked his head, finally cleared his throat regretfully.

"Hmm, I'm rawther afraid it's too small. Barely enough for two hundred people, isn't it? Hmmm—and this would be five hundred dollars, eh? I see. Hmmm—too small, I'm afraid. Not your fault, of course. Yes, I'd better get Town Hall or Carnegie."

So he had crossed the street and routed out a venerable man who allowed him to examine the dank interior of Carnegie.

"Hmm—These seats seem a bit out of line. You see what I mean. I shall be there—you see I like my piano a trifle to the left of the one there now. Hmm—Steinway—I shall want a Mason Hamlin this time, of course. Hmm—I don't know whether I can play in this atmosphere. A touch gloomy. Six-fifty, eh. Yes, it is gloomy. I only wish I had the little hall where I played in Paris. Van Deusen is the name. Hmm—A touch *too* gloomy. Not your fault, of course."

Outside he stood judiciously studying the bulletin board as if selecting a nice location for his own name, then he swung briskly round the corner. He could run into Dol's, of course, but then how much nicer to drop in later and lightly announce his concert plans definitely made; it would be a small triumph over that little group of Dol's that seemed so scornful of his ever really coming through with anything. Yes, he'd wait. In front of the Wellington he had a sudden vision of having done this same thing before, covered the same course; why, by God he had!—Steinway, Carnegie, Town Hall, then stinko for weeks till the whole thing was off and he had to get out of town for a season till friendly contempt had blown over and the hard-won backer been pacified. In that very minute he knew he would muff this chance, too, he might as well pack his bag right now. In fact the Brents were being very coolish lately, but then they were neither rich enough nor artistic enough to be out and out rude to a guest. In almost every country Van had cultivated a few average, unrecommended middle-class family friends for that very reason: they never threw you out, they never were sarcastic, and all you needed to do was feed them a good story once in a while about some big shot. It seemed to him that at every window along Seventh Avenue people were watching him, saying, "There's a man whose hands are shaking so he couldn't play a damn note if he tried, as a matter of fact this very morning he had the wheelies so bad he couldn't face Nora Brent and had to cower in his bed till she went out; yes, that's the man who thinks he's going to stage a big comeback."

To foil these imaginary detractors Van stood still and by tremendous concentration lit a cigarette with a magnificently controlled hand. There! On to Town Hall, and there he would see if the Green Room suited his intermission mood. He stole a look at himself in a window and followed himself with fascination through shopwindows for blocks. He definitely was a figure in a million, he thought, a man about to knock musical New York off its feet. Look out, Olin Downes, steady there, Lawrence Gilman! Van Deusen's coming back, that is if you grant he was ever there.

A lifetime of wholehearted drinking had done nothing to make him look less than his forty-five; his thin face was liverish brown and rutted, heavy pouches of extra skin hung under his eyes, though these eyes, brightly blue and ingenuous, looked out under the bushy brows with the direct false boyishness of a man accustomed to charm and to charm hard. His gray sparse hair and close-clipped mustache were carefully cared for as vanishing treasures, and his bearing was determinedly jaunty, slender hips swaying, step boyish and from the ball of the foot, the lithe firm tread of a man eager to prove he was perfectly sober, perfectly extraordinary fit and in full command of every faculty.

For no good reason Van had long ago adopted the manner of a petted, spoiled bachelor, a manner his one-time wife—none of his friends knew about Bessie—and the friends who regarded him as an intolerable pest did nothing to invite. Every moment he must act for a glamorous first impression on the world at large, and the role of the town bachelor pet pleased his fancy most. Women friends, used to nagging, bossing and abusing the fellow as a whipping boy for their own frustrations, were often nonplussed at the coy, sulky little-boy face he put up to them; instead of the nasty answers they deserved, he all but put his finger in his mouth with a shy, abashed smile, an air of I-know-you're-spoiling-me-but-I-love-it. Or he would burst into a peal of understanding laughter; exclaiming, "Now, Evelyn!" or "Now, Gwen!" as if he well knew the secret infatuation that gave rise to their irritability and was helpless to do anything about it. Could a man help his fatal fascination for the other sex? Oh, dear, this being the town darling was such a bore!

Before a haberdasher's Van paused to study a few hats, pulled his own a bit further over the right eyebrow, hunched his shoulders up, sucked in his stomach, and swung down the avenue, Van Deusen about to give Town Hall his business, Carnegie Hall, hmm—just too depressing, Steinway, hmm—obviously too small. Crossing under the El the public personality suddenly evaporated leaving only Van with a god-awful hangover, a most supercolossal thirst and a brilliant mental file of every fount in every city where he could charge things. The Fogartys, of course! If they were only still there! He followed the El at a run up Fifty-third, past the garages, looking for the little door that had been a gate to freedom in prohibition days. It was there! But would Papa and Mama Fogarty still be there? Yes, there was the sign across the second-story window of the little red brick building.

E. FOGARTY — OPTOMETRIST

This was the very sign behind which Papa Fogarty had conducted his alchemy in the dark days before repeal. Dear, dear Fogartys! Many a night he had sat in the backroom with Mama Fogarty, a fine-bosomed overripe lady, while Papa had examined people's eyes in the next room, thanks to some long-ago training. Van and Mama had drunk absinthe, the finest thing in the world for a hangover and pure as a baby's breath, for it was made in Mama's own kitchen from the freshest of crystal-clear alcohol with a mystic pill in it. How happy those dreary days were! There had been a whole winter, Van recalled, with no days to it all, just a sort of exquisite Arctic twilight creeping through the bars of the kitchen window! Mama made coffee from time to time or worked away at her postcard album, Van helpfully at her side or whatever point afforded the best view of Mama's beautiful jumbo bosom.

They never tired of looking at the postcard collection for Mama belonged to the postcard club, she had sent in her name and dues and exchanged cards with people all over the world. There was a beauty of a monolith to Lord Kitchener from Johannesburg, the Mannequin Pis from Amsterdam, the Taj Mahal; why the fortunate woman was in touch with the entire civilized world and moreover was willing to share her trophies with anyone, the merest acquaintance was free to look over her private correspondence. Even now Van's memory of Mama Fogarty was scented with licorice, he could have sworn that they had wandered in clear green fog through the hanging gardens of Peru, ridden in dahabeahs up the blue Nile, laid a wreath on a Polynesian queen's tomb, all in the carefree picture postcard age before repeal. His tongue knocking like an iron clapper in his parched mouth, Van reached the door, ran up the steps, knocked on the door. No one answered so he went in. The same room. Same apparatus. The printed wheel on the wall. The chart on the stand with the same challenge:

CAN YOU SEE

THIS LINE..............

Van rapped on the inner door.

"Come in."

Mama Fogarty herself as all was holy! And by her face, far plumper now, Van knew he still owed them plenty. She was cooking a stew, but among the vegetables on the wooden table Van's radio eye detected a heartening fat bottle.

"I'm on my way to Town Hall, Mama," cried Van, unbuttoning his gloves once more. "How good to see you! I'm going to have a concert in Town Hall, Mama! I had to tell my old friends first. Four years, it's been, hasn't it? Imagine! And the postcards!"

Mama was touched. She dried her hands on a towel and motioned him to a chair, waddled—good Lord, she was getting enormous!—to another chair herself.

"Ah, the postcards!" she repeated lovingly. "The club is no more. I haven't any new ones."

"Then let's look over the old ones," exclaimed Van. "Old time's sake! If we only had a drink!"

Mama shrugged. She pulled the albums out of the curtained pantry, opened it at Sunny Spain and left it on the table. She got out two glasses and wonder of wonders, a bottle of beautifully creamy green liquid.

"We still make our own, Papa and I," she said. "To the concert!"

"Thank you," said Van, clicking his heels, and the familiar fire shot down the old red lane, taste buds stood on their hind legs and roared, the Fogarty Joygiver coursed over his desert palate doing good, assuaging fever, a veritable Florence Nightingale to the quivering nerves. Mama, after the drink, was kinder. The i.o.u. for $56 faded gently from her mind. She showed him the prize of her collection, the sea gardens of Bali, and Van studied it carefully, for in a few moments he would be there, chamois gloves, shaking hand, and all.

"To my concert in Town Hall!" he cried, filling his glass again.

Mama Fogarty's bosom shook with laughter.

"It's so funny," she gasped, drying her eyes. "Last time it was Town Hall, too, remember? You were going down there so big and arrange for the concert! And you never went! And before that it was the same thing. I think Papa and I should call our kitchen Town Hall for that's where you always end."

"True," laughed Van. "By Jove, that is a coincidence." They both laughed till tears rolled down their faces and hours later when Papa came back, drawn by the smell of burnt stew, Mama and Van were still drinking to "My concert at Town Hall" and going into perfect fits of laughter. When Papa heard the joke, even he, mad as a hornet though he was, had to laugh.

*J*EFF STOOD in the dark alleyway beside the theater and smoked. Beside him there his play was unfolding; he stood pressing his body against the cold brick walls as if this was a blood transfusion between him and it, he felt it breathe and tremble and sigh with what he had given, while he himself felt drained and vacant with the loss; there was nothing in this lanky body, it was just an empty crate being rolled aimlessly back to a warehouse somewhere in Time.

Time was the thing. You would say that Life and Death were the ingredients of a play, but it was Time that was used, by the bolt, by the carload; Time cut up in squares, rolled in balls, distorted, braided, twisted, painted, now it was a flag, now a flag cut into bits, now magically it was whole again. So here was a play about a match factory, twenty years compressed into a hundred minutes, a feeling in a woman's breast twenty years ago transmuted intact across two decades and through a writer, a director, an actor, with no loss but multiplied rather in reflection. Here was a play made up of two hundred nights over a typewriter in a midwestern village attic, with sometimes apple blossoms outside the half-moon window and sometimes green apples, birds, reddening leaves, bare branches, snow; here was a play read aloud on an ocean liner somewhere along the Gulf Stream thus moving a match factory and the twenty years and the woman's feelings into a private stage in Ben Hyman's brain. Here was a play, made up as it was of all these rags and tags of Time, about to open and about to close, about to live and about to die; and there would be no more hole in Time than a pebble makes in the ocean when it would sink with all the hundred minutes and the two hundred nights and the twenty years. It was like a holiday, too, this play, for it belonged to no one person but to everybody; Jeff Abbott was lost in the shuffle, as abandoned as a stud once its purpose was served. Jeff drew his hands out of his pocket, started his feet going, walked himself to the sidewalk, and stared at the street, almost saw himself in the very bus station down the street where he had once arrived with his luggage of hopes for this play. His eyes had rested on this very theater, looking out from the bus station, there were undeveloped negatives of this very alleyway in his brain, now to be matched with memory.

Ben Hyman stood out on the sidewalk before the billboard on the other side of the iron, alley gates. The producer's moon face was bleak and yellow, the loose mouth drooping, the thick shoulders bowed, he held a cigar in his fingers but did not raise it to his lips. Time for him was ladled out in Morse codes, dotted lines, promissory notes, lies. He and Jeff looked at each other a moment, not recognizing each other but the same thing between them.

"Oh," he said, "it's you."

A man came out of the lobby and took Hyman by the arm.

"This is—" Hyman began but looked blankly from one to the other, unable to remember either name, author's or press agent's, and for their part they were too depleted to remind him that they did know each other as well as they cared to.

"A class house," said the press agent. "Prudence Bly and the café crowd, lots of Hollywood and Park Avenue."

"Cold as hell," said Hyman, "Not a big enough hand to get the last curtain down."

"Not cold," said the press agent. "Mad. Mad as hops."

"Downstairs don't like it," mused Hyman. "The gallery don't like it."

They did not look at each other. The calamity was on them like a war, wiping everything away but this one fly speck. The town itself of the match factory rose in Jeff's mind, a city about to be destroyed, he heard its dolorous chimes, he saw it as he had that first time many years ago, a structure for a play—the sulphur-frosted brook and trees, whitened fields year in year out, color-drained workmen with their charred faces and whitened hair and eyebrows, rows of them with dinner pails, their children growing up to be bleached like them, the town ashening under the fumes, and the woman factory owner herself as white as the Snow Queen in her manorial park where no birds sang, no leaf grew, no fish swam in the fountain; this was a village idyl where people were content, dully waiting for the Snow Queen to build more gallows for them, provide more white death for their young men. Jeff saw the village bloom and vanish in one moment, and suddenly he wondered what he was doing here; his part was over, he had served his purpose.

"Where you going?" Hyman called after him, not caring, as he walked stiffly away.

Jeff shrugged his shoulders. Hyman took a few quick steps and caught up with him.

"Look," he said in his ear, running along in little breathless steps to keep up with the long legs. "This don't matter. OK it's a flop. We gotta wait in this business. Once don't count or twice but the whole record. Maybe this is too good, that's a fault like anything else. But you got nothing to worry about, kid. You made 'em mad. It's a gift when you can make 'em mad."

"I know all right," Jeff said. "Sure."

He felt free now and he could breathe. He was alone facing Times Square; and now it was his city, it knew his whip, it recognized a new rider.

. . . bread and butter letter . . .

THE ROOM SMELLED of mutton and wet wash and reminded Jefferson pleasantly of Monday noon boiled dinner at home in Silver City. It was three stories above the Armenian restaurant, but the jolly shish-ke-bab penetrated the very pores of the walls. There was a mottled marble fireplace with a black grate holding a soupspoon or so of cannel coal, and Mr. Kajoolian had explained that nothing could be done about the flapping wallpaper since the Acme Hand Laundry in the basement kept everything damp. Skimpy cretonne curtains hung at the two windows, and they collapsed every time he tried to push them aside. The same blue cabbage rose pattern covered the cot and the china cupboard. Behind the ruffles of the latter was an electric plate, a toaster, three thick yellow cups, a cracked sugar bowl, four pretty claret glasses from Woolworth's, a few luncheon plates, three spoons, a knife, and a bent can opener. Mr. Kajoolian would try to

find a fork somewhere. Large cracks in the floor suggested rodent
opportunities, and the thought was borne out by the wads of cloth
stuffed here and there in the larger apertures. Anyway he could
breathe here, Jefferson exulted; and sunshine did come in these
rear third floors, though an occasional cloud obscured it caused by
a parade of family wash sliding by on its clothesline a few inches
past the window. It was rather cozy at that, looking up from your
typewriter and seeing a headless blue gingham lady blown by the
wind to full size smack against your window. Yes, it was a fine
place, Jefferson thought, as he sat at the folding table composing
his thank-you letter to Dol.

> I don't know what you thought, coming home last night
> and finding me an my way out with my suitcase. I tried
> to tell you I was leaving, but you got so upset and hurt I
> decided it would be better to go and let you know why
> afterward.
>
> The best way to begin, I guess, is to tell you
> about my mother. My mother is fifty-five years old, just
> ten years older than you. There are four kids. I'm the
> second, the fourth was born after my father was killed.
> He was a railroad engineer and most of the men in his
> family were railroad men, which meant at that time that
> they were smart men, men who'd been around all kinds
> of people and learned. My mother came from farmer
> stock. For twenty years she's slept on a couch in the
> dining room because she could get five dollars a week
> renting her own room to a schoolteacher. She's never sat
> down for more than ten consecutive minutes at a dining
> table because there were boarders who needed attention
> if the kids didn't. I've never seen her fondle any of her
> children and I've never seen her cry when any of them
> left home. She never had time. She hasn't had time to

talk to us much, either, even if she were a talkative type. But I know she saves to buy the farm she was raised on outside Silver City and hopes to go back there someday. When the Queenie Bly Flour Mills are running next door, she makes extra money serving lunch to the men. She saves out of that. Two sisters are married now and away from home. My brother's family live with her and pay her something. She knows I can't send her anything and she understands I may never be able to. She knows I can't work at home because the house is bedlam, and I don't like my brother's family.

What I'm driving at, Dol, is that when you give a party for me at a restaurant and sign the check for over a hundred dollars you only make me think how long and how hard my mother has to work to make that much. When you tell me I must learn to be more polite to "people who could be valuable to me," I think of my mother so busy teaching us to look out for ourselves in a tough world that she never had time to teach us to curtsey. When those lads around the place start comparing eight dollar neckties, and just for a gesture you give me a twelve dollar shirt, I think of the twelve dollar spring coat my mother buys herself every five years. I think of the years my mother put in teaching me to save, even when I was just doing odd jobs as a boy around the mill making three dollars a week, so that when I was ready to strike out, I had a few hundred dollars in the bank with a little reserve for her, too.

Anyway the bouillabaisse and champagne life just isn't my stuff, Dol. You've been darned nice to me, offering me your home and trying to show me the ropes. Looking around, I seem to think those ropes are for hanging the people that know them. They'd hang me, I know that. What I can't make you understand when I talk to you is that I'm not here to reap rewards for a few strokes of my pen but to go on working. I want to get my new play lined up and I've got to work hard, the hell with the valuable contacts.

I don't mean I didn't appreciate your having all those people to meet me my opening night. I'm sorry I wasn't there and I know it made you feel hurt but I got to thinking and, before I knew it, I was down in the Battery. I read the notices in a little restaurant on Staten Island by the ferry called Barkin's. You said I shouldn't be too discouraged by the panning they gave me, accusing me of brutality and bitterness—well, you saw what they said. I didn't tell you because I didn't think you would understand me, but those notices meant a lot to me. They meant I belonged in the theater. If my sword can pink that old pachyderm hide of the public, then I've got what it takes. I never set out to be a literary Schiaparelli, dressing up human nature to hide its humps. I'm not a writing beauty doctor who fixes up old chins and souls to gratify the customer's mirror. That's where my mother comes in, teaching us to work for the necessities. I find the playwright's necessity is neither to pacify nor please but to refurbish the mind, houseclean it, shake it up ready to meet problems, and not to feed complacencies. If the truth makes the critics squirm, OK.; if it satisfies them, OK, too. Those are secondary results. The primary obligation is emotional reconstruction. So, feeling this way, I didn't want your pity for my having a flop. For me it was a success. It's shown me that I know what arteries to cut, where to operate. With the world the way it is, that's about the only kind of success I can expect for a while—a few good people who know what I'm after and respect it and the critics stirred up for better or worse. And in your eyes it looks like failure. Your house and your crowd are organized for success, and I don't fit in. I don't want to. I hope I never shall.

If you'd like to have dinner with me, they turn out a fair Armenian blue plate downstairs here for forty cents, and you know I like to talk to you. Don't tell anybody where I am, because I'm locked up with the new opus.

Jeff stuck the note in an envelope, grabbed his hat, and set out to mail it. The hall was pitch dark, you had to find your way by touch and the crescendo or diminuendo of the lamb aroma. He had to pass Mr. Kajoolian, large, black-moustachioed, and oily, standing behind the cashier's counter of his restaurant. A warm flood of friendship came over him for Mr. Kajoolian, his first real pal in this town.

In the corner drugstore where he stopped for a stamp someone behind the counter spoke to him. It was one of Dol's young friends—Les Biggs, he reminded Jeff.

"They sure put you on the pan, didn't they, Abbott?" eagerly said Les. "I hear the *Sun* was even worse than the *Times*. I saw the show. Kinda queer, but I liked it. I like anything."

"Thanks," said Jeff, "thanks a lot."

. . . at home . . .

$\mathcal{I}$T WAS NOT without regret that James Pinckney had given up tea at teatime. In his own apartment he still wolfed a pot of English breakfast tea every afternoon when he was home, but now he was approaching forty, tea damned him as fuddy-dud. So he had vermouth at Prudence's, a "storm-tossed" this concoction was called, combined French and Italian vermouth with a twist of lemon. It upset his stomach frightfully like all *aperitifs* did, but James had come to the conclusion that in these days stomachs were going to be upset anyway, and, like army promotions, ulcers, gallstones and colitis were routine rewards of service.

Prudence was drinking planters' punch, which Nellie made very well, and, of course, Jean was drinking the same.

"We wanted to go to Bermuda for the weekend," explained Prudence, "but instead we're staying home and drinking planters' punches right here. Jean thinks we ought to have the turtle from the New Windsor Palm Garden sent up, too."

"A planters' punch does seem a little naked without the usual turtle," agreed James.

He was living in the future as always, phrasing the occasion as he would relate it tonight at Dol's. There were the two little dears, he would say, snuggling together on the sofa with their identical drinks and the same perfume—Ciro's *Surrender,* I thought it was, though it may have been *My Sin,* you know how often I've confused them—and it was "Jeanie, dear" this and "but Prudence, darling"; and then after Prudence kissed me—she *will* kiss me, God knows why, it's one of those formalities I detest like sleeping with your hostess on country weekends, *the* ultimate bore—well, there was little Prudence's lipstick smeared so the other little dear must take her gossamer kerchief and rearrange dear Prudence's mouth. It was too touching. What Stephen Estabrook must think is beyond me—playing the one against the other these years back and then finding he's been just the go-between, the girls are crazy about each other, kicked him right out, you know, when he interfered. But they do have him up once in a while, just the way they do me, and let him see how happy they are.

"Your lips are moving, James, dear," Prudence reminded him.

"Just keeping off evil spells," said James and regretfully returned to the present. He decided to make a psychological experiment and observed, "I notice Steve is lunching now and again with that Mrs. Brent Van discovered. Rather fresh-looking, you know. Athletic type, wouldn't you say?"

"Smokes a pipe, I hear," said Prudence blandly.

Jean was not so clever.

"That girl!" she exclaimed. "The absolute country-club-shorts type. However did Steve happen on her?"

"The boys were just passing her around," said James. "Neal had her, very quietly, of course, and only on Thursdays, then Van dug her out of the West Side someplace, and, of course, Steve had to see what this wild flower had to offer."

Jean was not helping Prudence's cool pose, James thought, pleased, for she kept looking at Prudence for confirmation of her own surprise and annoyance.

"I'm furious at Van," neatly Prudence stepped out of trap, "I get the manager, a press agent, provide the money for the hall—everything for Van to come back; and just the day he's to sign things and make final arrangements, he vanishes. Not a yip out of him. The place he was staying hasn't heard of him for days—out on one of those annual benders of his."

"We won't see him again this winter," prophesied James. "Allowing a fortnight for the binge, then the jitters accompanied by shame and guilt, the creeping out of town—oh, yes, we've seen the last of Van this season. No recital this year."

"We had everything planned," said Jean.

Oh, the *"we-ing"* of the couple, James exulted, relaxing into his anecdote again. The shy looks of possession, the silent understanding! Two little love birds, Jean in trailing royal blue chiffon and silver sandals on her large beautiful feet—platinum toenails, too!—and Prudence in white velvet pajamas, cerise cravat, oh, very boyish, very laddie-boy! And talking of "our" buying a sailboat for next summer and a trailer for "our" Canadian trip. *We-plans* for the future—possessions in common—well, James's lips formed the sentence, they're as settled as most married couples are at their silver wedding. What a joke on Stephen!

"I can't stay long, dears," said James, watching Prudence pour out his second storm-tossed. "Evalyn will be in town, and I have to do all those things she asked. The seats for *Winterset* and the Boston Symphony and *Tristan* again. We always hear *Tristan!*"

Evalyn was James's elderly female friend, the only woman in his life, combination of maiden aunt, mother, and Nero. When

she came to town from Philadelphia, James retired from all other
life, a tradition now so established that his friends recognized it.

"And Bert Willy, how is he?" politely asked Prudence. James
wriggled in his chair, rearranged his long skinny legs self-
consciously, and looked down at his hands. Everyone knew now
that he was one of the naughty boys, and he could not help being
a little proud, at least as long as Evalyn didn't hear of it and demand explanations.

"I feel terrible that he won't go see Dol," said James unctu-
ously. "Dol did so much for the boy, far more than I ever can. But
Bert says he won't go there. Isn't it too bad? Dol naturally feels
very bitter toward me, and I must say I can't blame him."

"What does Bert do?"

James looked vague.

"He just keeps up with things. Trends. He looks after Sebastian
while I'm away and then, too, he's gotten terribly interested in
cooking. He putters around the kitchen. I'm thinking of getting
him an electric range. I tell him he ought to work on a cookbook,
with his flare for that sort of thing. I want to help him make something of himself."

Prudence refrained from remarking that what he usually made
of himself was a nuisance.

"Steve and that Brent girl!" exclaimed Jean scornfully, out of a
blue sky. "Next he'll be out in Bronxville creeping in and out of
suburban family life like—like a Ludwig Baumann truck."

"Why, Jeanie!" sweetly reproved Prudence.

The dears, James joyously pursued his anticipated conversation,
actually have every thought in common, and little Jeanie-pie now
talks just like Prudence, every inflection, every phrase—it's divine!

"Pets, I must dash," he mourned, putting his glass down.
"Much as I hate to leave such a happy beautiful little pair!"

He collected his long body, adjusted his double-breasted jacket,
twitched at his lapels, all with the gravest concern as if his apparel

was too delicately made, fabrics too priceless to bear any but the gentlest touch.

"I'm wearing my Fortnum Mason today," he sighed. "The tie, of course, is from Evalyn."

The ladies cried out their enthusiasm, pretty arms around each other they followed him to the door, kissed him again.

And my God, Prudence is getting sweet, James added to his coming monologue; love has softened that adder tongue. He must tell all this in front of Steve, he thought happily; he must see Steve's face, for to be cuckolded in all directions by Amazons must be a bitter pill for the old Casanova ego.

"James," said Prudence, swinging on his lapels, "would you do me a favor?"

Now was the time, he thought and recalled that he had never gotten out of this apartment without committing himself to some embarrassing task, such as wangling an important invitation here or there, pursuing a reluctant male, begging some columnist for space.

"I'd like you to find out where Jefferson Abbott went," said Prudence. "Maybe Bert has heard about him somewhere."

"Now what do you want to see him for?" exclaimed James, quite annoyed. "His play was a terrific flop. The critics still rant about it. Personally, I thought it was perfectly brutal. Not an iota of charm! The boy is devoid of humor! You can't have all that death and bitterness on the stage without boring people to tears."

"It was maddening," agreed Prudence. "I don't know why it should have fascinated me so. But it *was* virile!"

"Oh, it was marvelously virile," said Jean. "Like blows on the heart! Really! I told Prudence so! I do want to meet the man."

"Please let us know where to find him," said Prudence. Suddenly James's heart leaped at the lovely picture of these two Lorelei set on the trail of the unsuspecting stalwart provincial. He would find the man, willy-nilly, he vowed, and his gray, kindly eyes shone with high resolve.

"That's true, you could do something for him," he said benevolently. "If you set your mind on it, Prudence, you could absolutely make that boy the Year's Genius."

"Definitely!" said Jean. "If Prudence would just take him up and get people to meet him! The play made me absolutely quiver! It wasn't good, of course, but it did make me quiver!"

Any other time James's and Prudence's eyes would have met here in a silent sardonic comment, but, thank goodness, James had savoir faire enough to know when to pass a sardonic glance and when not to. So he merely pinched each pretty cheek paternally, tucked his walking stick under his arm, pulled his fedora jauntily over one eye, and departed. In the elevator his lips were moving convulsively. Oh, it absolutely made me quiver! It definitely made me quiver! The little dear! The sensitive little pet! And the platinum toenails, thought James, above all I mustn't forget the platinum toenails!

. . . sweet vengeance . . .

*T*HE TROUBLE WITH REVENGE is that you have
to keep working at it, you can not relax and say "Well, that's
done!" so Prudence, getting at Steve for that galling disloyalty in
Paris, found herself so weary of punishing him, of forcing hate
where love had been that she wished to God she had just called
Jean a liar and let it go at that. She was furious with herself for
missing him so much, the late Sunday breakfasts in his big bed,
the perpetual game they played that kept them—she couldn't
think why—in convulsions of merriment, the game of being a
Mr. and Mrs. Hornickle of Rye. She missed their fights, his child-
ishly transparent fibs, his charming stupidity, his amazed enjoyment when she sliced up a friend. But all these things had
belonged to Jean, too. The dish was spoiled. She was sorry she had
ever enjoyed it. She wanted her three years of careless love back to
spend elsewhere; she'd been cheated, made a fool of by a fool like

Jeanie, worse luck. If Jean had only kept her mouth shut! If women would only stop confessing! But if most of them had to choose between kissing and telling they would pick the telling.

Jean had been in Prudence's apartment for only a month and it was already driving Prudence mad. For a while it served to protect her from relenting toward Steve, and it was amusing to think of his bewilderment at the two girls falling into each others arms instead of his. But now the fun was over, and Prudence only thought of what a nuisance it was to live with a woman and wondered how a man ever stood having one around.

Yes, Jeanie was as good as settled now. Prudence stifled an impulse to talk the whole thing over with James Pinckney, thought wistfully of a real showdown with Steve, but in these sissy moments she would find a full-page picture with flattering estimate of herself in some expensive magazine that would pull her together again. Would a public figure like that allow a man to weaken her? I should say not. So Prudence, the woman, was buoyed up by her own publicity and almost believed in herself as a woman of iron. When this person Bly set out to do something, if it was only spite work, she jolly well did it. So, chin-upping like mad, Prudence bought Jean another little present, an elephant-hair and platinum wrist band with a tiny crystal ball watch, and in return squealed with rapture over the blue leather Cross traveling bag from Jean—she only had three already. They had little dinners now in the apartment and showed their enchanted guests their latest presents to each other, and Jean played Prudence's records over and over till it was time to go to the Vedado for the supper performance when the guests were whisked off to listen to songs twice more. Jean now used her eyebrows the way Prudence did and said "oh, but *darling!*" with exactly the Bly inflection, and they had both gone from mahogany toenails to a deep tearose and smoked tiny Cuban cigars and said things were "divoon" one week and "gallicious" the next. When they raked over a mutual friend, they now finished her or him off with that cannibal's dessert "but there's something awfully sweet about her!"

Jean called Harvey regularly and begged him not to be too despondent and lunched with him downtown at Ye Olde Choppe House once a week. At night—more often daybreak—when they crept into their twin beds, creamed, netted, and lately in black sleep goggles to keep out the morning light, Jean's voice would drone on and on telling about Stevie, what he said that summer, how tender he was when she had that operation, how he thrilled her just talking on the phone; while Prudence, eager to go over silently a few romantic memories of her own, said "Umm-huh. . . . Umm-huh."

It would appear that what Jean was madly in love with was a summer three years ago when she was divinely thin and in Paris, and everywhere you went they played *Serenade in the Night,* and she preferred dwelling on her own romantic reactions of then to the uninteresting news of Steve of the moment. By the time Jean had talked herself to sleep Prudence had her anger at Steve sufficiently stoked to begin a new day.

Now the professional rivalry that had added sauce to her former passion could be completely released, she could read Nick Kenny's occasional cracks at Steve's program and crow; she could see Steve's radio rivals lauded and enjoy his certain discomfiture. Very likely, on his side, he rubbed his hands over Miss Merryleg's column, which made a point of disparaging the Vedado show, particularly since Prudence had added a new libelous number called *Miss Jollypins Gets the Sailor.*

In a racket that allowed only enemies they had been able to be frank only with each other. Now each joined the other's envious ill-wishers with a little sadness because it was their last bulwark. Once they might be downhearted with each other over the monotony of their business but only with each other; with anyone else it would have started fatal rumors that they were worried about their contracts, they were slipping, and a rumor in their world of intangibilities was enough to make a reality. Prudence dared mourn her lack of voice to Steve, for he in all honesty would console her.

"With a voice you'd only be another singer," he said. "This way you use what you've got to put over a personality not a tune. That little croak of yours socks 'em more than any bel canto, baby."

In a world of flatterers it was heaven to have one you could believe. And now Prudence felt lonely and lost and perhaps Steve did. When they saw each other at parties, Prudence waved all too gaily and was far too vivacious with other groups, while Steve was much too absorbed in the youngest, freshest beauty present. Each made a point of trying to leave before the other, mentioning important dates elsewhere, knowing how such mystery overheard would irritate the other. Whom is she meeting? Whom is he meeting? Their bitter curiosity would interfere with their exhibitions of indifference.

Prudence was always particularly gay when he found her wearing the gray lamb military coat and hat, for she knew how attractive he had always found this outfit, and it was a savage pleasure to see the reluctant admiration again in his eye and dismiss it. So you almost cried when Jean had that operation, did you, so you rushed to the American hospital with your arms full of violets and champagne, did you, leaving your unsuspecting sweetheart Miss Bly at home with a small adoring group of English pansies as your bouquet to her? And when Jean sighed, "It doesn't seem fair to Prudence," you said "Let's not talk about Prudence." This was all Prudence needed to recall from Jean's nightly monologue to make fury buzz through her head. "Let's not talk about Prudence!" That was something one couldn't forget, something to crowd out every sentimental memory.

"Isn't it gallicious, just we two?" Jean sighed at breakfast.

"Divoon," said Prudence and wished that Steve was as bored with his punishment as she was with giving it.

"Harvey still thinks I should marry Steve," said Jean. "But I shan't go through Reno a second time. It's too, too lurid. I think

Harvey is being too brave about the whole business. He doesn't seem to realize I've given up Steve. And marriage is so—so final! I may be old-fashioned but marriage seems *terribly* final to me.

Prudence said nothing.

"About Steve—do you really think I should marry him?" Jean toyed with the idea coyly as if, Prudence thought, all she needed do was to notify him of her decision.

A fat chance of getting that trained eel trapped! Then Prudence had an unpleasant second thought. Anything was possible. She would never have dreamed, for instance, that Steve would have fallen for Jean's too-cloying charms, but then he had. He might, therefore, even marry her. True, he and she had often derided the institution, laughed together over the chemical disintegration of the brain in marriage. Oh, it had seemed very funny to them, indeed, to see what smart alecks got themselves trapped. But what did such merry discussions prove, Prudence judiciously asked herself. Absolutely nothing. Lovers always talked that way to each other, and the next day the man was astounded to see the lady gladly accept some solid man's legal proposition; and on the other hand the lady, having schooled herself not to frighten her lover with hints of permanence, is appalled to see how easily he is caught by some dull little woman who has never heard of anything but marriage, and it turns out that all the time he was just waiting for a little Miss Right to give him an argument.

So Steve, in spite of his boisterous sneers, might be had. Jean did hang on, God knows, till a man gave in. Even if he was dodging her now as a sweetheart, he might fall for her as a wife. Good heavens! Prudence felt a suffocating despair at the thought of Steve in a wedding picture.

"Should I or shouldn't I?" repeated Jean dreamily.

"You could try," muttered Prudence. OK. Let him get married then and out of the way.

. . . visit to Olympus . . .

$\mathcal{M}$R. KAJOOLIAN was glad Mr. Abbott liked bib-ertouchou; it flattered him as much as it irritated Dol to have this provincial yell for "more of those gadgets."

"Three stews on sticks," ordered Jeff.

"Three shish-ke-bab," corrected Dol, "and arak later with Turkish coffee. Oh, yes, let's have kashar-tava."

"Naw," rebelled Jeff with that provincial stubborness Dol so disliked, that typical antagonism to anything foreign-sounding. Jeff would never be found in this Armenian restaurant if it were really good, Dol reflected, but this greasy little dining room with soiled tablecloths, loud stuttering radio, oily proprietor, and, at its best, a dishwater stench, was sufficiently like a bad railroad café in a midwest village to seem harmlessly homey to Jefferson.

"Kashar-tava is only goat cheese," persisted Dol. "You said before that you liked it."

"I like it when it's called 'goat cheese,'" said Jeff. "Kashar-tava tastes like an old silk petticoat."

This amused his new friend Kittredge enormously. Dol smiled patiently at this man's roar of laughter, a roar that ended always in a gasp of tittering and encored itself with a series of mouselike squeals that did not seem to come from the same mighty throat. Kittredge was a vast loose-jowled man of forty-five with gray flabby flesh sagging over his unbuttoned blue-checked collar. None of his buttons, vest or shirt, were fastened, so his rumpled maroon tie, daintily dotted in green, miraculously held his flying garments on to his person. His worn gray suit was shapeless; suit and skin alike seemed an elephant's hide that some smaller beast had appropriated. His close-set sharp little eyes and long hooked Pilgrim nose gave a lean rodent impression at variance with his great loose bulk. The nose itself was indeed his pride, a recognized and decent symbol of sexual competence but, even so, Dol felt it was hardly necessary to keep fondling it when ever he was pleased as if the feature were not already conspicuous enough. Kittredge banged the table with his fists in rage or joviality so that the dishes danced, the wine sloshed on the cloth, and Dol shuddered in sheer nausea. It was the second visit Dol had made to his young friend the playwright in these unsavory quarters, and each time the neighbor Kittredge had been offensively present, upholding Jeff in his sustained pigheadedness and clearly regarding Dol through hostile small eyes as a sinister unhealthy influence.

"Your nationalism can carry you too far," Dol said as amiably as his irritation would permit. "Think of arriving at a pitch of gastronomic chauvinism where you eat nothing without our national marshmallow on it and lunch daily on a tomato surprise."

"Ah, you don't appreciate this lad, Dol," said Kittredge too familiarly to suit Dol. "Jeff is simple, and we don't see enough of simplicity in New York. The old pioneer virtues have all gone to pot, what with these foreign pansies cluttering up the present-day scene. A boy like Jeff is refreshing. Cheese is just cheese to him, not *au gratin,* not *fromaggio* or *kashar-tava*—that's good, you know. That's good. Believe me, he's saved my faith. He showed me that a man *can* keep his head in this merry-go-round."

It was not a success, the little Armenian dinner, though Mr. Kajoolian sent sour red wine to their table and from behind his cigar counter nodded and beamed approvingly at every word of their conversation. Dol discovered that Jeff was seeing no one except this man Kittredge, who lived across the hall and who had unfortunately been an actor once, so that in any argument about Jeff's work Kittredge would place a large restraining paw on Dol's knee, "Excuse me, old man, you wouldn't say that if you knew the theater from the inside the way I do."

Dol wanted desperately to help Jeff, but the young man would give him no opening. He would have no smoothing of the road, Dol saw, but, perhaps, he would need praise and encouragement to go on in the face of his first venture's failure. This was a bad guess, too, for it seemed neither failure nor success could alter Jeff's concept of himself or his work. He belonged to that baffling group of confident writers who need no applause. For them a success is not a surprise but cause for wonder that it is less than international considering the merits of the work; a failure proves that a man is too good for his times. Public contempt merely proves that his talent is of such unquestionable magnitude that every man is stabbed with envy and understandable animosity. Thus Dol classified Jeff and Kittredge, too, whose own vaguely defined labors of the past few years had failed magnificently.

Dol felt bitter about this independent spirit, for he was sure his only value in the world was to help ripen what raw gifts the young man had. He had, and was eager to give away, all of the knowledge that he felt Jeff lacked and needed in his work. He had felt a purpose in life when he first met Jeff and read some of his work: here was someone who needed the background that

Dol could give. But whenever he made any suggestion of a smoother handling of a theme Jeff's eyes hardened as if Dol was the pimp emissary from a world of trickery above which Jeff and Kittredge flew like a pair of angry angels. Dol, after a few ventures, sank back depressed, convinced almost again that his life was futile; nobody, no one needed him; nothing he had ever learned was of any value to himself or anyone else.

They took their arak upstairs, at Kittredge's suggestion, into his room. Dol had wanted Jeff to walk over to the Prince George taproom for an ale, but Jeff seemed to feel as Kittredge did that all comfort must be fought as the enemy of integrity, so they sat on the humpy cot in Kittredge's hall bedroom, attempting to protect their anatomies from the iron ridges with two or three starved little sateen cushions.

"Everyone asks about you," said Dol.

"For instance?"

"Prudence."

There was a moment's silence

"I don't want to see Prudence," Jeff said slowly. "This Prudence of yours isn't the one I knew. What happens to people here? Does a person have to cut his guts out and hand 'em to the town on a silver platter to pay for having his picture in the paper? Prudence! I can't even talk to her anymore except through that stone front of hers. Is the stone inside, too? What about that radio guy Estabrook? Is that really a love affair—and how do two monuments make love anyway?"

Dol, surprised at this vehemence, attempted to explain Prudence but Jeff brushed him aside.

"The hell with her, who else asks about me?"

"Well, the Fellows. Neal has an opening next week, and it might be a good thing for you to go, be seen there, to show you're not sunk by your flop, and later meet their crowd. Those little things help."

"Think of seeing a Neal Fellows' play, boy," mocked Kittredge. "Civilized conversation in Long Island drawing rooms. Everything ladled out just right: a teaspoonful of wit, a soupçon of tragedy, a sprinkling of fox hunting and radicalism, wrap it up in chintz and take it out. Bushwah."

"At least Jeff can learn something from seeing how a seasoned technician handles his material, however shoddy the material may be," Dol said quietly, controlling himself with difficulty.

"That isn't how a writer learns, man!" shouted Kittredge." Let me tell you that's all the bunk, that technique stuff. Damn sight better for him to throw away his typewriter and keep out of the theater, go to China or Russia, work in factories, that's the way."

"I'd go to China like a shot," mused Jeff. "I hate the theater. Funny how I have to be in it."

"Most writers have found books and concerts and a certain amount of culture a necessary background to their work," Dol said stiffly.

"Neal Fellows is culture, ha-ha!" laughed Kittredge. "No, Dol, this lad won't learn from that kind of success."

Dol wanted to say if one learned nothing from success, one learned even less from failures such as Kittredge but he knew Jeff would disagree. Why did Jeff show that he thought Dol had nothing to contribute to his life whereas a man like Kittredge did? Dol looked over his superior with distaste.

Apart from having been an actor, Kittredge had written a novel once and had stewed around the edges of radical movements long enough to feel above both capitalists and work. Indeed he seemed to have no definite means of support and had long ago sold his typewriter. A few years back communism had entered his dreary life as coyly as a winged Cupid; it had brought more beauty than Love itself, and Kittredge had gladly given up the struggle for bourgeois triumphs to lie in bed all day sympathizing with the workers of the world. He was not a lazy man so much as he was a man who loved talk; he disliked work only as it was an interruption to good conversation. In the days when he was trying to write the book for which Brentano's had already given him a five-hundred-dollar advance, life had been very tiresome indeed. Each day he would, by tremendous flogging of his sleep-drunk brain, get himself out of bed and blearily attack his typewriter; but the thoughts that ran out so fluently in spoken words, backed up at the typewriter, and hours passed almost every day with nothing written but letters to surprised friends, corrections or arguments to the *New Republic,* the *Times,* or the *Saturday Review.*

In the hours of unfertile effort he had grown to justify his sterility by contempt for fecundity, particularly a rewarded fecundity; and this led to a warm love for any theory of society that would unseat these public favorites, as if their seats left free would at once be offered to himself, and why this adjustment should be more fair even he could not have answered. Evenings he wandered in and out of different radical meetings as he had, during his stage career, gone to fortunetellers and at one of these meetings he had been named for a committee. A committee, no matter what kind, was a wonderful chance for conversation; and there were committee discussions far into the night, often accompanied by beer, though this was considered frivolous and expensive by his fellow members. Kittredge would fall asleep, virtuous and exhausted, from these committee labors, and in the morning when the demon conscience tried to get him to work at his book he finally rebelled outright.

"The hell with writing!" he jubilantly cried. "I'm a politician now," and crawled happily back into bed.

He rearranged Marx and Engels for his own purposes, as a short-fingered pianist rearranges music for his own limitations, and as a consequence had in recent years found himself disowned by his comrades first as a "Fascist," then, worse, a "Trotskyite," a loose epithet that had by this time little technical connection with the old exile and meant only the ultimate adversary, though "Kittredgite" would have been a far better term for his strange egonomics.

Kittredge knew Neal Fellows. He knew everyone. When a name came up, he would startle all with a sudden cry of recognition, then as you waited for his comment, he would merely smile contemptuously into space, repeating the name with a short mysterious laugh, implying that what he knew about the person mentioned was enough, were he indiscreet enough to speak, to blow the fellow to bits. Dol managed to discover that he had once acted in Neal's first play, a flop. Neal was then a fairly decent sort, a "decent sort" being someone who liked you or at least tolerated you, said good morning if you met him on the street. But in late years Kittredge had found this world more and more crowded with snobs, Neal among them, snobs being people who did *not* like you, who did *not* say good morning if you met them. Dol was rather fascinated by Kittredgism as it was unfolded in the little Lexington Avenue room.

Kittredge, for instance, sneeringly referred to all assemblages where he was not invited as "literary teas." People who had seized the opportunities of travel or a new environment to drop him had "had their heads turned by success." And even when the public triumph of these deserters was not even visible, when it was absolutely nil, he found some obscure cause for snobbery in them if it were only a cousin who had married well. James Pinckney, for instance! Ha-ha! Old James Pinckney! Ho-ho! In spite of Dol's recent resentment against James he could find nothing in the latter's professional career to inspire envy; but Kittredge seemed to feel there was, for he sailed into him, chiefly incensed, it would appear, because Pinckney had once lived in this same wretched rooming house and was unbecomingly eager to get away from it. One deduced from Kittredge's indignation that if James had had an iota of fineness in his nature, any integrity at all, he would still be living in the eight-dollar room upstairs.

"A snob!" roared Kittredge, his little blue eyes blazing under bulging gray brows. "Can you imagine, my dear Dol, can you imagine, seriously, now——" and here his voice grew richly Harvard for he was from near Providence and had a perfect right, "someone you used to go with to the Automat, who used to put his ten pennies down for two nickels because by God he didn't have a dime—*pennies,* sir! Someone you've seen sewing up his pants before going to some party because they were so damnably shabby his wretched little bottom was half out—can you imagine, now I mean this, Jefferson, *can* you imagine such a person, I don't care man, woman, or child or your great grandmother herself, *suddenly* getting upstage merely because he got a miserable job as guide in the Museum?—That's all he is, literally, a twenty-dollar a week guide, I don't care what he calls himself, Assistant Horse's Thigh, hah! There's the ladies' room, ma'am. Czarina's jewels to your right, boys and girls! Pretzel exhibition downstairs, sir! A guide, no more, no less, and Pinckney gets high-hat over it! 'Sawry, old man, I'm just dressing for dinner,' he says when I call him up. 'Terribly sawry, I'm just off to the opera. *Tristan,* you know.' *Tristan,* for the love of God! 'The opera, Pinckney?' I inquire, 'Oh, that's right, tonight's bank night,' I say, and, of course, he burns up! *Tristan,* for Christ's sake! There's your Pinckney, for you!"

Jeff seemed perfectly content listening to Kittredge's outbursts as if blasting of smug New Yorkers made a clear road for the conquering stranger. He and Kittredge spoke the same language. It was Dol, who was the foreigner.

"Dol, I want to tell you, this lad here has so much more than O'Neill had at his age," declared Kittredge, relaxing at last after his busy annihilation. "I know the theater and I'm telling you. His new play is a tremendous advance over the last. Have you read the first act?"

"No," said Dol. He was hurt that his interest and undisputed taste should be ignored by Jefferson Abbott when any number of older writers were flattered at his criticism of manuscripts.

"It's the best thing I've done," said Jefferson placidly. No, this young man needed no sops to his vanity. Dol wished he could wash his hands of him, walk out to show his disapproval but there was his conviction that there really was something in the boy, some metal he had never yet encountered, something more like pig iron than gold, perhaps, but sound metal. It bothered Dol, as it had bothered the critics, to be unable to dismiss this curious vitality and power.

"What will you do if Hyman turns this one down?" asked Dol. "He's pretty decent to want it after losing money on your last one."

Jefferson lit a new cigarette and adjusted his lanky body to the humps of the cot, one leg over the other, a ratty little pillow wadded behind his curly black hair.

"Hyman may be dumb, but he isn't a fool," he answered calmly. "He knows there's nobody writing in the theater today that's got what I've got."

Shades of Shakespeare! Dol could bear no more, even from a young man who fascinated him as much as did this one, and he took leave without protest from the other two. A mink-wrapped young woman with a crown of golden hair brushed past him in the dark entry hall, and Dol was so taken aback at such a glamorous scented figure in the dank drab hall that he did not really place her identity for hours afterward and even then he could not quite believe it. He glanced at her attractive legs vanishing up the stairs and then, puzzled, walked over to the Vanderbilt for a highball and reflection on young Abbott. It would take a lot of success, he thought, to turn such a stout head, and he was both glad and depressed to be sure of this.

. . . Evalyn in Town . . .

BERT!" SAID JAMES Pinckney, satisfied that the interminable roar of the bathroom shower was at last ended, "Oh, Bert!"

There was no answer but the sound of water running out of the tub, then wet feet sloshing on tiled floor. James folded his Whitlock muffler, the cerise, placed it in his overcoat pocket, arranged the Chesterfield on its hanger, hung it in the living-room closet. With a sigh he shook Willy's wide-lapeled coat off the hook where it was dangling by its neck and carefully placed it on the purple hanger. A button off, dear, dear! And mud-sprayed hem, tchk, tchk!

"Bert," he said firmly in a slightly raised voice. "I wish to speak to you, Bert."

Silence in the bathroom. James's mouth tightened. He drew a deep breath.

"Bert!" he shouted, and this time his voice broke into a bray that rather embarrassed him. The door unlatched at this, and Bert Willy, damp-haired, barelegged, towel-wrapped as to midriff, stood scowling before him.

James sniffed.

"My toilet soap! My green toilet soap!" he said severely, "and the verbena salts. I told you that salts was not for every day, Bert. And a teaspoonful is ample! Especially when you wash it right off with a shower! Really! I believe you use a whole cupful!"

"Ah, nuts," said Bert Willy, and James sighed. "Evalyn is in town, Bert," he announced. "She will be here for dinner, and I want you to make that Mexican eggplant you made the other night. I do want you to make a nice impression on Evalyn."

"I won't be here," said Bert calmly. "I got to see Les about something."

Bert dried himself, fastened on candy-striped shorts that seemed perilously near to sliding off his thin white hips.

"Who the hell is Evalyn?" he growled.

"Evalyn is Evalyn Greer Vanderhoff of Philadelphia," said James, "and a very old friend, my very oldest and dearest friend. She gets to town very seldom but when she does, I put everything else aside. I think it is a very small favor, Bert, very small favor indeed to ask of you. There are not many friends I insist on your meeting." He saw Bert go to the dresser and rustle through the Pinckney shirt drawer and with an effort stifled a cry of real pain. When the new gray McLaughlin shirt came out, he merely winced for he was still afraid that any outcry would frighten the little bird away, a fear Bert was all too slyly aware of.

"What did you do today?" James asked, hungrily watching the delicious gray broadcloth slide over Bert's nasty little head. "I daresay Les was here all day. No need denying it."

"Les helps me type," mumbled Bert. "I was working." Working! James was mollified. He had been able to isolate a talent in his protégé and as the talent developed, the impresario was appeased. It was not only for Bert's sake James urged him on with his cooking and more recently with the writing of a cookbook, it was something of which James could speak aloud as an excuse for Bert. From the moment he had found the young man experimenting with cloves on an omelet at four o'clock one Sunday morning like the boy Mozart, James had breathlessly fanned the embryonic genius, inflamed it with a pious pilgrimage to the old master Moneta himself, who revealed the facts of pressed duck, fed him with the philosophies of Brillat-Savarin, Escoffier and legends of Sabatini. James underlined Horace's comments on food, in the Modern Library edition, for him and in public endeavored feverishly to draw Bert out on his "specialty" usually to the complete dismay of both patron and pet. Now James tiptoed reverently to the typewriter where "the book" was in process, the book that James had inspired the boy to write. A page was in the machine, and there was no honest reason for surprise to find it was only Page One and for that matter only Paragraph One.

James read with sinking heart:

COOKBOOK BY BERT WILLY

VEGETABLES. Vegetables ought to be fresh. Vegetables ought not to cook to death. They ought to only have a little water put on them as this makes them pretty mushy. If you put salt on vegetables too soon, it spoils the taste except in some cases. Vegetables are the following, lima beans, turnips, macaroni, baked beans, &.

James slowly put the lid over the typewriter and tried not to remember too bitterly the eight dollars he had paid for the Escoffier cookbook. Six lines! In five weeks of labor!

"At least you will be kind enough to make the eggplant," he

said in a proud, stifled tone. "There will be wine, of course. And a fowl. Therefore, hmm. Evalyn is very fond of Moselle—Hmm."

He pretended not to hear Bert muttering "A fowl, by Jesus, a fowl—hah!"

He went to the telephone and took his small gilt-edged engagement book out of the table drawer, leafed it over rapidly.

"Hello, Prudence. I can't make tea tomorrow, dear. Evalyn is in town. Give my love to Jean. So sorry." "Hello, Anna! I can't possibly make Neal's preview! Evalyn's in town. . . . Yes, I'll try to bring her in Friday evening but I can't really promise. You know Evalyn. Tell Neal I'm so thrilled over reports of the tryout." "Hello, Stephen. . . . James Pinckney. I'm so sorry about the broadcast tomorrow. . . . No, I can't possibly get in for it. Evalyn's in town. . . . Soon!"

Everyone who knew James knew of his Evalyn, and that a visit from the Inspector General could not cast a town into greater confusion. No one found her agreeable. Desperately James told stories about her to make her appear interesting, but she only emerged a more intolerable figure than before. As difficult to sell to his friends as any fiancée from another town, James decided to give up trying to paint her as clever and make her stupid instead with the limpid exquisite stupidity of the very rich but instead of stupid the picture came out hideously, incredibly cruel.

"How can you endure her?" friends begged to know even while they agreed that such shabby brains, shabby heart, and shabby manners must certainly spell royalty. "She's my oldest and best friend," James always answered. "She's a dreadful old woman, but I adore her!"

Even Sebastian hated Evalyn as James himself confessed.

"He knows her smell," he said. "It's that Philadelphia smell, a faint bouquet of scrapple and old Republicans. Sebastian won't eat his salmon and creeps under the bed and glares out the minute she sets foot in the house. My word, you should see those great yellow eyes glaring out from under my Candlewick spread. It's really frightening, and Evalyn gets quite hysterical in her Roman way."

Evalyn did not know about Bert, and James was secretly in a panic about the disclosure. Like most of his panics he enjoyed every single quiver and was already phrasing the anecdote about the dreaded encounter, the frenzy of possessive jealousy Evalyn would undoubtedly betray. It might go too far, of course. There might be murder. James sensed that. And she might definitely refuse him an invitation for the summer, and then where would he be? James thought, in view of what he was jeopardizing for Bert's sake, the least the boy could do was to be civil. He did not press the point, however. Never let it be whispered to Dol Lloyd that James Pinckney was a nag. No, he would say nothing further to Bert, exert no pressure whatever. But thinking of Salzburg his lower lip trembled just a trifle.

Every other year at this time James began to speculate whether Evalyn would take him abroad this year or whether it would only be the Bach Festival. This apprehension was enjoyed by the Philadelphia tyrant as much as it was by James. It was a game between them and had been for twenty years. Evalyn would drag out the suspense as long as possible, mentioning plans for Amsterdam or Paris or Mediterranean cruising until James's mouth watered. This baiting would go on all spring until one day James would be driven to declare that he had arranged to go to New Hampshire this time to visit his mother's people, the Shuggs. Last year he had almost been forced to do this, for Evalyn postponed her move till a desperately late date; and it was practically summer when she said—as she had said in substance many times before at this point, "James, I wonder if it wouldn't be a good idea for you to go to Europe with me. We could leave on the *Conte de Savoia,* spend a week at the Italian lakes, travel on to Salzburg for the festival and join my friends there, the Antonys!"

"The Antonys!" James cried, fastening on this barren old Baltimore family as excuse for his boundless relief. "Oh, I would love to see the Antonys again! And Miss Prague! I do hope Miss Prague comes with them!"

"She will!" cried Evalyn. "We will stay at the Hotel Stein!"

The Stein! Miss Prague! The Antonys! Music! Ah, bliss, and free trip, free meals, free wine—a summer for nothing unless you were stingy enough to count as cost a few pounds of flesh and a few quarts of mere blood and tears.

Tears now stood in Evalyn's fishy blue eyes for, as a matter of strict truth, it was as great a relief to her to have the little suspense game over as it was to her victim. It was part of the rules for her to act astonished at James's willingness to accompany her. She must offer obstacles, watch his last frantic gasps.

"But what about your mother's people? You really should visit them this year, James, since you didn't go last."

This James must weigh, frown over, hesitate, feign further doubt, prolong the delectable surrender a few more days until he heard from, say, his cousin Elmer in Washington.

"If Elmer goes up this year, of course that will distract their attention so I can postpone my trip till Easter," James finally stated. "But then Elmer is such a big man in Washington now, he may not be able to get away. If he could—well, one or the other of us really should go. We're the only boys left on the Shugg side. And Aunt Caroline is getting old. Grandfather, of course, is in his eighties! Yes, his eighties! After all, Evalyn, I'm forty!"

Not really forty! Dear dear! Imagine that.

The next step in the game was to berate Elmer for his selfishness in the event he should refuse to go. Elmer had always had everything, besides marrying one of the Bourney heiresses from St. Louis. A wicked shame if he took advantage of his position as judge to skip his family duties, forcing his younger, less fortunate cousin, to do the honors.

"And I introduced him to Gladys Bourney!" James cried.

"Without her money he would have been nobody!" boomed Evelyn. "Nobody! A little patent lawyer!"

This familiar grievance ran its course and served the usual purpose of drawing the soon-to-be-traveling-companions into the close rapport necessary to send them off happily together. Then came the amazing wire—as it often had before at this crucial moment—that Elmer, as usual, would spend the last two weeks of July on the Farm. Good old Elmer! Decent old chap, Elmer!

"It isn't that he's my cousin that I admire him so much," James explained again and again, "nor that he made that place for himself in Washington absolutely by his own efforts, it's that he's such a *decent,* such a *civilized* human being!"

Then they must celebrate with a wine supper and in a few weeks they were pacing a deck together and in no time at all quarreling and niggling over tips beneath sunny Mediterranean skies, refusing to speak to each other to the music of Wagner, sulking under the spell of Mozart, and enjoying themselves as only a female Nero and a sensitive bachelor can. The first few months after the return were mystery months, with James not sure whether Evelyn would ever speak to him again. Then there was the opening night this fall at the Vedado when Miss Vanderhoff, escorted by the anxious Pinckney, expressed her profound disapproval of Prudence Bly's songs, which, she said, would have been excusable if they were humorous inasmuch as the Vanderhoffs had excused humor for generations; but these were merely offensive, and the Vanderhoffs had never excused bad taste. Would she forgive James Pinckney for taking her there, he wondered, all aquiver? She would and did. She would be at his home for dinner; and unless Bert Willy made himself too obnoxious, it was to be a veritable love feast, the first step toward next summer's invitation.

"Bert," said James pleadingly, as Bert selected the finest Pinckney tie, a great English wool that encompassed Bert's skinny neck like a football blanket, "if you stay for dinner tonight you may have Les in tomorrow night."

"Huh?" But Bert, however inarticulate, was plainly won over by this simple offer of future treat. He and Les would spend long happy hours just saying "Huh?" and "Yeh" to each other, James suspected scornfully, and it made him furious for a moment. He was glad to see Sebastian modestly throwing up on the hooked rug, as excuse for rage.

"You've been feeding Sebastian chicken liver!" he accused.

"Aw," said Bert guiltily.

James, still ruffled, selected a five-dollar bill from his wallet, counted the remainder, and held the five out to Bert.

"Go to Baseys and get a bottle of Piesporter, Mr. Pinckney's Piesporter," he said, "and remember I shall expect change."

He did not really expect any change. What he expected and what he got was a bottle of Piesporter and a bottle of 100 proof applejack. The apple was not for Evalyn but, as James was perfectly aware, for tomorrow's party with Les.

At least this triumph put Bert in a more tractable mood, with his applejack stored in his valise—hiding it from me! thought James, mortified—and he set about his eggplant without too much complaining. The fowl itself was to be delivered fresh from Longchamps as the young Escoffier had proved untrustworthy as to what entrails were for the garbage and what for the table.

James bustled about, arranging seventy-five-cents worth of asters in his Ming vase, grouping fifteen lumps of cannel coal in the fireplace ready to be touched off the minute the bell rang, and finally arraying himself in his dinner clothes, while he hummed in a deep and quite new baritone snatches of the most expensive records. Surely, oh, surely, Evalyn would not be unfair about Bert; she would see his usefulness and after all she would have to recall it was she who had objected so violently to the occasional maid who had assisted in his hospitality in other days. That maid, colored, was named Whitepiece and had an embarrassing way of walking out at eight-thirty willy-nilly, her arithmetic under her arm, to attend night school. In vain had James pleaded, groveling before her implacable will as much as a polished host reasonably can grovel in the presence of distinguished guests. No, Whitepiece would *not* remain to serve the salad nor any part of it; the apron was already packaged for return to Harlem via the night school, and any obstructions Mr. Pinckney put out were so unfair as to incite possible race riots. So, often a dinner begun on a most gratifying formal scale would end with the host crumbing the table, a pink Cellophane apron over his pleated bosom. It had developed later that Whitepiece was a loyal angel in Father Divine's heaven, that her actual answer to James concerning her name had been "White. Peace!" Her insistence on finishing every sentence with the Divine salutation "Peace" had finally revealed the truth to Pinckney, but by that time she had been Whitepiece too long to change.

Yes, Bert Willy would surely justify his presence in the Pinckney ménage as an improvement on Whitepiece, if nothing else.

. . . the love feast . . .

𝒯HE ENTRANCES to any circus are not all made through the front gate; often those who value the performance highest have paid nothing, creeping in under the tent or cowering under a commodious apron. Just so, James Pinckney had made his entrance to society via the Dragon Women, and of all these monsters Evalyn Vanderhoff was the queen. James had known many and courted their favor out of the terrified conviction that creatures so formidable must have power; and even when one was merely the dictator of some inland city garden club, his conviction persisted that once he aroused her hostility back to obscurity he must scuttle. He had found these ladies, in spite of minor differences, alike in their rigid belief in their own correctness and in their monstrous passion for formalities to the exclusion of actual sensation. It had often surprised James that women whose virtue stood out like a buzzard's beak and whose honest horror of animal lust was not even forgivably Freudian, should thrust their bosoms so high and so far. If décolleté dress was formal, then they would out-formal the most formal by revealing as far down to the navel as their jaegers would permit. If Emily Post had declared bottoms up, James was certain these brave women would bare their very bottoms, garnished perhaps with a tea rose or bit of tired tulle, and in small groups would boom out sentence on lipsticks and modern music.

Evalyn arrived at the apartment so promptly at seven that James was forced to keep her waiting in the hall while he whispered frantic last minute instructions into Bert's indifferent ears. *"Don't* say you didn't make the chicken, *don't* say huh, *don't* talk about hangovers, *don't, don't, don't, don't."* He forgot to warn Bert against staring at Evalyn's bosom and therefore had to spend a deal of time kicking under the table in an effort to unglue the young man's eyes. For Evalyn was mad, and the madder she was the more formal she became, and the more formal she became—the more bosom. The most fringed prize of her fringed wardrobe haughtily exhibited her mighty forty-two, and she could not have been prouder if it had been bearded. New York always enraged her by its lack of awe to the Vanderhoff name, its crass catering to its own great names. James was usually sympathetic about this, but his delay in opening the door had all but subjected him to her gathering wrath. To add to her irritation his eyes were so constantly fixed on Bert, due to his apprehensions, that he made a dozen wrong answers to her remarks.

"What's the matter with that boy, is he wrong in the head?" she demanded in a loud clear voice when Bert, utterly speechless from the combined effects of James's "don'ts" and the lady's décolletage, stepped to the pantry for rolls.

"I'm afraid I've seated us wrong," said James in a hasty effort to cover Evalyn's dangerous comment.

"I don't see that three people could be seated any differently," said Evalyn, baited by such a nice point. "I'm on your right—he's on your left."

"But that makes Bert on *your* right, Evalyn—" James shook his head and studied the table judiciously, as if the seating of three people was a more scientific matter than met the eye, something to be worked out days ahead by the binomial theory.

Under the soothing effect of the Piesporter Evalyn finally decided to address a remark or two to the pallid, unhealthy young man on her right and by spitting out a sibilant baritone from her front teeth managed to raise Bert's hopeless gaze from her armpits to her chin.

"Williams, you say is your name?"

"Willy," corrected James, fearing Bert's silence. "And I believe you might start right in calling him Bert."

"Bert? You mean Robert?"

"No. Just Bert."

"But that is a nickname, a sort of gangster nickname."

"I tell him it is a nickname, oh, you're absolutely right, Evalyn," said James, and Bert's pallid pan turned from one voice to the other like that of some dumb beast. "But he says it's plain Bert. His father's name was Bert, and his grandfather's name was Bert."

"Why doesn't he call himself Bert the Third ?" suggested Evalyn efficiently.

"Ha," said Bert.

"Where are your family from, Mr. Williams?" asked Evalyn.

"Illinois."

"Where?"

"Illinois."

"My dear boy, of course I know that," said Evalyn impatiently. "Everyone's family spends a few generations in the Middle West, but I mean where were they from *originally?*"

Bert said nothing. The vital question hung on the air while

James blanched, and Evalyn watched Bert's calm carving of the wishbone he had given himself. He would not look up for James's warning eye.

"Virginia?" suggested Evalyn. "Massachusetts? There's a Williams in Baltimore, of course. There's Williams College, too."

"Willy," said Bert and filled his mouth grossly. "Bert," said James with ominous patience. "Evalyn asks where your family were settled before the Middle West period."

Bert gave in grudgingly, swallowed his food.

"Garden of Eden," he said and went into a fit of convulsive mirth that sent him choking and spitting into the kitchen amazingly unharmed by the poison rays from his two companions.

James hastily poured out the last of the Piesporter. They never had more than one bottle, no matter how dearly they loved it for part of the pleasure was in budgeting the last few golden drops, certain that they were the last drops.

"Bert's people were quite simple," he explained with a red face. "Sturdy yeoman stock. Professional in spots. At least there was a Dr. Willy, an orthodontist."

Then he excused himself to slip into the kitchenette to plead with Bert. Bert would not speak but stood licking the mayonnaise bowl with a horrid, sly little grin. It was all James could do to keep his voice down to a whisper, but the number of things he had to say even in a whisper, from pleas to threats, took so long that Evalyn had congealed into an ominous statue when he returned to the table. James took one look at the old senatorial face and quaked. He saw Salzburg vanish in a cloud of magic fire music, Bach's Bethlehem was further off than Joseph's; the pew at Town Hall, the gloomy dinners at the Plaza, the Christmas rum cake—all faded into the impossible. Desperately James asked about Trixie, the ancient poodle it had been his privilege to tutor on all their foreign travels, and the query faintly thawed the lady.

"Trixie is in heat again," she condescended to reply. "It's very troublesome. Of course, I put her in her Kleinerts every morning but she comes home from the park with the rubber all torn. It's outrageous at her age. There ought to be a diet. It's outrageous. OUTRAGEOUS! *Who is that boy?*"

James jumped.

"Bert. You mean Bert," he quavered. "Yes, his sense of humor is a trifle low, I'm afraid. Do you mind if we miss the first group tonight? It's Scarlatti. Not our dish, at all."

"Low, indeed," was all Evalyn said, and they made no more reference to the third person, who did not emerge again, hiding in the tiny kitchen even during the coffee with its minute drop of cognac, which was probably just as well as James didn't want him to know about the brandy. But the worst happened, as James had fearfully anticipated. When he returned to the apartment late that night, the offensive lad had fled bag and baggage even to the applejack. Empty bed, empty dresser drawer, the valuable thesis on cooking cruelly yanked out of the typewriter—ah, that hurt! Not even a note, not even a snapshot.

"Bert!" called James at first commandingly and then coaxingly as if the boy, like Sebastian, would come creeping out from under the sofa. In the same manner he ran to the windows and looked out over the rooftops, rushed to the hall and looked up the stairs, then down, frantically remembering an old saying that cats run upstairs, but dogs—and, perhaps, boys—run down.

"Bert! Oh, hoo-oo! Oh, Ber-ert! Yoo-hoo!"

Gone!

"Damn Evalyn!" shouted James at the top of his voice, and there were real tears in his eyes. "Oh damn, damn, DAMN Evalyn!"

. . . West to East . . .

*T*HE BRENTS AND the Fellows were like *that*.

Everyone talked about it and one member of the foursome, namely Mr. Eugene Brent, of Central Park West, did considerable grumbling over the new friendship. For one thing its effect on his wife was to make her petulant and bored when they were alone. In many other ways it changed her nature. If he prided himself on talking her out of moving to Greenwich Village—an old house with garden on Twelfth Street was her whim one day—she consoled herself by taking up tap dancing, which, God knows, is the first step toward psychoanalysis or divorce. She wanted to go to Nassau and then again she didn't. She thought she'd "go to Columbia and study journalism but I don't know." She thought they'd take a house in Wood's Hole this summer and then again they might go over for the Coronation. She thought she'd dye her hair. She thought she'd ride in the Park every day. She thought they'd store the furniture and move to a hotel. Oh, anything, anything to break the monotony!

She began replacing their respectable Macy furniture with "pieces" from decorators' galleries. The sets of Thackeray, Dickens, Scott and Dumas that had once conveniently filled their book-shelves were now a source of mortification to her. Rather than sets, horrid mark of a Mind-of-the-Month, she would have the shelves bare, or dotted with ugly toy animals in Meissen or Chelsea, with a chic literary flare indicated by a volume of the young English poets and a Babar book.

Brent was well aware that this was all his own doing. It was he who had feared domestic boredom first and had insisted on his Thursday freedom. It was he who had, on such an evening, brought that agent of the devil, Van Deusen, into their simple honest ménage; and after that it was Van who had opened the cage for the little bird and introduced the new world of the devil. Since that day, only a few months back, the little West Side couple had been passed down the line like a football, they had been in many of the best houses once and, while seldom invited themselves, were often the guests of invited guests at glamorous functions. They gave a fresh note to any occasion, Nora with her clear brown face and athletic grace and Brent himself so sensa-tionally average looking. How refreshingly dull they were, everyone agreed! In Prudence Bly's group they shone as the only persons who did not talk or try to talk like Prudence. Indeed their lack of conversation rose to peaks of brilliance, while their appalling lack of malice made them seem quite inhuman.

It was Neal Fellows, who took the Brents when Van deserted them and promoted them from party appendages to the position of family friends. This was an old custom of Neal's known well to everyone in town but the Brents. When Mr. Fellows began to tire of a lady, he sloughed her off onto his wife and left the easing off of the affair to the unwary Anna. The wife and the girl became inseparable; they lunched together, listened together to Neal's manuscripts, together they disparaged any new flirtations he might essay. In time this female friendship tapered off, as so often happens and the girl never knew how painlessly and easily she was let down, nor for that matter did Anna know what had happened.

In the case of Nora Brent, Neal found himself in an odd position. Nora was taking this first affair very seriously and sighed every other minute. "We mustn't! We really mustn't!" and it was all exciting and dangerous and wonderfully naughty. Nora enjoyed it all tremendously and knew Neal must be seriously in love with her, or he wouldn't want her to stay all night; and she felt terribly sorry and kind toward Anna. The charm of such a naïve relationship can wear off for the man, at least and Neal was soon anxious to drop it. But for some odd reason he found himself jealous. Nora's normalness was taking men by storm, and many of them were far better known than Neal, an irksome thought to even a bored lover. Stephen Estabrook, for instance, sent her flowers, and heaven knows flowers from a radio favorite are far superior to any from a mere writer.

So it was that Neal, harassed by play rehearsals and maddened by the suspicion that his latest discovery was herself being rehearsed by better men than he, became very much interested in the problems of Butternut Biscuits and in no time at all had his little charge guarded in his absence by her husband and his own wife. It is easier for two couples to keep out a stranger than for a lone, busy man, so Nora's time was quite taken up by the new intimacy with the Fellows. She was able to see just why Neal needed her by observing Anna's calm complacency; certainly the social life opened up by the Fellows' circle was more entertaining than that of Brent's college and business set. Brent himself did *not* think so. He did not like sitting in cafés till they closed and he did not like being in the doghouse as his faux pas were constantly sending him.

"There are the Dukes," Anna would murmur. "Second table."

"What Dukes?" said Brent, thinking of Windsors and Duke Ellington and even when the millions connected with the name were explained to him, he still was stupidly unimpressed. That sort of stupidity amused people for a while but embarrassed Nora, who was rapidly acquiring a Park Avenue mind.

"Don't say *who* and *what* and *never heard of it,*" she scolded him. "Nobody in that crowd ever says he never heard of anything. Do the way they do. I don't care if it's a book or play or person you never heard of in your life, say 'oh, yes,' as if it were all old stuff to you. Honestly, Gene, you might catch on to a *few* things for my sake!"

Anna and Nora lunched together, they shopped together. Anna enjoyed showing Nora what a name she had made for herself in shops and restaurants and could not have been more self-righteous about her fame if it had come justifiably through a father's bank account or some little labor of her own. Her genius in pinning a high school beau in Gloucester to a youthful engagement warranted recognition, she seemed to feel. Neal paid her for her blindness to his activities by allowing her to ride his name day and night like a pet pony. Nora grew uneasy over the constant loud repetition of this name. Anna waved the name as boldly as if she were only a friend of a friend of Mrs. Fellows instead of the lady herself, who should have calmed down about it by this time.

"Mrs. Neal Fellows's table, please, captain. . . . Charge to Mrs. Neal Fellows! . . . Tell the chef lobster a' la Neal Fellows, he knows what I mean! . . . Seats for Mrs. Fellows!"

Under such constant pressure Nora could not help despising Neal a trifle for enduring this megaphone wife. Anna bragging of her doll husband made Nora see only his faults, she wanted a bigger doll of her own, so it was into this role she put Steve Estabrook.

"Mr. Estabrook's table, please. We are guests of Mr. Estabrook, captain." Even Anna was sometimes routed by the deeper bows of the waiters over the radio name.

Nora was really more excited over being in the swim, even if she could only float, than she was over any man. Much more fun than the parties of her new friends were the evenings in Pelham or Forest Hills with Gene's business friends where she could quietly boast of these parties waving great names, revealing in any number of ways that she was far above the old contract bridge crowd. And Brent gave grumbling evidence of her promotion by his sour comments on "your friend the radio star"—"your admirer's new play!" It had reached a point where the Brent dinners at home were almost silent for Nora could talk of nothing but her new friends or, if she was disappointed by their neglect, her restless plans for some other kind of life. Brent could not open his mouth without derogating the new gods. He saw that his wife now lived for the not-too-frequent commands from court and when the telephone merely offered cocktails with some flour men from Minneapolis, her very voice and eyes lost luster, and you would have imagined that a fortune had been lost. Her excitement in dressing for an evening with the Fellows goaded her husband to scornful slurs.

"You're just not interested in the theater," Nora rebuked him coldly.

Brent *was* interested in the theater, but his interest took the banal, unprofessional form of discussions of plays and acting instead of box office or chic little amusing tattle on advance sales, angels, and managerial losses.

So, bristling with domestic antagonism, Mr. and Mrs. Brent left the rococo splendor of their red-plush, mirror-walled, broccoli-scented lobby the night after Neil's play opened and taxied over to the apartment hotel in the East Fifties where a few intimates were dissecting the latest success.

It was not as pleasant an evening as one might imagine. Anna Fellows always felt that in the cause of her husband all hatchets were buried, and even the Montagues and Capulets must embrace today over the newest triumph of their dear Neal. This was not at all the case. Even if Neal had failed, men would still have disliked him for his collection of women and the ease with which he hoodwinked his wife, always unforgivable in another husband. Moreover he made a great deal of money and invested it shrewdly, never an endearing virtue; and critics had formed the habit of praising his "superb craftsmanship," his "sharp uncompromising satire," and his "magic touch with the box office" so there was no cause nor need for love on that score. Nor did Neal give his friends any reason for loyalty nor defense: he never drank to excess, he never got in trouble, he never made a fool of himself, he never gave anyone reason to feel superior, an elementary rule in friendship; he was not even a target for political attacks from left or right, since his visit to Russia two years ago, a feted guest of the Union, had made him ok with the left and admired for sheer bravery by the right. His satires on both manners and politics were marvels of diplomacy; he pointed out glaring flaws in the regime, then showed what lovable, excusable, thoroughly delightful flaws they really were, so that the word for these works should have been *flatires* instead of satires.

Therefore, rejoicing over his new hit, the Brents found about thirty poker-faced friends, not including half a dozen beautiful boys who followed any parade and who were now wooing Neal by slavish worship of his wife. There was Stephen Estabrook, Nora noted quickly and was hurt that he had not called her for over two weeks but seemed perfectly unaware of neglect, glancing at his wrist watch constantly like any other contented guest, and in the same vein acknowledging introductions with a warm handclasp and an eager look over the shoulder of his vis-à-vis. There was Dol Lloyd, fastidiously perfect as to his gray with black accessories, long slender face sloping into gray-blond hair that of a tired old faun's. Pinckney was there, his pale eyes fastened gloomily on Dol imploring silently, "Where is Bert? Please bring up his name. Have you got him? Where, oh, where is our little pet?"

As Anna bustled about whispering instructions to the waiters, the party wove itself without reservation into a perfect web of dislike for the host. Unpleasantries about the play overheard in the lobby last night were gleefully passed around. Mr. Pinckney spoke of watching the leading lady's nice play of muscles as she tossed the epigrams about, report was circulated of a foreign minister's wife's miscarriage induced by the second act curtain line.

Into this wasps' nest Mr. Fellows himself walked at eleven o'clock, still beaming from his conference with the BO and comfortably happy in the animosity of his guests. He had concluded long ago that it was better in this town to be hated and sought after than loved and avoided as a sweet failure. He looked about for his little West Side couple and was glad to see Nora safely engaged by her husband, so that he might pay court to Jean Nelson, whose lovely white sheath gown was so shoulderless, backless, sleeveless, and chestless that every man present was eager to probe her mind. Neal was pleasantly reminded that nothing was more piquant than discovering the charms of an old hitherto-untapped friend, particularly for a lazy man. He was the victim of a habit, too, of using a new love to tide him through the writing and production of each of his plays, then allowing the curtain to fall on both play and love at the same time. If he could just get Mrs. Brent settled, he would be ready for his new courtship but he did not like raw edges and there was still the unexplored about Nora. Certainly he had never been so annoyed by jealousy before, speculating spasmodically whether someone, say Steve Estabrook, really would get to first base one of these days. The puzzle held him much longer than did the lure of her healthy beauty.

"Darling," Jean said to him, a cloud of divine incense floating toward him from her fair hair, "you are so sweet not to let your head be turned by all these people. Such character! You're absolutely *too* strong!"

Even Neal could not fail to overhear the snatches of flattery to which he was so marvelously immune: Why didn't the tightwad loosen up with his profits and take a good house instead of a dinky hotel-decorated suite at a second-rate hotel? The least he could do was buy a painting of his own, give a few good artists a break, but not he, the blue-plate art furnished by the management was good enough for him—Cape Cod Doorways, Venetian canals, Godey prints. And why couldn't he buy Anna a respectable diamond bracelet instead of those bangles made by the Fred Harvey Indians between trains? How about this smiling Scrooge giving a real party, too? . . . Yes, that was why he lived this way, so he wouldn't have to return handsome dinners, he could return champagne with lousy martinis or Grade B highballs. What did he do with his dough anyway? Try and borrow fifty from him and see how white he gets; how was it that no pennies were ever lost in transit to his sock? No, Neal's head was not turned by these whispers of his intimates, nor did he give a damn.

Standing on one foot then the other, by the bartender, was Eugene Brent glowering around the room. He wished to heaven Nora would get over liking these people the way she got over the journalism course and the Santa Fe notion. He would never be any better at it, that he knew. He did not remember faces nor names nor what it was that people did that he should be impressed by; he did not remember authors' names, just book titles and never the ones written by the author to whom he was speaking. He did not know anything about Palm Beach; his subject was fishing off the Keys. He had dimly learned one lesson, which was that if someone was neither attractive, clever, kind, nor chic but was loudly applauded for these qualities, it meant he was Society. But this scrap of intelligence did not help him get through an evening.

Anna stopped to chat with him but Anna depressed him with her earnestness, and usually she brought him some dud, beaming as if she had located a pearl in her oyster instead of vice versa. He saw her bearing down on him presently with a toothy, bejeweled apparition in green velvet, a small feather in her hair, which could only be—and indeed was—Miss Evalyn Greer Vanderhoff, the girlfriend of James Pinckney, whom the latter had finally induced to meet playwright Neal. Guests had been passing the Philadelphia Nero around like a wet baby and Anna was forever finding her scrapped in a corner with a fixed awful smile. As one doomed, Gene saw Nora slip away before Evalyn's advance; the picture stamped itself on his desperate memory of Nora's apricot satin on apricot skin, amethyst sandals on bare feet. Oh, he was definitely sunk for the evening now; for he was not clever enough to be rude. Good-bye, dear ones, he silently prayed as he surrendered, good-bye oh, darling nasty people, good-bye dear lady foes of my wife, good-bye gentlemen so fondly measuring me for horns! Good-bye again and again!

"Would you like a glass of water?" asked Brent and realized with dreary resignation that his voice and accent had changed. Over this he had no power. It always happened at times when a roomful of varying cosmopolitans' twitter rebuked his native accent, and words in his throat were so frightened that they tottered every-which-way when he finally conjured sound. Wooja lakka glarsa worter? Wud ye lark a glossa wotta? Wurja—

"Nayoh," said Miss Vanderhoff, and Brent was hushed.

Miss Vanderhoff gave him a penetrating look through lorgnette, for she herself was one who counted on speech as the one banner of breeding. No matter how banal the thought, how vulgar or trivial, if it was uttered in her own rigid conception of a cultivated voice, the speaker was—well—possible. Miss

Vanderhoff's own speech was not quite Philadelphia nor East nor South nor Hahvad nor Oxford but something more wonderful than all of these; for she had invented it herself, and the more baffling it was to others the more satisfactory it was to her own ears. For instance, Evalyn did not fasten on the *r* as the key to culture but sounded her *r*s firmly, unafraid, even allowing them to detonate like a cheap village bell. Nor did the *a* broad or flat interest her; her *a*s varied, sometimes it was so flat it turned quietly into a short *e,* yet in the very next word came out as pear-shaped as anything. The *s* was her triumph, however. She thrust her lower jaw out until the lower teeth were a bare eighth of an inch past the uppers and through this latched jaw she whistled.

"Issssint thet interessssting?"

She kept her teeth together with the resolution of a virgin keeping her knees locked and, apart from her "Oah isssint thet nayasse!" and other favorite *s* ejaculations, her articulating stance gave her entire vocabulary a genteel sibilance that was unfailingly impressive.

"Zzzhreally?" she said to Brent again and again and he could not figure out how she did it, even though he concentrated with the aid of six whiskys neat. *S* was in everything; like a cockney *h* it was impossible to conceive just how or where it had crept in. Miss Vanderhoff clearly felt that a word without its *s* was a word without its pants, and the odd part of it was that no one could converse with her for five minutes without catching it. Simple, rugged fellow that he was, Mr. Brent, in no time at all cockeyed, found himself trapped in sizzling sentences, utterly unable to get back to his own language. He signaled Nora, who was happily oblivious to all in Stephen's conversation, he appealed to Pinckney, who had finally engaged Dol Lloyd in deep conversation but there was no help anywhere, no one to rescue the poor sinker in the swamp. As to Anna—smiling sunnily at them from a safe distance—

"Izzzzint ssshe sssszwheet?"

"Yissss."

"Ssssssoah nayasssee."

"I ssssink ssssoah."

When James Pinckney finally tore himself away from Dol to take Evalyn off to her train, he found them fizzing away at each other like a pair of seltzer bottles. Mr. Brent shook *s*s out of his hair like confetti after the ball, and for days afterward feared his tongue was between his front teeth for good and all.

The evening marked the revolution of Eugene Brent. He left these occasions to Nora alone hereafter. And Evalyn Greer Vanderhoff did not speak to poor Pinckney on her way to her train until the very last minute when she informed him that she was through with New York, absolutely through! She had been neglected, abused and left to a dolt and she was very surprised at James, very surprised indeed!

. . . the run-around . . .

PRUDENCE RECOGNIZED Anna's hourglass figure wedged in the rolling machine at Arden's and was inclined to dart swiftly into the next booth, but Anna had sighted her in the mirror.

"Prudence!" she cried, flinging the Christmas *Tatter* to the floor with all her strength. "Where have you been keeping yourself? No one sees you, why didn't you come to us Friday, did you see the play, didn't you think it was Neal's best, especially the summerhouse scene, the poor darling, will you come up for badminton at four?"

"Hello, Anna," answered Prudence.

She looked ghastly. Anna was the only woman in New York who would not notice it, and that only because she was forever wrapped up in Neal. Look at the puffs under her eyes from insomnia, look at the shoulder bones popping out, look at the drawn mouth, if anybody looked like a girl that had been given the run-around, that was Prudence. She was enraged at this external evidence of ordinary feminine heartache.

"Is Jean here?" asked Anna and extended a knee and heavy thigh into the machine maws to be kneaded, balancing herself on one large flat foot.

Was Jean there? Of course, Jean was there. Jean was everywhere. There was no escaping her. Wherever Prudence ran, this sweet Doppelganger was right behind her. She had gone into the beauty shop alone, but in fifteen minutes Jean had sent a message from a turquoise satin floor pad in the exercise room, and Prudence must stop in just a second to watch Jeanie practicing the scoots.

"Isn't it divoon?" said Jean while a victrola played *My Hat's on the Side of My Head* to Jean dragging her fanny jauntily across the mattress. "It's the scoots."

"I call it worms," said Prudence and half a dozen exercise girls in varying pastel satin rompers broke into chimes of toy mirth. "Sofa does it every day."

"Shall we take a peek at Valentina's for negligees? Shall we stop at Le Mirliton for a bacardi?" Jean burbled. "Darling, if you insist on staying for badminton, do you mind if I take Sofa and run up to Nora Brent's for dinner? I know you can't stand her, and it will be so boresome; but I simply have to show people I'm not jealous because Steve likes her."

Did she mind? Oh, divine, divoon freedom, Prudence thought happily. When she encountered Anna Fellows, she was considering getting in touch with Harvey Nelson, begging him to forgive and take back his erring wife. Or must she escape by taking a foreign engagement? But then Jean would follow her to London or Paris. So this is how difficult it is to get rid of a woman, reflected Prudence, so this is why men have learned to be so wary! And this elation at having just a dinner's freedom was just what any husband felt!

"I wish," said Anna, as they rode down the elevator together, "you would dine with me. It's Thursday, you know and Neal is out."

Anna had many comforting virtues, but she was definitely one of the half-people, a type Prudence always found uninspiring. Whatever they were in themselves was lost in the imprint of another's pattern and was as unsatisfactory as a fifth carbon copy.

"The girls are coming in for cocktails," said Anna. "They're so anxious to meet you."

The Cosies! Of course, Anna's old bunch, the Cosies. "I have a tentative dinner date with Jefferson Abbott," lied Prudence.

"Bring him along," urged Anna. "I'm so interested in him. Neal might be able to help him, you know. Hyman says the boy is having a bad time, not eating and all that, and so proud! Do bring him."

Not eating, yet that was more agreeable than calling on his youthful girlfriend, Prudence thought, puzzled. Of course, her date was not at all a date, since he refused to telephone after she had sent telegrams. It was maddening when he was as aware as she was of the attraction between them; it was a perpetual thorn that he was obstinate enough to resist her when his every gesture and even his scorn indicated interest. She and Jean had found him at Dol's recently, and again he had been insulting about her mode of life. Prudence was annoyed for days over this rock she could not move. Jean's gasps of wonder at such hostility did not help.

"Do bring him," repeated Anna, climbing out of the car in front of her modest hotel. "Do you think he'll mind five or six women? The Cosies may stay."

"Oh, he'll adore it," said Prudence and leaving Anna, asked the driver to go downtown slowly, so that she might consider a new plan of attack—anything to break this monotony of Jean, anything to make up for Steve, anything to show Jeff Abbott who was the stronger.

. . . the old peaches . . .

O<small>NE BY ONE</small> the ladies flew from the elevator, pitter-patter down the velvet-floored corridor to Room 1174. The door opened—Surprise!—arms flew out, squeals, twitters, coos and cackles scattered on the air like flying feathers, and the Cosies were together again. In the fifteen years these ladies had been in constant touch with each other, they had never ceased to be amazed at meeting each other of all people, and their ecstasy over each other's hats, gloves, complexions, wit, and general perfection had never waned. Can women be loyal, can women be fair, can women be friends—oh God, and how! Two of the five Cosies had husbands, and the group ecstasy flung itself on the associate-Cosy as ebulliently as if he was a new fudge cake. All of the girls were simply crazy about Neal, and they attended matinees of every one of his plays and loved them, I really mean that. True, they were a little frightened when he barged in on their teas with Anna; he was

a little too gruff for the gentle creatures and he would never discuss the points in his works with them, which was hardly fair since
four out of five had majored in English and were especially crazy
about the Drama—Beaumont and Fletcher, Marlowe, *Voyage de
Monsieur Perrichon, The Trimplet,* Moscow Art, and intimations of
Jacques Copeau!

"Neal's so shy!" they gleefully decided and teased him no end.

Neal was shy of them, true enough. It took far more courage
than he could muster to face this little group, suspecting rightly
as he did that although he did not know one from the other,
every one of them knew all about him: what size underwear he
wore, what curried shrimps did to his liver, what gargle, what
mineral oil, what contraceptives he used, how long he sat in a
tub, and the very state of his bowels. The girls were dominated
by Anna, who had been a Big-Girl-on-the-Campus—YW president, Try-Phy, Junior Prom chairman, Glee Club manager, Best-
Liked—when they were only Little Girls.

The last to arrive today was "Tommy," who came in from
Bronxville especially for the party. "Tommy" was a pinched,
sallow brunette, with sunken black eyes and a thin red mouth.
She had on a new skunk cape and hat, which caused a tremendous squealing. "Tommy" had once been engaged at college to
an Incompetent, a blue-eyed jolly nobody soon sent flying by
"Tommy's" mama. Ever since that brief romance she spent her
time in sanitariums, in quiet hotels in the Bavarian Alps and
even more with a psychoanalyst, a Dr. Pen, who was a perfect
darling and recommended sports. Therefore Januarys usually
found her skiing carefully at Kitsburg or Sun Valley, autumns
found her in Carolina or Arizona earnestly cooperating with
horses as per Dr. Pen, and in between times she wrote long
heavily underlined Round Robins to the Cosies. If Anna was
queen, "Tommy" was the fortunate princess; for fifteen years
almost her only happiness was in the sad reflection that at least

her life *looked* glamorous and full. "You lucky rascal!" the Cosies accused her.

After the first cries had subsided, a waiter wheeled in the canapés and the favorite cocktail of the girls, a "Debutante" consisting of gin, orgeat, grenadine, lime, and probably meringue. Anna announced her "surprise," for there was always a glorious surprise, which was that she had invited Prudence Bly to join them.

"Why, you regular old *peach!*" they all rejoiced. "Prudence Bly! Oh, how *adorable!*"

There was a bustling air of Alumnae Day about the place; the women had slightly frozen, wizened masks of their young faces, not the serene middle-aged faces of their own mothers at that age, but the eager restlessness of eye, the still frantic seeking for *What* that preserves and shrivels youth far into the fifties these days. It was almost the truth, their boast, that they looked exactly the same as they had fifteen years before, in some lights even better; but in crueler glares incipient wrinkles, drooping mouth lines popped into view, and their faces became what they would be twenty years hence. The eyes would always be eager, though each year the look of hurt astonishment increased that fewer and fewer things were peachy, people were more likely to throw than to *be* old brisks.

At these reunions Anna bloomed. It was as if her life with Neal, her everyday routine, was not real but a fairy story to be related to the wide-eyed girls. Neal's coldness to the Cosies made them all the dearer and more exclusively her own, her private pleasure, just as his carefully timed absence made him all the more respected by the girls. Nor did Anna ever include the girls in her theatrical or generally social activities. They never met Prudence Bly nor James Pinckney nor Van Deusen nor Dol Lloyd nor Stephen Estabrook. They never met them but they knew them well. Every weakness, every intimate detail of these personalities was known to the Cosies through Anna's faithful reporting; certainly James Pinckney would have been amazed to know that the two modest ladies who asked his help at the Museum one day on a Semi-Precious Jewel paper for a Stamford Club knew all about his Aunt Hepzibah Shugg in Oklahoma City and considered the letter he wrote home from Capri in 1931 very amusing indeed. They knew, these perfect strangers, that although Prudence Bly's picture was in the *Bazaar* with three practicing duchesses and a prince, there were extant candid camera shots of her dancing in Harlem with a few definitely untitled characters; they knew that Jean Nelson's "family estate" on Cape Cod was named SHORE DINNER, and their own simple observations were overshadowed by the marginalia of more spectacular figures. The Cosies were really the Friends of People, each member derived color from an absent personality and at their meetings you would have thought they were five stand-ins for personages too high up to attend. After all the hats and coats and lipsticks had been tried on and an amazing number of "Debutantes" imbibed, an order for chicken à la King and crepes Suzette was sent downstairs. At the same time a telephone rang, and Mr. Neal Fellows cautiously inquired of his wife if it was all right to come home yet.

"Come right home this minute, darling," cried Anna. "We're all alone—just 'Tommy' and 'Buzz' and 'Winks' and 'Boo' and me."

. . . The perfect wife . . .

OF COURSE, Anna, the Old Brick of the Cosies, was not the Anna of Neal's world. The Cosies, in spite of their fondness for each other, were so absorbed in demonstrating and articulating their mutual devotion that they had no genuine knowledge of each other at all. Their exaggerated admiration for Anna was offset by Neal's friends' pity for the same, for her resolute dignity during his noisy infidelities was certainly deserving of pity. Anna baffled them, however, by sedately assuming the role of a protected, adoring, and adored little wife, and it was difficult to pity a lady who basked in such a role, however imaginary her good fortune might be. Friends who had just left Neal candidly and hilariously in bed with possibly a mental equal would look shiftily at the floor, while Anna discoursed plaintively on Neal's jealousy, his uxoriousness, his stern rules for her conduct.

"Oh, I must not take another cocktail, Neal hates me to take

more than two except martinis, isn't he mean? . . . Yes, I know my
other hat is much smarter but Neal simply won't allow me to wear
a red hat, isn't it a pity when I love red? . . . I'd love to stay later,
but Neal will be so cross if I'm not in the house when he comes
in. . . . Oh, goodness, is it really ten! Neal will make such a scene if
he has to come into an empty apartment. . . . Yes, I know he may
be out all night but he insists I should be home anyway to talk over
the casting. You know he leaves absolutely everything to me!"

Some men became attracted by this demure Victorian wifeli-
ness and paid court. Unfortunately Anna was so healthily sexed
that she was likely to succumb all out of character if it was conve-
nient—that is, too rainy to go home or too early to go to her dress-
fitting; but all stigma of sin was removed in these rare episodes by
her running chatter of Neal as she undressed, boasting loyally of
his witty faults, bragging in a dozen strange beds of her perhaps
old-fashioned chastity and of her husband's unshaken worship,
until often the intruder's momentary lust gave way to irritation,
he was likely to expostulate that this overpossessive husband of
hers had not been home for a week, was, as the whole town knew,
baldly pursuing some well-known belle with minor scampers on
the side. If, however, the would-be lover's infatuation was enough
to tolerate Anna's wifely pangs, then he could continue in favor by
adopting the role of wholehearted admirer of Neal. He must up-
hold Neal publicly, must flatter him, urge on his anecdotes, praise
his work, his *mots,* his drinks, his habits, and scourge his critics.
No different from other lovers of wives of celebrities, he must defend Neal's very virtue, must retort when gossip began about the
master's amours, "I happen to know all about that affair. Neal
was perfectly frank about it to Anna and me. He says E........ is a
gorgeous-looking girl, and he liked to take her out just to look at
her for hours at a stretch. He says it rests him. He thinks she's terribly dumb, as, of course, she is. He likes her but as for sex he
quite frankly says he'd rather sleep with a wax dummy."

"Yes, Neal always has to try everything," someone might murmur and, of course, be properly rebuffed.

There was the unvoiced compulsion to free his own relationship to Anna from the taint of mere consolation and to make her seem desirable rather than forlorn the lover must clear her as best he could of the unalluring label of betrayed wife. Indeed the admirer of Anna—there had been several and all short-lived—had such a shameful role to play that none but inferior men were content to play it and were never properly thanked by Neal for their enforced loyalty but more than likely held up to private ridicule, ridicule that Anna ungraciously enjoyed.

Eventually Anna's unwavering faith in her own happiness broke through other women's claims to Neal like a soulless mighty tank. It is impossible for other women to rejoice in a lover whose wife is so conspicuously complacent, so suspiciously content, who gently smiles at his open flirtations as if this was all charming child's play well-understood and often discussed between the happy couple, so customary that the wife could well afford a benign indifference, touched, perhaps, with pity for the new, alas only temporary, slave.

So Neal's women—and for that matter even Neal—were mystified, and believed Anna was cruelly, diabolically clever, while Neal, fairly shallow himself, respected Anna for her deep devotion to himself, always an impressive and moving thing to a man. Anna was neither clever nor deep but so thoroughly narcissistic she honestly did not see how any man could fail to see how superior she was to all other women in looks, brains, and general nobility. The Cosies had done this for her and fed her vanity week by week. Betrayed sweethearts had tried to emulate Anna's successful technique of possession, but genuine emotion ruined its effectiveness. Clinging and confident, Anna held her husband because of her brave, unwincing stupidity. She was too egotistical to admit he was lost so he never was.

. . . Mr. and Mrs. Hornickle of Rye . . .

$\mathcal{I}$T PROBABLY WAS NOT a good idea going straight to his room. He had not asked her there, and she had been obliged to ask the address of Dol. If he was broke, he would resent someone from his hometown witnessing his poverty. Prudence thought this over and, having arrived at no decision, dismissed the car a block north of the address to allow more time for thought. She did not want to leave anything unfinished in this life, and Jeff was still to be finished. It preyed on her. Was his antagonism genuine or the sign of a strong sex pull? She could not leave this problem unsolved.

Near the drugstore on the corner a large man was tenderly urging a small dog to function. Prudence saw next to the drugstore the Armenian restaurant mentioned by Dol with the dark entrance beside it to the upstairs rooms. The large man, at last successful, pulled the dog on its leash toward this very doorway a few steps ahead of Prudence, and it was then she recognized the dog as her own Sealyham.

"Come on, Sofa," said the man.

For some instinctive reason Prudence did not cry out but watched dog and man disappear in the doorway. Sofa here! Why, Jean had taken Sofa! Jean and Sofa! Then with the fatal intuition of the guilty Prudence realized that Jean, too, must have obtained Jeff's address. On her way to the Brents for dinner, was she, so that no one would think she was jealous! Boresome, was it! It was incredible that a stupid girl like Jean should be as deft a liar as a smart girl like Prudence. She was suddenly furious, remembering Jean's exclamations of the last few days. "Isn't it strange that Mr. Abbott dislikes you so much, when you say he was such a beau of yours years ago? Isn't it odd when any other man would be so flattered to have you run after him, because you do, don't you, dear? Do you suppose he just happens to dislike your type, or is it a pose? But fantastic! Utterly fantastic! I never saw anyone so strong-minded and so virile! I'm really rather intrigued."

Oh, yeah?

Prudence tiptoed up the stairs, listening for voices. A door opened two floors above her and a man said, "I brought Sofa back, Jeff, and I'll run along now." The door closed, and the man lumbered down the hall to another room. Prudence flew up the next flight. She heard Sofa's merry bark and stopped short. No other sound inside the door for a moment, then a chuckle, a thoroughly amiable chuckle from that most unamiable of young men.

"I can't get over your coming down here to cook supper for me," Jeff was saying. "It's the last thing I would have expected from a girl like you. I swear it makes me laugh."

"But I adore cooking!" It was Jean all right, even though the sentiment was startlingly foreign-sounding. "I'm just a small-town girl, darling, there isn't a thing about a house I don't love."

"I'm damned," and the appreciative chuckle again.

"If you knew how bored I get with my life," sighed Jean.

Dumfounded, Prudence stood still. When she finally crept downstairs, her knees were wobbly and the hand grasping the banister, quite clammy. This must be the way any deceived husband felt, not half so much jealousy as astonishment that any creature so inferior to himself could be so much more clever. Never an inkling that she was after Jeff! The "boresome dinner" with the Brents! Oh, it was too much. Prudence, out in the street, felt her head swelling and boiling with conflicting furies. To be fooled a second time by such a little idiot as Jean! Steve first and now Jeff! And Jeff was hers, whether he knew it or not, he was the whole part of her she had hidden, he was hers to neglect or love or destroy. Jean knew that. She wouldn't have gone after him if she hadn't known it. Jean could not love a man unless some other woman's perfume was still upon him. That was Jean. Prudence stumbled along the curb, not caring who saw her, dimly meaning to flag a taxi but forgetting as they flew past her. Things were too confused. She felt afraid as if her invented façade was cracking up, she could not count on herself anymore. She had a moment of lucidity wondering why her bond with Jeff Abbott seemed more final than her affair with Steve; it was because Jeff was underneath everything, he was the props under everything she had built, he was Silver City, he was herself. He was her secret candy box that she had put aside for some dark day and then found rifled.

She got into a cab presently and knew she should go to Anna's as she had promised to meet the Cosies and then go home to put on her new dress for the Club. There was a new dress waiting from Bergdorf, a shell-pink thing under gauze, demurely indecent and she had in her purse this minute the innocent ribbon she planned to wear in her hair. At this instant she could have wished the ribbon was a revolver, for never had murder seemed so necessary.

"The hell with the club," she said aloud. "The hell with Anna. I'm going to Steve."

That was the ticket. Begin all over from scratch. If things had gone wrong since a certain date, set the clock back; erase the intervening hours. She knew this was a mistake but she wanted to make a great crashing honest-to-God mistake. She wanted to even when she walked through the ridiculously pretentious modernistic lobby of his apartment hotel and thought that nobody but a radio star would select such a bleakly tasteless place to live. Funny, she never thought that when she used to come here, infatuated. Here, too, the help was conditioned by the clientele; radio, nightclub, and cinema stars were what the porters lived by.

"I hear you got some fine new songs, Miss Bly," said the doorman. "That last record was a pip."

"Well, stranger," said the elevator boy happily. "Sure looks good seeing you back. Mr. Estabrook said to say he was out to everybody, but that never means you."

Well, that would be one on Steve, then.

Steve himself opened the door. He was in handsome new yellow pajamas with a black Chinese coat. She didn't know why it looked utterly silly to her but it did. And the long carved cigarette holder! No, he was not surprised. It had been four angry months, but he was not surprised.

"Come in, Mrs. Hornickle," he said, with a courtly bow. "And how did your little talk go at the Garden Club?"

He took her furs, her hat, her bag.

"The ladies found it very stimulating, Mr. Hornickle," said Prudence. *"The Happiness of Flowers* was my subject."

"You couldn't have chosen a nicer theme, Mrs. Hornickle," he said, leading her firmly into the next room. "So much discontent in the world, so many buttonholes without a flower. Take the freesia!"

Four months since she'd been here. There was Dinky in his rocker, in a tiny replica of his master's pajamas. There was the same victrola playing one of his own recordings of *Moon Over Miami*. Everything the same but—

"Were you able to do much on the genealogy, Mr. Hornickle?" she asked.

"Very little, I'm afraid, Mrs. Hornickle, very little indeed. I was so upset by the material on the Choctaw Hornickles. Fancy one's grandmother on a reservation, Mrs. Hornickle!"

"Better on than off, Mr. Hornickle, if you'll pardon my taking the long view. Could I trouble you with this zipper, Mr. Hornickle?"

It was perfectly hopeless, of course. Even in each other's arms she knew so well it was hopeless, there is no magic for tired love. This was why she had come, but it wasn't going to help. Murmuring in the dark, she thought how silly, silly above all else, were the movements of love when the reason for them had fled. Here she was in his arms but wondering why and why she had ever found them sufficient. As bad as pansies, these professional he-men, the same elegant small-clothes, scents, little luxuries. This was the man who had had the power to throw her life off its organized tracks, upset an applecart that had taken her years to construct. She saw the careful part in his beautiful sleek black hair, recognized the barber by the scent. She recoiled from the big muscular hands, so exquisitely cared for were they. The even shimmering tan of his fine body only made her smile, knowing it came from a faithful regime under the sun lamp at Health Center. Everything that she had, in love, loved about him seemed ridiculous now, even his eagerness to renew relations with her, an eagerness mingled, she sensed, with the apprehension that owing to too recent dissipations he may have worn her welcome out before she arrived.

"Hopeless," she thought. "It's made everything worse." Jeff Abbott was the man she wanted, that was all there was to that. If she had dared, she would have leaped out of the place, said "Goodnight and thank you," and rushed away forever. But lovers reunited have roles they must play, and they were both seasoned troupers. Both knew, when they kissed good-night, that never had time been more wasted. It could never come back. Three years of love and jealousy were definitely lost. No, you could not turn back.

"It's eleven, darling, and you've got to dress for the club," Stephen said. "I'll drive you straight home, or you'll be late."

"Let me go alone," said Prudence. "I'm considering doing some thinking."

What did it matter whether she ever saw the Vedado again? A lousy restaurant where she sang lousy songs. Jeff knew that was unimportant. Jeff knew it didn't matter whether she had a pink new dress or whether the Vedado closed or shut. She was be-witched, Prudence thought unhappily, her brain was no longer her own, it said things Jeff Abbott was thinking, not what she had so carefully taught herself to think. She went straight home. Three years of Steve! What in God's name had been the matter with her? Why couldn't Jean have had him and welcome? Silk pajamas! Cologne! Dinky! The top hats and white ties emerging from her elevator when she reached the River Hotel made her sneer. All right, maybe she was going crazy, maybe Jeff Abbott had turned her brain upside down. Anyway she was not going to the Vedado tonight. She brushed the pink dress off the ruffled counterpane and went to bed. She heard the telephone ringing frantically; the Club was on her trail, but she did not answer. Hours later she heard Jean come in and felt Sofa's warmth at the foot of her bed.

"How was your dinner?" she asked carefully.

"But dull!" Jean answered readily. "Just Gene's business friends. I simply suffered agonies! And guess who was there!"

All right, who was there, liar?

"Who?" Prudence asked instead of obeying her first impulse.

"Harvey Nelson, no less! We came home together and stopped at the Vedado for a drink, but you had just left there," blithely pursued Jean. "I heard the new dress was positively sensational!"

"Really?"

The shamelessness of her! It was fantastic.

"Of course, Nora Brent is really such a fool!" said Jean.

"How nice for you," said Prudence and turned her face to the wall.

She heard Jean humming in the bathroom. The pink dress had been a sensation, had it? And Harvey had been at the Brents, had he? And that left her with something to sing about in the bathroom, did it? Dear, dear Jeanie! Prudence fell asleep and, when she woke next day, she heard Jean's voice instructing Nellie in the next room.

"There will be four guests, Nellie," Jean was saying. "Be sure to serve the armagnac with the coffee; I'm so tired of Prudence's Courvoisier. And use the orange bitters in the martinis, they're so much better!"

Prudence came sleepily but grimly to the living-room door.

"There will be no guests and no dinner, Nellie," she said. "I'll have poached eggs in bed."

Jean was arranging giant lilies in a huge vase and stood transfixed at Prudence's interruption.

"Why—why, Prudence, what is it? What in the *world*—"

"Maybe Miss Prudence feel like being alone," suggested Nellie blandly.

"Exactly," said Prudence and banged the door. "But I've asked people!" Jean cried helplessly. "Prudence, darling!"

"Have to take 'em down to the restaurant," Nellie said briskly. "Miss Bly ain't in no mood."

"But Prudence!" Jean wailed against the locked bedroom door. "Something's happened—what is it? Prudence, please tell me—oh, dear! What have I done? Oh, Prudence! Oh, *dear!*"

She continued to wail softly against the door while Prudence's voice rang out sharply from within.

"Is that you, Harvey? . . . Harvey Nelson?" she was shouting over the phone. "It's Prudence, Harvey. Harvey, I'm fed up—for God's sake come and get it."

. . . Harlem to Bay Ridge . . .

$\mathcal{S}$OME FORTUNATES have souls of cork so that no matter how many times they sink to bottom it is only a matter of time before they are popping blithely about again on the waves. New York is full of these cork-lined robots, up and down they pop through every one of the ages: Great War, Freud, Proust, Depression, Marx, and Streamline; they far outlast the sturdy swimmers and the periodic dunking to the bottom seems to keep them fresher than the steady labors of the faithful; their constant somersaults keep them wiry and young. Van Deusen was largely cork with asbestos trimmings. His misadventures might stun him momentarily, but in good season he came back lighter than ever. Intimations of his recovery were now coming to him after an unusually long blurred period. He had spent several days trying to figure out how it was he had ended up in Brooklyn this way at his long lost or rather long unclaimed wife's apartment. At one time in his life these blanks in his memory when he seemed to have functioned somewhere, somehow, and with God knows who, as a human being of sorts, disturbed him frightfully. He was never sure when strangers spoke to him just what his relations with them might have been; he tormented his mind trying to discover remnants of whatever this experience with them might be and he dared not ask. Finally, when it became habitual, he began to be amused. There was his own life, and there was his zombie life. Within him, he fondly concluded, was a mysterious stranger. He was Mr. A, and the zombie was Mr. B. The two never met and it was only occasionally that Mr. A had any record of what Mr. B, using the Van Deusen name, had been up to. This last adventure of Mr. B's had ended up in a bedroom in Bay Ridge and must have been a prolonged abuse of the family name for A was still trembling so much that he could not hold a glass, and his whole soul felt purged and wan.

"Van Deusen in Bay Ridge! Van Deusen back with old Bessie! Can you imagine that!" he mused, lying on Bessie Van Deusen's—she had kept his name—best pink sateen bed, coffee and crumb cake in hand, since as soon as Bessie went to her shop, Van enjoyed *petite déjeuner* in bed, a luxury forbidden by her on account of the crumbs. "Brooklyn! Old Bessie! Good God, how fantastic!"

It would have entertained him vastly to know that Bessie's shop help considered him a calamity as colossal as any war. Bessie's Beauty Parlor, Croquignole Wave, Rejuvenation Facials, Manicure, with its smirking wax head graciously decorating the window, was over a Swedish delicatessen store on Fourth Avenue in the Seventies. The help in both of these places and even in the markets next door now knew the whole unpleasant story of how poor Mrs. Bessie's husband had had the nerve to turn up again after all these years. Mrs. Bessie was hard-working and well-thought-of, and everyone shook his head over this undeserved blow.

"There he was in the vestibule waiting for me," Bessie told over and over, "so what could I do? Twenty years since I seen him, and I wouldn't a known him if it wasn't for the bow he gives. Clicks his heels and down he bobs like an actor. 'Wife,' he says, and I just give one look and says 'My God!'"

It certainly is tough luck when a woman's husband turns up after two decades of blessed amnesia, especially if the lady is an honest, hard-working little woman who really can't afford a husband, especially such a high-class one. But Bessie was fair-minded and felt it was her cross to look after him, once he did turn up, though God knows why he had come to her with all his society women to turn to. It had been on his account, after the premature crash of their marriage, that Bessie had moved to Bay Ridge. Van had often boasted in her presence that he would never set foot in Brooklyn, so Bessie, born a Brooklyn girl anyway, concluded that Brooklyn was just the place for her. Her brief sojourn in New York as a hotel manicurist had brought her nothing but trouble anyway, especially Van Deusen. And now here he was again, claiming rewards as if he deserved them and being intolerably amused about it all.

"Back to Bessie!" he chuckled a dozen times a day during his lazy convalescence. "How Prudence would laugh!"

He began to have dim fugitive recollections of a dark closet bedroom at the Fogarty's, of Papa Fogarty shouting a great deal and pushing him outdoors; of long fuzzy walks in strange neighborhoods and then—fishing around in his memory for clues—he recalled a dismal period of hideous remorse, shame, suicidal mortification in a Harlem hotel bedroom. As in a photoplay he saw shots of himself following crowds aimlessly, standing with a silent, grave group of men before a blackboard in a stockbroker's office, standing with a silent, grave group of men before a blackboard in an employment office. He even read in chalk on the board "Crucible Steel . . . 109 ½" and then the letters dissolved into "Dishwasher . . . $14." He saw himself or rather he saw Mr. B, in an undertaking parlor in the Bronx, assuring a pale gaunt bald man that he would be delighted to begin work at once as undertaker's assistant. He had always been interested, he said.

"It's an opportunity in a thousand," admitted his employer.

Mr. A, sitting up in Bessie's bed in Bay Ridge, mused morbidly on the past activities of Mr. B.

A funeral parlor! he thought with something of a shiver. Good heavens, B!

All there was to this opportunity was to sleep in the Parlor at night, watching over any stiffs that chanced to be held there awaiting burial and to receive any new ones that sought admittance during the night. Van pictured them stalking with marble feet down Lenox Avenue like the statue in *Don Giovanni,* banging on the plate glass windows, bellowing forth orders for their burial. Not a bad berth at all that B fell into, reflected Van: room free, bed free, true a mat over a stone bench at night might not be too cozy, but there was surely no fault to be found with the room, a beautiful baronial place with wax flowers in great stone amphora, giant ferns in every corner behind which plaster angels hovered. No objection surely to such comforts. And by sliding open the middle doors you had the benefit of a little alcove— chapel, piano, organ and all. Was there any objection to the assistant practicing his repertoire to while away the lonely evenings? None, whatever. All this luxury, mind you, and nothing to do but be there from 6 P.M. to 6 A.M. with five dollars a week besides as pure velvet. A chance in a million.

It was rather cold at night in the Palm Grove Funeral Parlor. That may have accounted for the twinges of rheumatism now afflicting the convalescent Mr. A. The piano, too, was sadly out of tune; but even so, the brave sorties into the *Military Polonaise* all hours of the night brought little groups of curious faces to the front windows. It amused Van to step back from the piano, part the rubber vines on the latticed doorway and bow to this mildly surprised audience.

"I will now play a nocturne by Chopin," he would announce in a ringing voice, "by special request."

The undertaker himself deferred so politely to Van's advice on the dressing of the dead that Van vaguely suspected a lack of legitimate preparation for the profession. No novice could have listened more eagerly to the itinerant musician's suggestions on special colognes, coiffures, and the use of a color rinse in the embalming fluid, than this grave bald professional. It was to Van Deusen that the success of Mrs. Hiram Bomberg's funeral was due, and the embalmer freely admitted it. The so-called Dr.— whether Reverend or medical was always a question—Grunt, with his assistant Mr. Van Deusen, worked out an entirely new personality for the dead Mrs. Bomberg. Gold was dusted through the dank grayish locks, false curls and false eyelashes added, an inviting smile stenciled on the lips, eyebrows re-arranged to neat surprised arcs, the whole creation drenched with an alluring perfume named "Cuban Kiss." The bereaved husband, who had been able to endure his loss with some indifference before, now took one look at the vision created by the two artists and would scarcely allow the beauty to be buried, so desirable had she become.

Dr. Grunt was a music lover, too, it developed, and discovering Van's gift, begged him to play duets with him at the organ. Van obliged politely, although the doctor's only pieces were *Carnival in Venice* and *Pomp and Circumstance*. The doctor lived at an obscure hotel named The Marvella and it was on a social Sunday call here that Van found incentive to break with the gentleman. The doctor's dingy suite was filled with ancient medical books framed sepia prints dealing with all grisly phases of death and sickness hung on the wall; a nice pair of marble hands, clasped doubtless in a death-vise, stood on the walnut mantelpiece. Limp lilies and other funeral flowers were in the lace-curtained window seat, and from brass bed to green-plush settee the home was no more cheerful than the embalming parlor. Van's face fell on seeing a glass plate of Woolworth fudge set out beside a cigarette box. Candy meant no liquor and although he was tapering off now, accustoming his raddled system to merely a constant 50 per cent intoxication instead of a hundred, nevertheless, he saw no reason to waste a Sunday afternoon on a fudge orgy.

The doctor was newly shaved, bathed, and reeking of some heady bath powder. His bleak head was polished with unguents and sat in its collar like a Brancusi on a block. Across the skull lay a half dozen wistful black hairs, lovingly coaxed and brushed all the way from the left to the right ear. He evidently had very little social life so that even a visit from his apprentice was in the nature of a festivity. He spoke of the weather, he passed out photographs of a blooming brunette who, he said, was his wife but who had vanished years ago in a St. Patrick's Day parade. This reminded Van of his own matrimonial error, and he too sighed over a Brooklyn heiress named Bessie, who had loved him too well. Once these polite overtures were over the doctor offered Van a cigarette, and it was then that Van's uneasiness began. With the first few whiffs a vague alarm penetrated to the depths of his cockeyed consciousness.

"Odd flavor," said Van, smoking, and to his immense surprise began to giggle.

"Marijuana," said Dr. Grunt, and gave a pleased smile. "Do you really like it? I grow it myself, you know, in a window box. I rather thought you'd like it. Homegrown and all. What have you been using?"

Using? Van looked blank.

"You ought to shift, whatever it is," advised the doctor. "You shake all the time. Look at your hand this minute. I shifted to reefers last year. Not that I was ever a real snowbird before. I never took more than five grains a day, actually. The way these reefers are working out I don't need anything else, to tell the truth."

Van left the doctor's suite coughing and giggling behind his hand and uncomfortably aware that if the world looked curious under alcohol it was completely disheveled under marijuana. He did not like this new shakiness added to his old. That night he had the ague: The angels and the waiting coffins made him shiver and the reflection of his own face, liver-spotted, full of a new line of pouches and ruts, alarmed him. He even sobbed quietly for over an hour, sitting on the ivory wire settee, just because he could not make head nor tail out of his newspaper. He felt himself grow pitiful and small, and it was unbearable. He thought of his step-brother in Oil City, a sarcastic enemy but he desperately needed someone to whom he belonged, for he was afraid. The pit opened up by Dr. Grunt appalled him. Was that next? He thought of the doctor's blooming wife, lost these twenty years and that made him think of his Bessie, abandoned that long, too. Bessie was his, anyway; she might be dead and gone but she was his, and he needed her. Hardly two hours after the thought had come to him, he was standing in her vestibule seeing his own name on the knocker: *Bessie Van Deusen*. So this was Home. So this was Brooklyn. He was relieved to feel intimations of the old ego re-turning at the mere sight of these dowdily respectable surround-ings. Here at last was a background to which he could feel superior, here he could revel in his unique traits rather than be crushed by them. The fever and tremors, which in any other surroundings would have made him sobbingly abject, here made him assume the role of spoiled child; and fortunately for him he fainted almost as soon as he had set foot in Bessie's kitchen, so that she could not do otherwise than put him to bed. She had a dim suspicion that he would occupy this bed and allow her to squirm uncomfortably on the living-room couch the rest of her days if she didn't watch out. But her first duty, while he was sick, was to look after him.

"Poor Bessie!" Van chuckled, watching her sweeping up the ashes he had left scattered all over the hardwood floor. "Good as gold! And what did I ever do to deserve it?"

"You left me," Bessie was stung into replying. "That was something."

She seldom gave vent to such sarcasm, however. She was a talkative enough woman in her own shop, to tradesmen, fellow workers, and neighbors but she had nothing to say to this husband, anymore than she had ever had, anymore than a person had to say to a merry-go-round. They had met at Long Beach to begin with on a Fourth of July; and young, in bathing suits, laughing on the beach, their essential differences had not mattered. Van was broke and at the time disgusted with his own friends; she was making lots of money in the hotel near Times Square; the boys were returning home from the Great War and rushing her, and she was beginning to see a future life far above her past connections. It was only a brief period for both of them, however. Van's ambition returned, and Bessie's vanished. After a week's honeymoon they found themselves complete strangers. Bessie refused to chatter for the mocking edification of any man, and in her subsequent silences Van adopted the debonair role of an artist who has married his housekeeper, retaining his bachelor freedom yet with all the domestic privileges. As far as he was concerned, it might have been an ideal arrangement on this basis and he might have gone far, but Bessie was not quite stupid enough. She was shrewd and she was stubborn and she did not worship him, a necessary anesthetic in being ridiculed. She thought he played the piano like no human being she had ever heard, so far as she knew he was better than Paderewski but if the world did not think so, she was perfectly ready to admit she knew nothing about piano anyway. Any Coney Island musician was as good as Paderewski to her. If he couldn't make a living at it, he must be no good. In a few weeks Van had given up the effort to fit his marriage to his ego and had vanished into another world, which Bessie took no trouble to investigate.

Her brief fling over, she settled down into the modest niche her Scandinavian forebears had made and was content. For a while she kept a dog to satisfy her desire for affection; she kept it in little woolen jackets and nice little beds and had it beautifully altered but it died after ten happy spoiled years. She went to church or lodge picnics once in a while with a German widower but refused his offer to wed and share her earnings with his four growing children. Her youthful prettiness was short-lived, and even at twenty-two the blond hair had become drab, the roundness of her body had become thick and stolid, the hands rough, the eye lusterless, and from then on she looked like her mother and grandmother before her. After the dog died, she took over the son of her sister in Canarsie as her special protégé. He was a fat amiable boy who had always adored her because she had made a practice of giving him five dollars every Christmas, something he appreciated far more than the scratchy underwear, rickety bed shared with younger brother and general hard tack supplied every day of his life by his harassed parents. When Aunt Bessie took over Chunkie's future, he rewarded her by being honor pupil at high school. Later, studying to be an electrician, he spent every Sunday in the Bay Ridge apartment, while Aunt Bessie fussed over him, mended and darned him and talked of setting him up in a shop by himself.

Into this idyl Van's appearance threw a monkey wrench. Neither Bessie nor Chunkie got the point of his barbed merriment, but that it was ridicule they did know. They found that there was no combatting it and no ignoring it, either, so all they could do was to leave him the apartment and take quiet walks around the block or down to the candy store for a soda, where Bessie poured out her bitterness.

"There he sits in my bed with his bad stomach and his headache and his dizziness, me waiting on him hand and foot as if he'd been a good husband. Yes, and he gets something to drink somewhere, too. Lord knows how, because he hasn't any money, unless he's charging it to me. And he talks about his music and how he's going to do this and he's going to do that, then he makes his cracks about the beauty business as if it was just too comical for words. At least I work at my business, I tell him. At least I have a home, which is more than he's got."

Three Sundays were almost too much for Bessie's patience, depriving her of her quiet celebrations and gossip with Chunkie and alarming her with the possibility that this was to continue forever.

"Chunkie! Oh, it's too delicious!" Van laughed. He was almost himself again after three weeks of Bessie's grudging care. "And that lovely Brooklyn accent of his. 'I sor a gazz stove.' No, I can't even approximate it. Bessie, you say it—perhaps, I can get it. How do you say—g-a-s again?"

Bessie, scarlet with suppressed indignation, shook the crumbs out of his bed. Van, in her bathrobe, sleeves up to his elbow, swaggered about smoking his cigarettes, waiting to get back into the warm nest and chuckling at his private little joke.

"You can heat up that veal stew for your supper," said Bessie grimly. "I'm going to a movie with Chunkie."

"Veal stew! Now, if I were at my friend Dol Lloyd's I would have a nice Chablis with that stew—or perhaps a *vin rosé*—a matter of choice, yes, a simple claret, perhaps—hmm."

"There's a can of beer on ice," said Bessie and walked out with stolid indifference to Van's peal of laughter.

"There's a can of beer, she says," he mimicked her accent. "Oh, wonderful Bessie. Oh, priceless Bessie!"

It was lonely when Bessie went out, leaving no one on whom he could lavish his wit; and by the time he got into his clothes Van felt well enough to sally out toward the Shore Drive, swinging his cane briskly to the surprise of the local residents. His legs operated well enough for him to strut even more than usual, and he laughed as he walked at the delicious irony of Van Deusen, international artist and pet, being in this humble background. He stopped laughing a couple of hours later when he returned to find Bessie's door locked and a simple note pinned on it for him.

> Go where you can get your wines. I'd rather put my sav-
> ings into Chunkie's future or my own shop than take
> care of a souse in my old age.

Yours, Bessie.

"Chunkie!" Van twirled his scrappy mustache and burst out laughing. "Really, Bessie is superb. Ha-ha. Chunkie wins out! Bach is defeated by a permanent wave! I must tell that to Dol, I really must, and Prudence. It's too priceless."

Not having a single dime in his pockets Van hailed a taxi. He would ride from the Bridge to the Bronx if need be, calling on friends until someone paid his fare. That friend he would reward with his immediate company. He knew this much: that people will pay a taxi bill who would not lend you five dollars for some worthier cause.

"The Ritz Towers!" he cried in a clear ringing voice as he set-tled back. No point in going back to the same world. No, this time he would aim a rung or two higher. He would call, to begin with, on an old love named Hannah Fitzbaum. He would inform her he was just this minute off the *Queen Mary* and had been impelled to look her up first thing, before rushing straight to Hollywood. If she wasn't in; he would try the old singer at the Ansonia again; he would try the Astors, the Whitneys, the Guggenheims—the sky was the limit!

He was still smiling when they crossed the bridge, and he saw again the challenging spires of New York. Mr. B was lost and forgotten. A finer, better Mr. A was in complete charge.

"Van Deusen rides again!" he chuckled and then rapped on the pane with his stick. "Faster, driver! People are waiting for me!"

. . . the routine . . .

"HEN YOU'RE TERRIBLY crazy about me, aren't you, pet?" Prudence asked.

They were shooting ducks at Coney Island. They had had their pictures taken with their cheeks puffed out wearing each other's hats and they had had their palms read by Zorayster the Astrological Wizard, and peered into boarded-up palaces of wonder, so now there was nothing left but to shoot ducks. Jeff had won an extraordinarily ugly beer stein and a pocket comb.

"Not really," answered Jeff, squinting through the gun. "A boyish infatuation for an older woman that will pass when my voice changes!"

"But I was your first love," she insisted as the shots clicked out, and ducks wafted by on their perpetual belt cheerfully unharmed. "I'll be hard to get rid of, too, don't forget that. Remember Sappho. So light to carry the first flight but after that—"

"Here. Your turn."

She took the gun and aimed. Two ducks quivered.

"How would you like to go to Scotland and kill real birds?"

"I'd rather go back to the hotel," he said.

"You say the nicest things," Prudence said. "Do you suppose it's Tuesday in New York, too?"

"A different week, that's all," he said.

They went back to their roller chair. Prudence wanted to hold hands as they wheeled along the boardwalk, but Jefferson carefully placed the beer stein in her arms and moved out of reach.

"I wonder if the Club truant officer was after me again last night," speculated Prudence. "Funny, when I'm with you it seems so inane to break my neck getting to that place every night, as if it mattered whether people heard a song or didn't."

She waved merrily to a mufflered old gentleman bundled up in plaid rugs in his roller chair.

"Want to race?" she yelled. He shuddered and rolled on.

"I'm sure he's the same old man I saw rolling around the Marlborough Blenheim last Easter in Atlantic City," she said. "He probably just gave the chair its head, and it rolled straight up here. Darling, it's really true, then, you never loved anybody but me?"

"Hush,'" he ordered. "You know damn well I'm not sure of anything—you—me—love. How do I know whether it's love or experiment? I'm not sure whether I like this feeling of being sold."

"Sold? Not *sold,* Jeff?"

"Why not? All your affairs, for instance. The routine. Coney Island. Let's be kids again. Let's be crazy. Let's go on a roller coaster. Let's kid everything. You start every affair that way, don't you?"

Prudence looked shocked and hurt, for it was quite true. She'd forgotten. Jeff was so different and difficult, and everything had seemed so new.

"Always writing your play," she reproached him. "You make up characters for me to be and believe it. You know you mustn't crack down on me so much, or I'll be convinced you're in love with me."

"I'm trying to nourish my reservations," he said gloomily. "Nobody will ever make me as mad as you do. Nobody will ever interfere with my work the way you do."

"Darling," said Prudence gratefully.

It seemed to her she had never been so happy, so deliriously free in her life. Nothing mattered but hanging on to Jeff every minute. She couldn't remember even feeling this way before, probably because no one had ever been so stubborn as he.

"You do admire me for making something of myself?" she coaxed.

"There's not a thing about your life I admire," he said. "The only reason I don't cut loose from you is that I'm always thinking if I go on I'll come to the real you. I think I find it sometimes making love to you but afterward I'm not sure. I wonder if you haven't cut out for good whatever was real."

I wonder that myself, thought Prudence and was quiet, a little afraid.

"Want me to prove my mettle?" she mocked.

Jeff shook his head.

"You wouldn't. I'll go back home in a few weeks and work like mad. You'll go back to Estabrook."

"I won't," she said. "I'd go with you—*dar*-ling! You know that."

"Don't make me laugh," sneered Jeff. "You fit people into your life here. You never try to fit into theirs. All this is you. There isn't anything else. You wouldn't give up one step in your routine for anyone, love or money. Love is a racket, just a part of the picture. You wouldn't lose an eyelash over it."

"Would you, either?" she had presence enough of mind to retort, but that would start another quarrel so she hurried on.

"Is there anything I could do to prove you weren't just routine?" she asked him humbly and she did seriously wonder what in God's name he expected of her.

"Come back with me to Silver City," he said. "That's all I can offer. An old farm. Work. Love. Faithfulness—I'm a fool about that, if you don't mind. I'd write all the time and be mad over the newspapers and never funny. And if there was any choice between you and my work you'd be the one to go. That's my proposition, so good-bye."

"Certainly a very attractive offer," said Prudence, wide-eyed; The picture of herself in a bungalow apron putting up quince jelly came to her—a publicity picture for *The Ladies' Home Journal,* "Prudence Bly, Just-a-Home-Girl-at-Heart, Her Favorite Waffle Recipe"—she laughed.

"Laugh," said Jeff bitterly. "I knew you would. I'll think of you laughing and get you out of my head all the quicker."

He got out of the chair, produced a dollar for the porter. He stalked on to the hotel, without looking back at her. Prudence could not stop laughing. Down on the sands a fat man in a bathing suit shivered, waiting for an audience before he leaped debonairly into the frigid waves. He took Prudence's laughter as derision and plunged gasping.

"Jeff!" she called, controlling her hysteria, and running after him. "I'm not laughing at that, at all—you're always so sure of what I'll do and what I won't do—darling, I think it would be an absolute lark—wait, please—Jeff, please wait."

He wouldn't believe her. He wouldn't even turn around. She sighed.

. . . it isn't Benny Goodman . . .

Dol woke up in the kitchen, fully dressed for the day, standing by the china closet with a glass of cognac in his hand and a coffee cup beside him on the table. The bottle of Martell was at his elbow and judging by the contents of the bottle it had taken two inches of this to bring him to his senses. He decided that he must have been carrying on a perfectly plausible conversation before consciousness came to him, because there was the maid Mrs. Miller calmly scrubbing away at the green-lozenged linoleum, her backside a picture of honest endeavor. This was happening more and more in the last few years; he got up quite as tight as when he went to bed but went through the motions of bathing, shaving, dressing, looking at the paper, until the cognac brought him to. He wondered what he said to Mrs. Miller on these occasions. Nothing out of the ordinary, obviously, since she seemed perfectly calm. Very likely to Mrs. Miller a man was not drunk until he picked up an axe. She was still uneducated in the gentleman-school of drinkers who became more gentlemanly with each drop, applying these drops at steady intervals as if they were oxygen, until eventually the subject turned into a store-window dummy with an equal incapacity for movement. The third glass of brandy was poured with trembling fingers into his coffee, and this really set the dummy's mechanism to working. He could see: there was the jolly little Kuniyoshi lithograph over the icebox, placed there deliberately during a conversation deploring the isolation of art to the showplace living rooms when it should be used, like the radio, to brighten the dull routine of daily life.

Whether Mrs. Miller's routine was brightened by this bowl of slightly mad apples was not apparent from her phlegmatic rear, which, as a matter of record, now seemed a dour disappointed art critic's face demanding for even this simple spot more of a museum pet than Kuniyoshi and if it must be Americana, a Wood or Benton. Dol saw the kitchen clock, an electric marvel recording in ebony on ivory twenty minutes to two. He had other sensations now, too, that showed he was awake and alive—a slight headache and a faint intestinal rebellion. He could even hear, so magical was Dr. Martell's Snake Oil. The gramophone was going in the living room.

"Good morning, Mrs. Miller," said Dol cautiously and then reflected that he must have said good morning to her a dozen times already, but she showed no resentment or surprise at his insistence.

"Mail," she said and raised her head to nod toward the kitchen table where the usual stack of letters and papers lay waiting. Dol flicked them over without interest. By this time he knew there was seldom any message really for him, personally, even though his name was on all the envelopes. Invitations, thank yous, begging letters, excuses—all might have been mimeographed notes to any other local bachelor; but there was nothing, nothing really for Dol Lloyd, the man who belonged nowhere, who never belonged in Des Moines, who never belonged in Paris or New York, the Dol Lloyd, whose friends understood him even less than his family had. A note from Jeff Abbott he tore open first.

> Sorry about the opera tonight. Thanks so much for asking me but I'm working every minute. I know you think I need music and someday of course I will but right now I have to work like mad. Hyman has come round to the new play. Come and see me again.

Dol smiled wryly. He had counted on sharing that night one of his favorite joys with this young man who would not be helped. He had counted on an expansion of soul, a mellowing that he was certain must always result from hearing Flagstadt; he had counted on a miracle, of course, as if a young wine could suddenly be aged and enriched by a hurricane instead of the passage of years. It was another proof of how little you could do for those you were positive needed your help. For a split second Dol experienced such a futile despair he could gladly have cut his throat with the pretty carving knife lying in the sink. A vista of ten thousand mornings like this loomed before him: mail, Martell, Mrs. Miller, disappointments, periodic testimony to the waste of his life. The booming of the gramophone in the next room rescued him. Bert. Bert was back again. He had forgotten that one comfort the way he often did, the way you forgot the cat or the dog until left all alone by your own kind you bethink yourself and fling yourself with passionate gratitude on the little beast, crediting it with all the virtues you missed most in human contacts—brains, loyalty, stability. Bert! Dol pushed open the door. He felt better. The sun was pouring in the high studio windows, a mighty baritone was booming out *Le Cor,* Bert was back and tonight he would hear Flagstadt. Life was worth living.

"Bert," he said and then saw that Les Biggs was there, too. Of course. Before the four steps that led down to the room Dol pulled himself together. Either you had Bert and Les or no Bert at all. He must keep that in mind when the sight of Les's pallid face got on his nerves too much.

"*I love a hunting horn . . . and the fox is far away . . . oh the sounding horn . . . boom-boom . . . and the fox and the fox and the fox . . .*"

"Oh boy," Said Bert.

"Boy, oh, boy," agreed Les.

This meant they liked it. God knows they liked it, for they had had the repeat brakes on for hours yesterday, too, and the day before while the instrument siphoned off the essence of masculinity in sound.

"I wish you'd stop playing that, Bert!" fretfully exclaimed Dol, meaning only that he wished Les would get out and save the place from looking like a problem boys' schoolroom, for the two lads, so blankly, imbecilely pretty, sat spellbound, jaws agape, a picture of arrested development before the Capehart.

"It isn't Benny Goodman!" resentfully answered Bert. "You only said to stop Benny Goodman."

"It's classical!" said Les. "It isn't Benny Goodman."

"First you say to stop Benny Goodman," said Bert sulkily, "then I stop Benny Goodman, and now you say stop this, too. Say!"

"All right, all right," Dol hastily pacified him, for in his annoyance at seeing Les and the emphasis this shadow put on Bert's own weakness, and for that matter his own, he had forgotten to note that this was a friendly overture from Bert. Bert was trying to show that he liked something good in music just the way Dol was always wanting him to. Bert *tried*. No one could say Bert didn't *try*, but Dol wished he could also talk. It was too embarrassing to be forced to explain to his friends how secretly gifted the young man was when the boy could hardly put a sentence together.

"How was the show last night?" Dol asked, remembering he had bought tickets for them for *Red, Hot and Blue.*

"Oh boy!" answered Bert.

"Oh, me, oh, my!" echoed Les.

"I'm glad you enjoyed it," said Dol. "I hope you will like *Fidelio* tonight as well."

"Aw!" groaned Bert.

"Aw, gee!" said Les.

"But that's only fair," expostulated Dol. "It's my favorite opera, Bert, and if I let you go to what you like one night, it's only fair you should go with me to what I like the next night."

"Have a heart!" said Bert.

"Aw, gee!" sympathized Les.

The baritone continued to chant his love for the sounding horn—and the fox far away.

"Very well, I shall invite Jean Nelson," said Dol as smoothly as he could.

"Hot dog!" commented Bert.

"Oh, boy!" said Les.

"You might call up the Warwick and see if she's there yet or if she's at Mr. Nelson's apartment. I rather think I shall call Harvey to make sure she's quite recovered from her breakdown."

Dol saw that Les was wearing the beautiful beige sweater he had ordered for Bert from Jaeger's while Bert wore a shabby shrunken high school blazer, indeed the very thing that Dol had ineffectually sought to replace. "I see my gift arrived," said Dol. "Perhaps I should have ordered two."

Bert scowled.

"Les hasn't got any clothes," he said. "He catches colds standing at that soda fountain by the door all night. He had pneumonia once, too."

"A pity," said Dol.

He smiled brightly at Les.

"At any rate," he added, "you are fortunate in being able to take a day off any time you like. I doubt if even the manager fares that well."

"Ah," said Les, suspiciously.

"You leave Les be," muttered Bert and turned the phonograph to its loudest.

"'I love a hunting horn . . . and the fox . . . and the fox . . . and . . .'"

The two boys sulked silently like two scolded children, shutting Dol out of their life as if he was the unpopular dean. He despised himself for minding this so much and for feeling old and ridiculous before them instead of enviably mature. Alone, always, he thought again, and something about the contented amœbid pleasures of the two lads drove him to the desk in the corner where he seated himself with his back to them ostentatiously leafing over his notes on "Artists as Critics and Critics as Artists," for this was the work begun at least twenty years ago that gave him, in his lowest hours, a sense of purpose in his life. The great red velvet-bound notebook with its gold clasp was drawn out of the desk, the key turned, the carefully hand-written pages spread open with an impressive rustle, a sign that here at least was *not* an amoeba, here was a man with work, here was a man with a legitimate excuse for scolding idlers. No one had ever seen the inside of this book and so no one could jeer at its pretensions. Even Les and Bert were silenced when the pen began scratching busily over the pages. For some days past it had done no more than copy over and over one sentence of Théophile Gautier regarding "utilitarian prose":

I have an intimate conviction that an ode is too light a garment for winter, and that we should not be better clad in strophe, antistrophe and epode than was the cynic's wife who contented herself with merely her virtue as chemise.

However the intentness with which the distinguished figure bent laboriously to this task of copying and tracing made its effect on the two boys, and reluctantly Bert switched off the machine.

"Anything else you want of me?" Bert gruffly asked.

The busy pen paused presently.

"Please don't disturb me when I'm thinking, Bert," said Dol.

Les signaled Bert with his eyebrows.

"Can we take the car then—while you're thinking?" Bert asked and, prodded by a second glance from Les, added, "We could drive over to Liberty and see if those records you ordered from London have come yet."

Stay—Dol found himself silently imploring—oh, for God's sake somebody stay, and he almost said he would give them each ten dollars if they would only stay; but then they would stay too eagerly, humiliating him even further by their opportunism, and after a few minutes they would be on pins and needles to be off celebrating their wealth without him, two children with a dime apiece. So he wrote down carefully once more, "A hunting horn is too light a garment for winter and we should not be far away—"

"By all means take the car," he said. "By all means, do."

No one, no one, no one, he said over and over, no one, no one, and when he sat that night with Jean Nelson at the Metropolitan, it was even worse, for if none could share your few pleasures, it was better to be alone than to have a woman's perfume between you and it. So presently Dol left Jean to her hand waving and smiling and kiss throwing and whispers of "Isn't it divine, Dol? Truly divine, I mean!" He stood at the back of the house a little drunk but gloriously alone with music and he forgot Bert, Les, Jeff Abbott, his mother, Jean, Gautier, and the fox—all the people who had ever disappointed him in wondering what made the difference between a fine voice and a magic one? No difference in tone, in quality, in attack, but as Fidelio the Swedish singer's simple great voice flowered and soared and was enough to fill with joy a million hearts. It rose through the ascending glittering tiers, the great hall was not large enough, it flowed through the checked patterns of light marked EXIT, it roamed the halls, consorted with old echoes in shadowed corners, it visited the old caged attendant in the ladies' check room, floated kindly over her proud book of autographs—Sembrich, Schumann-Heink, Caruso, Jeritza, Patti—and was reined in again by silence, the splendid echo left quivering on the air like an abandoned cloak, warm from recent use.

Dol looked about him at people, his head was held high, he looked at them proudly as if "see, this is what I have, you, who think my life is futile, that I have no reason for existence, look, listen, this is all mine, no one can deny me this one fortune." He thought of Beethoven as an example of how warm personal charm could pervade great music and wished Jeff Abbott was there to hear how it could be done, how love, humor, and wisdom can be so blended as to need no words, of how revolutionary sympathies in the sense of understanding the simplest human common denominator can be projected in formal, correct pattern, so that the message and the pleasure both come through precise use of line color, canon, and fugue. In the *Leonore Overture,* for instance, what could be more completely said, without words, detaching it from its operatic connections? Here was musk military and rich, not of the army but of simple people affected by the army, here was a charm, almost acuteness of form, a tune to be swung on the roof of a baby carriage to keep it from crying, then the same toy charm swelling, growing, no-no-no—YES—WAR!—all flowering from the tiny rattle, and then the toy world swelling into the machine world, the Terror World, WAR, and the military roll dying off into a little swinging tune in a baby's carriage, a music box, something to keep the child from crying.

Dol was excited and happy now translating music this way, and looking about the opera house, he thought why this was his home, this was where his happiest hours had been spent, these walls surely loved him as he loved them, here was where his noblest thoughts had been born, here had taken place his first superb moment—yes, it had been Caruso's Samson, and he knew it had been worth living for. Here was his home. When he died, he would be brought here to die with Tristan and Isolde; he would die to great music. He walked about smiling during the intermission, not recognizing those who spoke to him in the lounge, hardly knowing Jean, who shook a reproachful finger at him from a table of friends sufficiently respectable to be in the process of being snapped by a *Journal* photographer. All the rest of the evening Jean kept her hand through his arm, and his whole body recoiled from her fragrant proximity. He looked about him at boxes of debutantes in pretty pastels set like Easter baskets about the Horseshoe and he hated them all, their colors screamed above the singing, he hated all women for they are the enemies of peace, they must crash through beauty with a shrill cry of "Me! me! little tiny me! listen! look! me!" He forgave Jeff Abbott and Bert for not coming with him, for at least they had the taste to stay away when they were not interested rather than coming to compete. Indeed he loved everyone who had stayed away tonight, for at least they did not obstruct his present joy.

"Where shall we go now?" asked Jean, snuggling back in his car. "Didn't Mary Whitsey's hair look marvelous? I wish you could have seen her before Guillaume took her in hand!"

"I'll take you home," said Dol.

He could not wait to get her out of his sight. He wanted to go home, even if Bert was not there, even if the fresh case of cognac was not there, he wanted to get home quickly before a pretty lady's chatter had pecked to bits his lovely evening.

. . . Sunday night games . . .

$\mathcal{T}$HE ORCHESTRA PLAYED *At Maxim's Where I Dine* at ten minutes to seven thus losing Mr. Pinckney's fifty-cent bet that this selection was always played at six-thirty. In the café James produced two quarters from his pigskin change purse and laid them at Prudence's glass. They were drinking cassis and playing kubito under the handicap of indifference to both of these sports.

"The only thing I can really play," said Prudence, "is the slot machines. I wish now I'd gone down to Miami."

Pinched-looking, thought James judiciously, yes, sir, Prudence was beginning to look pinched and now and then downright angry that fun wasn't fun, people weren't amusing, drinks weren't good, life wasn't life.

Just beginning to realize, mused James, that what she's worked at all these years isn't at all what she liked, and Fate simply sold her a bill of goods because it didn't have what she wanted. Now what would that have been?

Prudence shook the kubito board and the little men toddled patiently into place.

"Of course, you should have gone to Miami," James frankly agreed. "Goodness knows what you've lost by staying here. Everyone's saying the Miami-Biltmore didn't even want you, in spite of the publicity about your refusing. You should have pacified your public by going to Hollywood at least. People in your profession ought not to be seen in town this time of year. Riding around town with Jeff Abbott on Chinatown buses and sightseeing boats, playing chess with him in Sportland like some lady barber!"

Prudence smiled reminiscently.

"I liked it" said Prudence. "I like loafing in New York."

"Loafing in New York!" scornfully repeated James. "You know perfectly well there's no such thing as loafing in New York. There's either work or out-of-work in New York. And we don't want to see our gay entertainers hanging around town doing nothing, expecting everyone to like them as if they were *people!* An actress out of a play, a columnist without a column, a singer without a contract—they're absolutely worse than nothing in this town. You know how bad it looks, Prudence, for you to be seen just anywhere and with just anybody."

Prudence shrugged her shoulders.

"You think you don't care," admonished James. "You think you're established and can do anything. Just wait till next week when the Vedado opens again without you, and everyone asks if Bly is really through."

It was true enough. No one would believe that it had been Prudence and not the Club that refused the four-week spring contract. You paid dearly for such independent gestures. James suspected that the Club had not pressed the matter for this time, either.

"Don't croak, darling," begged Prudence. "We're having a lovely time, and if you make so much noise about my giving up my job, everyone will think we're Greenwich Village lovers, and you know how you'd hate that."

James decided to let the matter drop, but he made a mental note for history's sake, that at 6:55 P.M. on March 10 in the Café Lafayette he had tried to warn Prudence Bly that she was skidding and had been rewarded with shoulder shrugging and a skeptical smile. Very well, said Mr. Pinckney to himself, and planned the anecdote. Why, she had even admitted that Dolores, her pet astrologer by whose name she swore and who had guided her these last ten years, had said last Monday to beware the Ides of March!

"Dolores is such a fool about her stars," Prudence had laughed. "Just because I pay her she thinks I really believe in them."

Oh, yes, Dolores was a fine prophet when she was flattering but a quack when she predicted doom. To tell the truth James himself could have predicted some doom without astrology by just watching the change in Prudence's public façade. Anyone could have done so, he reflected, the fall was only unforeseen by the clever subject herself. Skids were always being mistaken for skates till one tried to do a figure eight or triple fleur-de-lis. The skids were always so obvious to every stupid bystander; probably not a friend, bellboy, nor bootblack who could not red flag the doomed one ages before the final slide because it is for this they have all waited. It is for the crash the crowd watches the aircraft exhibition, it is for the fall they watch the daring young man on the flying trapeze. This is one's public, these patient waiters for calamity.

The only thing, privately deplored James. I shall have to spend my old age trying to console her for the injustice of it and will not for a minute be allowed to say "I told you so."

"Don't look now," he whispered; "but I believe that Jean Nelson and Steve are just creeping into the dining room."

The whole triangular mess was over—of course it must be—but James wondered if he were right when he saw Prudence quietly push the kubito board aside and open her vanity case.

"I am not interested in either Jean or Steve," she said loftily, laying on a rich ruby lipstick, a female preliminary to open warfare that James observed with a sinking heart. "Jean and I are through. I'm a *little* surprised she's gone after Steve again. You told me she had a nervous breakdown. Is this part of it?"

"I can't keep up with her, my dear," lamented James. "You ladies are so wiry these days. It was only last week I took a gardenia bush to Lipincott's for her, and here she is out."

"Why Lipincott's this time?" grimly inquired Prudence. "She's always had her breakdowns at Miss le Roy's."

"I know," agreed James. "Perhaps it's the beginning of a new cycle. But I truly did see her lying pale and wan in the hospital last Sunday, and here she is today all rosy with love and old-fashioneds."

"And Harvey?" asked Prudence.

"Harvey is resigned. He enjoys being unfaithful to Jean more than he does to any other woman, so he always takes her back."

"I can't understand what I ever could see in her," pondered Prudence. "I swear I'll never have a word to say to her again. So hideously dull, James! Unbelievable."

"She had her own mattress and her own silk sheets and her primrose puff brought right into the hospital," said James. "It was a beautiful breakdown, I must say—the whole thing sprayed with Chanel Five. Trays sent straight from the Colony, and the wan little figure in aquamarine velvet, lying there so bravely with her book, *Lust for Life,* again. The poor darling doesn't know she's read it four times."

"What did Harvey give her this time?" asked Prudence. "The reconciliation gift was a small jade doodad for her charm bracelet," said James with satisfaction. "Each one gets less valuable than the last."

"When he's fifty, he'll start taking them all back, one by one," prophesied Prudence. "Did they go in or out? Be a lamb and look."

"Steve's in the hall so—" But before he could give further details Prudence had leaped from the table and made a dash for the hall. Open murder, probably. One never knew what to expect from these two girlfriends, especially since their bitter parting. Well, there was nothing a man could do in these cases but sit tight and try to pray that the darlings would confine their abuse to each other.

James regarded himself with pleasure in the wall mirror. He had recently attended a rather special dinner at the Explorers' Club, and the honor had stung him into raising a fragile Van Dyke, which even in the bud made him look, he felt, fully as distinguished as Dol Lloyd. It was this beard as much as a certain boredom with his usual circle that made him affect Sunday night supper at the Lafayette, dallying an hour or so over the French newspapers, essaying brief skirmishes in French with the waiters with many a "C'est ca! . . . Tiens, tiens . . . vraiment?" and other intelligent observations. One of these days he planned to bring Evalyn, no less, down here, and by Sheer cosmopolitan magnetism force her to invite him on her Balinese expedition. He had had difficulty persuading her away from Majorca since she had been there before and was absolutely confident that all this nonsense about the Spanish war reaching there was pure newspaper rot. In vain he showed her the pictures, the newspaper stories. "But my dear boy," she insisted implacably, "I've been there. I know the place. It's the quietest spot in the world. I *know.*"

James had viewed himself in the mirrors at all angles, consumed several small sausages on sticks and contemplated the menu with a view to ordering the *vol-au-vent* of lobster with a delicate Chablis when the orchestra's sally into *Kiss Me Again* brought his eyes to the clock again. Seven-fifteen? What had happened to Prudence? He looked inquiringly at the waiter, but the latter merely nodded toward the door and shrugged. Ladies were always being lost in cafés. It was nothing to worry about. James pushed his glass aside and stood up. If she had found Jean, perhaps the best thing for a man to do was to pay the check and slink out before the feathers started to fly. It would never, never do to be confronted by both ladies—perhaps reconciled—with what he had said to each of them about the other. No sooner had this wisdom been revealed to him than he had followed its mandates. He was tiptoeing out the door when he collided with Steve Estabrook, who had evidently reached the same decision, for he had his hat and coat and was looking cautiously behind him as he crept.

"Oh—Oh, Pinckney!"

"Yes, it's me, Steve."

They stood looking guiltily at each other. "You knew Prudence was here with me, Steve?"

"I saw her in the café as we passed and tried to keep Jean out of sight. But then Jean disappeared."

"I'm afraid we won't see them for hours," said James. "They're in the johnny."

"Oh God," said Steve mournfully. "We might as well have a drink. What is it women have to say to each other in cans that takes so long?"

"I suppose they're having it out," said James complacently. "They are throwing everything up to each other that they so lovingly once confessed."

"I might have known!" groaned Steve.

"I don't suppose we could sneak out," said James. "They might make up their minds to jump on me for what I've said here and there."

"I may have said some things myself," reflected Steve. "How about a whisky neat?"

They sat and had a whisky neat. As no one interrupted, they had another and for appearance's sake decided on a third.

"Shall we dine together, Pinckney?" suggested Steve at seven forty-five.

"Splendid," said James eagerly. "I had practically decided on a *potage santé,* a *vol-au-vent* of lobster and a nice Chablis. This is really a lovely surprise, Steve. How much nicer just the two of us!"

"You don't think we ought to send a tray up to the ladies' room?" doubtfully asked Steve.

"Never," said James. "If they've killed each other, we won't want to be mixed up in it, and if they've made up, they will certainly kill us."

The *potage* could not have tasted better. James told Stephen how much his friend Evalyn Greer Vanderhoff, of Philadelphia, enjoyed his radio program, a lie, but pleasant to hear. Stephen told James what a success he would be if he ever cared to go on the air himself.

"Now, now you're just flattering me. Still, my talk for the Museum was very highly praised—a certain quality of voice, you know—"

"Damn those women," interrupted Steve.

"Poor dears," sighed James. "They live for their feuds. If one would only decide to take you and the other one Jeff but, no, each must have both of you and God knows what else besides."

In the ladies' room the pretty little French maid understood not one word of what it was all about, but she eagerly sympathized with both ladies. They were pretty and young and talked all at once, that much she did know; and so she smiled and agreed with whichever one seized her by the shoulder for corroboration of statements. This did not serve to close the discussions by any manner of means.

"So Harvey is going to start you up in a little shop," said Prudence, combing her hair. "A gigolette agency?"

"Prudence, you know Harvey would not allow me to go in business."

"But your mother was," Prudence reminded her. "Your father got over it and ran off with the telephone girl in Hyannis, didn't he?"

"I don't know where you hear such lies," said Jean and accepted the comb Prudence handed back to her to run through her own golden halo.

"Why do you tell people I haven't a radio personality?" inquired Prudence ominously and added, "Let me try that banana powder, will you?"

"It makes you look like an egg," said Jean, handing her the vanity case, "but you're more than welcome. I never said you didn't have a radio personality. Never. But it really is true."

"Thank you," said Prudence. "I see the sanitarium has restored your bad humor."

"My figure, too," boasted Jean, smoothing her hips tenderly. "I've lost two inches from bust to hips."

"Your thighs are still too thick," Prudence said. "You should try my Sigrid at the Park Central."

"Never heard of her," said Jean.

They each retired silently to separate booths where Jean hummed *Afraid to Dream,* and Prudence whistled something entirely different. When they came out, each seemed to have made a vow never to address each other again for they washed their hands in chilly silence, offered the roller towel in icy politeness to each other's inquisitional fingertips.

"Prudence, why are you so angry with me?" quavered Jean. "Haven't I always been a friend?"

"I'm not mad at all, silly," said Prudence. But she thought she would always be mad at Jean, not for what she did to her but for showing up her own foolishness by her patient imitation of it. No one loved a magnifying mirror, after all.

The little maid beamed with delight as the two young ladies, now arm in arm, went out like lambs. At the foot of the stairs Mr.

Pinckney and Mr. Estabrook met them apprehensively.

"We were just sending a light supper up to the powder room," said James pleasantly.

"All right, girls, say it," saluted Steve. "I've been on the pan the last hour, and now let me defend myself. What was the verdict?"

"Your name never came up," said Prudence.

Baffled, the two men went back to their brandies while the ladies ordered a dish and amiably exchanged artichokes and sprouts from each other's plates. And even when the chairs were being piled on the tables at midnight, the little party could not have been more friendly.

At Prudence's door James tentatively remarked, "I daresay Jeannie will be moving back here again?" and then to cover his too sympathetic disparagements of the girlfriend in the past he hastily added, "Jean is really rather a darling, isn't she?"

Prudence stared at him.

"That viper a darling? Honestly, James, you men are the most two-faced bastards."

Mr. Pinckney was still reeling from this riddle when he reached the street. Peeking in the Plaza bar on the way home, he was not at all surprised to see Steve seated alone in the dark baronial Men's Bar drearily engaged in getting thoroughly tight. Mr. Pinckney tiptoed away and left him there.

. . . So it is true there is someone else . . .

$\mathcal{W}$HOEVER HAS FOLLOWED a lover through the rain or blinding snow knows how barren are the rewards. She finds he is actually meeting the one she suspected, and then what? So it is true, she says, as shocked and numbed as if she had not suspected, accused, reproached, every day for weeks. So it is true, and she stands, perhaps, in the doorway of the tailor shop across the street watching the windows of that apartment as if whatever was to happen would happen in full view. Somehow, certain as she was a few moments ago that he was there having a rendezvous with *Her,* no plan was in her head as to how to use the proof, once obtained, so that even though her head knows the truth, her heart is a fool, her heart continues to believe something else. Nothing to do but say, "Ah, so he did; so that's the way it is, eh, just as I thought, and just as everyone said, and just as I might have known," then

shiver under her fur coat, cold rain whipping through silk unheeded right to her skin.

It was thus that Nora Brent had spent her evening, knowing
and yet not knowing that Steve Estabrook was out with Jean,
that he had taken her—as he used to take Nora for pure mischief's sake—down to Neal Fellows's studio on University Place.
She saw him take Jean out of Anna's cocktail party with a
whisper to Neal—and surely she saw that key slipped from hand
to hand—but she had gone on smiling at something else, something Anna was telling about the Cosies; she had gone home to
Gene, still smiling stiffly but sufficiently weak from the operation Gene didn't know about, to go straight to bed while Gene
went out to dinner alone.

In bed the conflicting miseries of the last few weeks rose up—
that wretched business of using Neal—of *all* people's bed for
Steve, and detesting everything about Gene for no reason except
his blind permission for her to be in this desperate confusion. Now
all confusion was lost in one overwhelming jealousy. She should
not have come home. She should have rushed right after them and
burst in upon them. "I just want you to know I'm not being a bit
fooled, thank you." Then, having proved how shrewd she had become in these new worldly affairs, she would have endeavored to
endure his disgust and the other girl's quiet triumph. Women sitting pretty can afford self-control, they can beguile with their good
taste and womanly modesty as if modesty was anything but the
public overflow of a colossal conceit, the crumbs from a well-fed
ego! No, she would make a scene and scream that he was hers, he
had no business wooing her away from Neal if he wasn't hers, or
for that matter why hadn't they both left her with her perfectly
good husband if they only wanted her on a list? No, no—that
would be a dreary exclusion, the thought of being on no list, of not
knowing the breathless whispers of worldly love, the wild danger
of locked doors, secret meetings. Yes, she would make a scene and

after the scene she would weep like a fool; he would be cold and superior as if he were the one to do the forgiving, as if what he had done was at least done quietly and inconspicuously, as if only her loud screams were the offense to sensitivity. No. She would not go inside. For that matter could she twit him tomorrow with the evidence of the keys? She could not to any advantage, certainly but, of course, she would. She would cry, "But how can you say it's a lie when I saw you with my own eyes? I saw Neal give you the keys, I saw her squeeze your arm. I saw you go in the door of the studio!"

"So what?" he would say, and she would stumble, "Oh, it isn't that I mind your taking her there; I know you were once her lover and might be again; don't think I don't understand men like you; and I know of course you don't take our affair seriously. I'm not dumb; but it's just that you *lied* about it that I mind, when I saw you with my own eyes."

"I lied because you would make a scene," he would say, and then what?

She might as well have stayed in her bed that rainy night, might as well have fought that insane impulse to jump out of the covers the minute the door closed on Gene, dress with trembling hands, rush outdoors, glad it was raining in torrents, glad to drive across the Park with the lights quivering like great tears from the heart of the city, glad lightning was slashing the black sky and thunder bellowing, glad she had a fever—all these hazards she welcomed, all the cruelties of nature that dulled the cruelties of love. If the taxi would only slither into death off the gleaming curved driveway, if the thunder would only bowl down the whole city, let the towers topple like ninepins, let the end of the world roar over her shrieking heart.

There finally she stood, hours, wasn't it, in the tailor's dark window, waiting, watching, with the red and blue electric card in the window flickering on and off—CLEANING—DYEING—TAILORING—and with that poster of Academy of Music, Melvyn

Douglas-Robert Montgomery-Claudette Colbert in *I MET HIM IN PARIS* — ONE WEEK and the other poster EIGHTH ST. PLAYHOUSE — *THE BIG BROADCAST* — FRI. SAT. SUN. Of course that was the one he had wanted to be in but NBC wouldn't let him off for Hollywood yet. Supposing he did go to Hollywood, she would go there too; and there they would be away from all this torment, just they two; but already she saw Dietrich and Loy and Hopkins and Henie all getting him away from her and she would be there in beauty parlors all day being thumped and dyed and waved and peeled to bring him back instead of standing in the rain watching his window wanting to find out and not wanting to find out.

"It's too stupid of me! Too stupid!" she cried aloud, furious at the tears running down her cheek, shaking them off as if they were mosquitoes, certainly no tears of her own but something palmed off on her by an enemy just to humiliate her. Then, she saw she was watching the wrong window, the seventh instead of the eighth and the eighth was dark, he might not even be there, so now she ran over and spoke to the door man.

"Did Mr. Fellows's guests arrive?" she asked brightly.

"He wint up there, miss," said the doorman, "and nobody else has come in."

So they hadn't even been there. So she had been wrong. So— ah, nothing of the sort. They'd gone to Jean's place or else to Steve's—though Steve's address was a little too well-known for discreet wives to invade. No profit, then, in following the lover, nothing could be proved, and no proof used to one's own happiness. Angrily Nora ran out to a taxicab, back through lightning and thunder, back to corroding night—thoughts, to futile despair, to tears smothered in a twin bed, to the peace, the still, murderous peace of Home.

. . . ghost party . . .

$\mathcal{J}$F YOU VALUE my opinion as much as you say," said Dol Lloyd to Jefferson Abbott, "you will take my advice once at least before you go back west."

"What?" asked Jeff so brusquely that Prudence pinched his arm.

"You've been here eight months," said Dol carefully. "You've had your production, your promise of a second one, an assurance of a foothold in the theater, and you've learned your own power. But you're going back to live on that little place you've bought without the faintest notion of ever having been away from it. You've never tasted New York, even. You live in a cell, eat in cellars, work all day, run out in little alleys at night for food or company. You won't meet people who can help you, you might just as well have been in Silver City all this time, you have absolutely refused to take what New York has to give. I have never seen such deliberate self-flagellation. Do you enjoy handicapping yourself? When you get back home, will you have anything to remember—will you have anything in your mind that Silver City couldn't have put there?"

Jeff laughed.

"I'll be thinking of what Hyman said about my new second act," admitted Jeff. "And that's really what I came for, Dol, not to see the sights."

"But darling," said Prudence, sorry again that she had used *darling* so indiscriminately that it no longer meant anything, "you ought to try out one typical great party, you ought to at least know what you've been sneering at all these months."

"I haven't been to a really swell party since—well, since the Soviet Embassy entertained Ilf and Petrov," said Kittredge, rubbing his hands in frank anticipation. "What a party that was! White tie, of course. I rather enjoy a good stiff party, whets the mind, whither civilization, and what not."

Prudence and Dol knew then it was purely for Kittredge's amusement that Jeff finally consented to come to Dol's annual farewell party, but at least it was a concession.

It was too bad it rained that day. It was too bad so much bitterness was unleashed before the party opened, too. Jean Nelson, it seemed, was to assist Dol as hostess so that Prudence half-decided not to come even if it did leave the field to Jean. James Pinckney had called up to say Evalyn was in town, and he couldn't come unless he was able to persuade her, too; but Bert Willy, answering the phone, said insolently, "Oh, no, you don't bring that one, Pinckney!"

Mr. Harvey Nelson was annoyed that his newly returned wife should be so suspiciously taking under her wing for the day a handsome young import named Mr. Browne, though Jean's interest in the lad was due to Prudence's allergy to him, since Woftely Browne was the monologuist, with tap routine for descriptive effects, who had taken Prudence's place for the spring term at the Vedado and was—unfortunately for Prudence's future but much to the delight of her friends and the management—doubling the house profits. Now that the club had a leg to stand on, it could forget Prudence Bly and her recently undependable appearances and was purely for the sake of the young Englishman transforming the Vedado's recent Latin background into the breath of old England in the shape of Tudoresque taffy sculpture, chintz and kidney pie.

"You're sure you won't fall in love with some dame and go haywire on us like Bly did?" earnestly inquired the manager, hovering over the dotted lines where Browne's name was to nest

"Quaite sure," said Mr. Browne, "Oh, *quaite* sure, my dear." So the Vedado strong man lowered his eyes with a blush and hastily signed.

All day long Jean's maid was busy trying to get slippers dyed to match her trailing violet chiffon, Harvey's secretary was using the brand-new reconciliation roadster to pick up Jean's amethysts at the jewelers, Dol Lloyd himself was sternly applying simple Dubonnet to a system that screamed for brandy, and Bert Willy was dispatched to Steve's to borrow his houseman for serving, to the caterer's, to the florist's, to Liberty Music Shop for the new Yvonne Printemps records. After all this trouble it had to turn into a raw cold rain, there had to be an elevator strike so that traffic was choked with parades of picketers, strikers, skyscraper-bound office workers, and there were no taxis to be had, a day of rain, wind, revolution, hats blowing off and rolling in flooded gutters, umbrellas whisking inside out, old ladies knocked down, commuters panicked, so that by five-thirty only nine of Dol's hundred invited guests had arrived. Not one of these nine was of any consequence whatever, and each was furious with the others for being so unworthy of a trip out in such foul weather.

Jean wafted in, flowers in hand, turning her adoring face up to Woftely Browne, so recently the toast of London, but finding moments to breathe anxious apprehensions into Dol's ear. Dol could find no way to breathe life into a party, still-born, except by ordering Bert to change the Capeheart every time the long faces of the assemblage suggested it. Nor was anyone going to unbend through drink, though the long table was laden with fine whiskies, martinis, and champagne; it was as if they had looked at each other's horridly unpublicized faces and decided that to share wassail would commit them to some undesirable fraternity and so they preferred to sit parched and cross, watching the door for an Entrance, while the chafing dishes of mushrooms and shrimps and sausages steamed in vain invitation, and the rosettes of caviar and slabs of smoked turkey were shunned as if they were so much reading matter. Steve's man supervised the four caterers in doing nothing, and Mrs. Miller, in cap and apron, was there to check cloaks—though so far she had only a couple of seedy basement silver foxes and a half-dozen domestic felts, all embarrassing evidence that the party was a flop. Jean looked with frank scorn at the loyal few who had shown such bad taste as to come. Eyes lit up when the bell presently rang and four gorgeous boys from the world of music and movies entered, but these were soon canceled by three mere ex-wives of Names asked to come as a special treat. Even Dol looked somewhat appalled as the bare bones of the party showed through, the gorgeous boys were usually decently lost in a crowd, but here they were all too obviously basic—the press agents, the photographer, the head of a Loan company, the great psychoanalyst so embarrassingly on familiar terms with everyone—here was the fringe of a party, the last twenty names on the least exclusive list, meant to be lost among celebrities and here they were, exposed to the naked eye, naked nobodies.

At six-fifteen a dozen splendid people finally arrived, with Jeff and Kittredge right behind but it was already too late, the party had been christened a flop and no matter how vivacious the conversation now that guests worth talking to had come, the doom was already spelled; someone who didn't understand the gramophone's exquisite mechanism had thrown a lever unexpectedly and broken eight Greta Keller records; they slid on the plate like vaudeville pancakes with a sputtering of *"du-du-dus"* and *"sehn-suchts"* and *"liebes"* and *"schatzies,"* and crashed. This was the signal for general surrender to liquor, which meant that Bert and Les and the swelling number of beautiful lads ganged up around the refreshments amid squeals and Schrafftish chatter.

"You see what we've been missing?" Kittredge snickered to Jeff. "You see how easy careers are made?"

Prudence finally put in an appearance and saw at a glance she should have stayed away. There were Jeff and Kittredge standing in a corner, neither drinking nor talking but openly sneering at the party. Kittredge presently set about definitely to have a good time in his own way by being disagreeable to publishers' ex-wives and, what with strident references to such indecencies as the war in Spain and the c.i.o., soon had sent more than one sensitive woman scurrying for her wraps. Jean Nelson was so glad to see her that Prudence might have known there was bad news someplace.

"Meet Mr. Browne," cried Jean. "He's simply packing them in at the Vedado, darling, so maybe you won't ever have to go back there. He is so *clever!*"

Mr. Browne was smoothly good-looking and assured, but even so Prudence saw nothing in his every remark to set the company off into such wild paroxysms of laughter. It occurred to her now—as it never had when the applause was for her own *mots*—that laughter is far oftener a tribute to success in the world than in the word. The group that ordinarily surrounded her with great delight still did so but with wary eyes and ears for Mr. Browne's every gesture, and when—to illustrate a remark—he went into one of his descriptive taps, all went over to him and there was nothing Prudence could do but pretend equal rapture until she realized this was all part of Jean's plot and rushed over to Jeff, soothed by his muttered condemnation of the whole place.

"I am so deathly sick of it all," she said, and it seemed to her the truth and a great relief to have said it, and she glowed in the new approval in Jeff's eyes.

"I supposed it would be too late to expect any sense from you," he grudgingly said.

No one had invited Arch Gleason; surely it was nothing but evil chance that brought him reeling into the room, spreading consternation on host and guests alike. Those who never had seen him before were shocked to see the ragged gray man with no necktie stumbling down the living-room steps and those who recognized him looked quickly around the room to see whether anyone else was speaking to him, though heaven knows the man could scarcely expect to be recognized after all these years, and it would be awful to find yourself the only one speaking to him and so stuck with him the rest of the evening.

"Wouldn't you know? Wouldn't you know? As if everything wasn't bad enough already," Jean lamented in Neal Fellows's ear and could have wept for the dreadful initiation she was giving her Muriel King chiffon. "Well, Dol and I shan't speak to him," she added, with mysterious authority for one of her vanities was in referring possessively to the Doubtful Men as if her own femininity had been too powerful for their natural inclinations. "I shall tell Dol to put him out."

It was on Neal the ragged visitor finally fastened and his hoarse whining voice could be heard above the suddenly subdued conversation around them.

"I thought I'd pick up a little money working," he was saying and mere contact with the room made him revive a long lost British accent. "The elevator men striking gave me a chance, see, so I happened to be put to work in this building but they were beating up the scabs—ha-ha—imagine me an elevator scab!—so I ran in the first door and what do I find? Old Dol Lloyd and all the old crowd."

An elevator man suddenly the guest of honor would have been grisly enough but a mere scab! And reeling, too, quite as if he was drunk, reeking of some inferior brand of Bowery alcohol, for no better reason than that for thirty cents he preferred to be in a blessed daze than to budget his pennies and have five hot dogs at intervals and see life with wretched clarity. A creature drunk merely because it was a relief from hunger was so obscene and sordid a spectacle that the guests were scarcely able to enjoy their champagne.

One was drunk, as Dol himself was at that moment, because of intolerable boredom or because one's play was a flop or success, one's lover was lost or regained, one had won or dropped a fortune—any one of these was legitimate excuse for excess; but to be drunk—and on such vile-smelling etherish chemicals, too—merely out of poverty was more than decent people could bear and the young English guest of honor, Woftely Browne, found himself shaking hands in farewell with people who had barely arrived. Above this polite murmur Archie's voice went on and on, describing his long illness, the pains of his recent pleurisy, his pericardial twinges, the abscess in the lung, the difficulties of getting false teeth; it was incredible that this very society had ever found such a dreary wretch so witty, clever, so chic, so "worth knowing" that they had once shamelessly begged for introductions.

"So that's what happened to Arch Gleason," Kittredge kept murmuring to Jeff. "Fifteen years ago he was the darling of the debutantes, why he was as much a fixture in the entertainment racket as Bea Lillie or Helen Morgan or Prudence here. Tops. Never spoke to me, of course, though I saw him around with

Pinckney and Fellows and the rest. Snobs, all of 'em. Now look at him."

The ragged pest moved about the room recognizing long lost friends until they were all slowly backing out of the room, wishing walls would melt behind their frantic retreats.

"The odd thing," Jean Nelson was whispering to Jeff, "he was always like this, really just a dreadful bore, only we didn't realize it when he was doing so well. You know when people are properly dressed and have some sort of standing professionally, they are quite different. I really smile to think how we were taken in. He *always* talked about his aches and his doctors, and we were simply amused. We were just wrong about him."

"Something was wrong somewhere," said Jeff, and everything he had ever hated in these crowds, everything he had ever feared in buzzards came over him. Prudence looked at him and saw what he saw—that all these guests would end up haunting other parties just as Arch was doing; she felt frightened and ashamed that before Jeff came, and when she was more of a focal point, she had never seen the tawdriness of these parties. Even now she was not sure her obsession with him was not betraying her, making her lose a world she had won for one she wasn't sure she could get. But when she saw Jean scolding him tenderly for his neglect of her, she had a rush of conviction that whatever he said or thought was the truth, and her feeling for him was the truth, not a game between her and Jean the way Steve had been.

As usual at these affairs Dol sat in the big yellow wing chair by the fire, smiling fixedly and ignoring his guests. But today of all days his smile was too fixed, his stupefaction so obvious that Neal and Jean came over to nudge him into consciousness and found that he had not passed out as they had unfairly suspected, the man was merely dead. The afternoon had gone so wrong from the very beginning that for the host to drop dead was exactly what might have been expected. Stifling her first outcry, Jean

Nelson remembered her manners in time to summon the caterers and they lifted Dol as inconspicuously as possible into his bedroom, and the guests were not subjected to any mortification other than the usual one of seeing their host seemingly pass out before they did. Bert Willy was the only one to sense something wrong and run into the bedroom, bursting into helpless baby sobs at the sight of the haughty purple face on the bed among all the silver foxes and sables. "Hush, hush," Neal kept saying though this only brought more and more rasping cries from the thin, fair-haired boy.

"I won't hush! You—none of you were good enough for him, that's what! I don't care, he was good, and I was going to tell him about cracking up his car last night, honest I was, I was going to tell him tonight I was sorry. Now he's dead! I won't hush!"

Even with the doctor's entrance explained as merely precautionary, the whisper crept around that something had happened, something almost as dreadful as Arch Gleason's presence, and one by one Mrs. Miller yanked out the furs and purses from under the still head and passed them out the door to the disturbed ladies scuttling away from the vaguely sinister place; the fires still blazed under the chafing dishes, Les and the boys had started the endless repetition of *"I love a hunting horn,"* the waiters doggedly passed their trays of dainties to the remaining few, but no one ate, no one drank except Arch Gleason, and he wolfed whole platters, he drank from bottles unable to wait for service, and his wheezy rasping voice went on and on telling of bigger, better parties than this where he had been the host, and people listened, waiting with eyes on the closed bedroom door to know the story, something to tell at dinner, something sensational.

It was bad enough to have Dol die, they felt later when the truth was out, but to have him drop dead right in the middle of a party—even though it was his own, and he had a perfect right—and make so many people feel uncomfortable was so un-like him, so gauche, so lacking in taste as to be almost unforgiv-able. Everyone pretended to understand that such accidents can't be avoided but it gave everyone a nasty turn, it was a long time before they could say anything wholly kind of Dol. If he knew he had a bad heart, he should never have drunk himself stiff; it was a reflection on the whole group. And the least he could have done was to keep out the awful man Gleason, who—as the guests were finally tiptoeing out, leaving only a half-dozen grim old friends, the waiters, the sobbing Bert Willy, and Mrs. Miller—leaped to the table, sausages, bottles all about him—oh, the man was definitely mad but still—and shook his fist at them, screaming, "Look what you've done! Look! And you won't even stay to mourn him, you won't be bothered with anyone honest enough to die before you've buried him! Liars! Lice! Go on home before your lousy stomachs get upset, save your hides, run, don't be seen in a scandal, don't be seen talking to a failure, don't let them know you saw a dead man—"

And then, as they fled into the hall like natives before the tidal wave, he jumped down and ran after them, still shouting his epi-thets, shaking his fist, he ran down the stairs after them, all eight flights, for the elevator strike was still on, and as he whipped them across the lobby and out into the cold raw rain, the pickets saw him, the scab, and closed in on him; presently an ambulance bell rang ting-a-ling through the roaring storm and a bundle of rags was shoved into the wagon with an intern beside it, and the blocked tooting cars all along Fifth Avenue were squeezed even further while the bell raced ting-a-ling-a-ling down the great street, up and down the city, make way, make way for Arch Gleason!

. . . and the fox is far away . . .

PRUDENCE WROTE long letters to Jeff and frequently referred to love and how insipid life was when the true love was out of reach. Jeff's answers, written from the fastnesses of the little house that his mother's death had left him outside Silver City, were not comforting. "Don't be silly," he said in sum; "you know perfectly well I was just a new thrill to a jaded appetite."

She wrote:

> Neal Fellows's play hasn't sold to pictures after all, so he has turned quite Red; and you know how sour that makes people, like going on the wagon. He hates to see anybody else having any fun. Naturally Anna turned Red, too, and studies a little magazine that she recites, and even though they still give parties, they are for the

benefit of miners or orphans or a cause and there's an admittance charge, so they not only feel divinely noble but
don't lose any money besides. It keeps Anna busy as a
bee what with the rest of her time being taken up at
Arthur Murray's learning the Big Apple with the Cosies.

To this Jefferson austerely replied:

For God's sake, Prudence, what do you believe in if you
can't believe in your own friends? What fun do you get
out of being so damnably wise? Please remember that
your remarks on paper, without benefit of your personal
attractions, are frightening and make me suspect I fell in
love with a witch.

Prudence reflected on this warning, judicially pondering her
impressions, finding them no different from those of anyone
else she knew, a language everyone spoke, X-ray lenses they all
used for detecting motives in each other, a panning for sham
as if it were gold nuggets to be triumphantly declared when
found. Trying to disguise her trained reactions now from Jeff,
since he found them ugly, baffled her. Experience became a
hump, her truth a deformity that was a barrier to love. She tried
to disown it, practiced privately wiping her mind clean of all
asides but simplicity only confounded her, and for goodness she
had no clue. When she saw a benign old lady, she dismissed
the instinctive comparison with Grandma Queenie Bly and,
watching her cling tenderly to her old husband's hand,
Prudence's puzzled surprise was in itself a contamination. The
wisdom she had was for human failings, of sin, corruption, and
betrayal; none of these surprised her, and she loved the world
accepting this. But now, with Jeff's recoil from her, she wondered about the other knowledge beyond this, a superior sophis-

tication, warm confidence in human goodness for it struck her that it required more bravery to bear that simple banner in a world of sin than to go forever wisely armed. Even alone she examined her thoughts now so trained to seeing money or publicity prizes for every unexpected heroic deed and watching people cry over martyred heroes in books or plays or movies she found herself envying this infantile acceptance of surface nobility, the feeble-minded faith in leaders, the joy their sentimentality gave them; and even as she envied them, she reflected that their satisfaction in exhibitions of human virtue was in inverse proportion to their own misdeeds, made them able to say proudly, "Die down, conscience, see how fundamentally good human nature is in general."

At least if there was no cure for doubt, there were disguises for it so Prudence took to laboring over her letters, going over each one to cross out anything that sounded worldly wise, naughtily oversexed or cynical, and presently a letter would emerge that pictured a Prudence dewey-eyed and filled with naïve joy in her friends' successes, rapt in baby adoration rather than horrid lust for the big strong mannykins who lived all alone on a farm and did his own cooking.

Sounds as if I had my finger in my mouth. It positively lisps, thought Prudence in disgust, reading over her final drafts. One more revision would have me playing with my toes.

Town was duller than ever in June. Dol was dead, and no one mourned him, for an elderly banker with artistic frustrations, a yacht, and a penthouse near Carl Schurz Park had taken over the Lloyd goodwill and guest list and if his parties had more visiting Hollywood and other foreign exiles than Dol's, at least the principle was the same: no one whose picture had ever been in the papers could say that he was turned away from the Commodore's thirsty. From the depths of Des Moines a vigorous, austere mother and two sisters had appeared to claim Dol's remains, and he was hustled back to the despised land of his fathers like a bad boy back to the reformatory. The wistful paragraph in one of his letters that he should like his ashes scattered around Caruso's monument was regarded as sheer nonsense, cremation was granted only to his notes and life work "The Artist as Critic and the Critic as Artist." This work, on examination by the three ladies, seemed such a revelation of lunacy in the family that they lost no time destroying it. The pallid pair, Bert and Les, who had hung around the apartment weeping were sent about their business, having given all the evidence needed that the dead man was better so. "Poor old Dol," everyone said and forgot him except when they missed his favors.

Prudence had an offer to go into a small noisy place on Fifty-second Street in the fall, but she haughtily dismissed it as unworthy of consideration even though the Vedado had made her no overtures. When she returned from her summer cruise, she would choose her place—the Rainbow Room or Versailles, the hell with the Vedado.

Miss Merrylegs wrote in her amiable column:

> Few nightclub singers can adapt themselves to changing fashions. Prudence Bly has proved no exception. In times of war and stress such as these, threatened on all sides with communism and fascism, the American public is not content to listen to risqué songs even when sung by such a personable young woman as Miss Bly the accordionist singer, and the Club Vedado was very wise in dropping her. The American nightclub set is as discriminating as that of London; and after generously giving its evenings over to the various charities and war benefits now occupying society's time, it seeks afterward entertainment more in the spirit of those graver matters. That is the demand Woftely Browne has so happily met with

his splendid original art. Small wonder that patrons cry again and again for his tapologue—*Wooojy-woojy Boo, didja-woncha?*

At least Kittredge was a safe subject to write about so Prudence wrote Jeff:

I saw your friend Kittredge the other day. I went down to see him, darling, because I wanted to know what you were doing, and the postcard sentiments you toss me from time to time do not appease. There was your friend Kittredge, the intellectual giant, with a stack of letters from you all pouring out your little heart—but never to me! There was also a prospective Mrs. Kittredge, a purple, toothy sparkling little party of about forty named Georgia, in a green hat and rouge and button earrings. I'm sure you would like her since she is a writer, and you would find her more worthy of your confidences than a mere performer like me. Kittredge acted a little squirmy about her talk of marriage but bragged about the big Federal Writing Project he was going to handle down in Washington. It has something to do with bird migrations; I believe he's to prevent them by his pen. He had a new giftish-looking tie, a clean shirt with buttons, so he's as good as tied. She's something or other in Washington and gave me her book to read. It's her own autobiography, all about a perfectly ravishing woman journalist named Georgia, who shakes scoops out of every bed in Europe.

There was no answer to this letter and Prudence lay awake nights thinking of some finer-spirited way she should have broken her news. "What an interesting woman Mr. Kittredge is engaged to, not just a pretty face but a real conversationalist, a real helpmate. One never tires of hearing of her adventures, and by her book it is plain to see how well-thought-of she is in the highest international circles—"

Prudence spent considerable time working herself up into a defensive rage at Jefferson for his perfectly calm acceptance of their separation. After all they had been something to each other, and you did not expect young men from the provinces to walk out of an affair as if it was a village romp. That was the lady's privilege. Then she decide to wash it all up and look on it in the debonair manner of which he accused her. She went to parties only to find herself looking on all her friends' activities with Jeff's hostile eyes and, as she herself was being more and more moved from the center of attention, she was able to perceive how empty their adulation of each new figure was for there is nothing like getting a perspective, even though, like old age, it's forced upon you. Now that she was agreeing with Jeff, she was angrier than ever that he found his bleak little farm so pleasant without her when her own crowded pleasant life in New York was so bleak without him. Why should one person's contempt of her life spoil every pleasure for her, throw her so completely off her elected track? Anyway, there must be some girl back there, some rosy cashier at the mills, some berry picker maybe who said she loved the soil so that he believed it. He was always so ready to believe in the simple tastes of his own people and so sure all New Yorkers had to have four orchestras and a diamond gardenia when it was quite the other way round, the New Yorkers were avid for simplicity—would spare no expense to get it.

Everyone was going away now. She could not understand why she was fool enough to keep delaying her own summer flight. There were farewell orgies on liners, and in the June sifting the summer people came to the top like bad beans. Underneath the protective layer of winter habits, winter friends, and selected activities lay the summer people, lost in the churning of teeming seasonal life but only lying in wait to spring out in pairs and strings the first hot spell. These faces of people once known and abandoned now were laid bare in restaurants and on the forgotten streets where summer in town sent one. Faces met on steamers, in prep schools, in bars long ago, In ladies' rooms, fraternity dances, forgotten proms, family reunions, out they all sprang from the now strange population with the dramatic familiarity of a recognized name on a passenger list. By September they would be crowded back by the returning intimates, vanishing wanly into the city shadows, their names blessedly forgot, their telephone numbers torn up, their very faces once more unknown.

Arden had veiled half of her house, and in the enforced intimacy of one floor for massage Prudence and Jean pretended not to see each other as they took turns being weighed or squealed over the Scotch hose in adjoining baths, heard the fond spanking of each other's flesh in twin booths, and listened attentively for the gossip each might impart to her masseuse. Now, why, Prudence asked herself suspiciously, is *she* in town after Decoration Day, there's more to this than Harvey being unable to get away so soon; and she wondered suddenly if Jean had heard from Jeff, if she was waiting to swoop down on him in his farmhouse with a garden hat and a southern cookbook someone had said Jean was feuding with Steve now that Prudence herself wasn't interested there, and since Charlie McCarthy had put Dinky's nose out of joint. So powerful was Prudence's curiosity over the devious activities of her ex-chum that she permitted herself to look up as their dogs paused simultaneously at a pet tree at the Park entrance.

"How big Yes and No are!" Prudence offered flatteringly as Jean's twin Boston bulls involved themselves seriously with their leash.

"Yes," sighed Jean in amiable acceptance of the rubber olive branch, "but they are so strong, and my arms get so tired and really they haven't half the personality that Sofa has. They take after Harvey more. Woozywoozywoozy, Sofa," and she snuggled Sofa in her arms while her two bulls growled jealously.

"But so divinely virile-looking, they are!" said Prudence. "One wouldn't be surprised at *anything.*"

In a few moments all three dogs were tossed in Jean's car to the care of a frantic chauffeur and the two ladies were seated on the St. Moritz sidewalk with a mint julep in each hot little hand, and cautious conversational checkers were being moved to and fro and jumped. These began innocuously with the summer lives of Manhattan dogs, poor dogs locked in ghostly shrouded apartments with their meal sent in all piping hot on napkined trays by a tender public service, their wistful promenades on roof and garden behind livened footmen while their mistresses roved the seas with only a furred memory. From dogs' summers the step to their own plans was easy. Prudence was determined not to mention Jeff's name. If his presence in America was all that was keeping Jean from her annual foreign travel, let Jean betray this in her own stupid way and this Jean presently did.

"Tell me, darling, I value your opinion so highly, do you agree with everyone that Woftely Browne is the best artist in the entertainment field?" Jean inquired and, burying her charming face in a mass of mint, she waited for Prudence to recover.

"Absolutely," said Prudence radiantly, "but he'd be so much more amusing if he worked in blackface. Why doesn't someone tell him? You are so close to him, Jean—"

"I know," said Jean, lowering her great eyes now so laden with brand new eyelashes that the ordinary winking process was a sheer exhibition of strength. "I *am* so close to him, if you must know—I always tell you everything. Yes, Woftely and I are—well, it's the biggest thing in my life, Prudence."

"But I thought he was just one of the boys," said Prudence.

"Everyone thinks so," said Jean sunnily. "All the husbands think so. Woftely says he finds things are made much simpler for him that way. The idea was original with him. He says he wouldn't dream of going into a new set without his red handkerchief. It frightens off the boresome hostesses and gives him a little time to pick and choose without being rushed right upstairs."

"He sounds darling," said Prudence.

"You won't tell anyone he's really—I mean—normal, will you?" begged Jean. "I mean for Harvey's sake."

Prudence's eyes widened.

"As if I'd ever spread such a nasty story!" she exclaimed.

It seemed Harvey had been able to get the gifted tapologuist a radio contract, and he would be in town all summer so that by an odd chance Jean, too, felt that New York was the greatest summer resort in the world.

"He's so amusing," sighed Jean. "I can't tell you how amusing he can be. After that Abbott man! Oh, that grim, grim Jeff Abbott!"

"Isn't he?" Prudence was reassured. "Still, Jeff is quite male if you don't mind that sort of thing."

"There's no sense in a man being male unless he's going to do something about it," said Jean firmly. "You could take every stitch off and he'd go right on explaining Pavlov or Einstein. I simply can't be bothered with a man who wants hot dogs and pie at a time of night when other men want normal things. But I don't need to tell you, dear, you've been through it all."

"But no!" Prudence said peacefully. "He never mentioned hot dogs to me. I never guessed that he preferred them."

Jean's face fell.

"You mean he really—well, dear, you are so much stronger than I am."

"Oh, I didn't use force," Prudence replied. She had never been so happy in her life. So Jean hadn't gotten around Jeff at all. What a dear he was. She even forgave Jean.

"He's gone back to the sticks, I hear," said Jean. "Of course, he may be the great playwright that Brooks Atkinson says he is but he never belonged in our civilization. He just doesn't fit. How queer for him to rush off and leave you, darling!"

"He expects me to come there, too," Prudence bethought herself.

"Of course, you won't," said Jean. "He must have known you never would."

"Why not?" Prudence found herself saying and for the first time realized that Silver City it would have to be, then; she would have to prove to Jean and to Jeff and to herself that this was the real thing.

"But the Middle West in summer!" protested Jean. "All hot and icky! And you know how everyone will talk in a little village—call it a free love colony and send the sheriff after you."

"One could get married," said Prudence.

"Prudence Bly! You couldn't! You'd never go through with it. Never. Not you."

Prudence was as amazed as Jean at her next remark.

"If your friend Mr. Browne wants to sublet a terrace apartment tell him about mine. I'm going to Jeff next week."

Now she was done for; she would have to go, and once there Jeff might not seem half as desirable, and she would be trapped. Maybe she would get the same old creeps passing Queenie Bly's house but at the moment she wasn't going to have these fears, she only felt a wild free exhilaration that was like being at the top of a hill with a glorious slide down before her and, oh, the freedom of sliding instead of climbing!

"Why, Prudence Bly!" Jean kept saying over and over, staring at her, speculating what had made that man so firmly friendly with her and so loverlike to Prudence and finally deciding it must be that she had started out on too intellectual a plane. It was a pity. If it hadn't been for her mistaken lead, it might be she who would be giving a fresh twist to her life by gloriously sacrificing all for love in a cottage.

. . . the little celebration . . .

𝒯HE BRENTS WERE HAVING their anniversary dinner in the Terrace Room where they had had their first dinner together six years ago. Eugene kept fussing with his tie until Nora cried out, "If you don't stop doing that I'll scream!" adding with restrained calm, "I don't see why you dress up at all if you feel so self-conscious about it."

"Well," stammered Eugene, "I thought it would please you. You had your new evening dress, and I really don't mind."

"I didn't get my new dress to wear in a hotel dining room, thank you," blazed Nora, though it wasn't Gene's fault there was a big convention on, and parties of people in paper hats kept strolling from table to table tootling on horns. "Why did we have to come here anyway?"

"We always come here for our anniversary dinners," said Gene blankly. "Don't you remember we had our first dinner here with my uncle from Detroit?"

Nora, looking far too lovely in her quaint flowered silk to be so cross, did not answer. No, she would not have any champagne at all, she would have a stinger, that's what she would have.

"It's an anniversary, and we'll have champagne," said Gene, getting mad. "Put a magnum of Veuve Cliquot '21 on ice, waiter."

"You and your wine dates! You'd drink it no matter what they brought," sneered Nora. "Furthermore I shan't touch a drop of it."

"Don't have to," growled Gene, "and while you're having your stinger, I'll have another old-fashioned."

"You'll be so full of Bourbon you won't know whether it's champagne or dishwater," said Nora, who had whipped Gene into being a wine connoisseur by being openly impressed when other people fussed about brands and labels and dates, so at her outburst now Gene felt quite righteously abused. "I'll have another stinger."

Gene was about to say something very nasty but she did look so lovely, and he was sorry for the way the Fellows had let her down. Even if she was a little in love with Neal, which he vaguely suspected, he wasn't angry, just sorry he couldn't go up to the man and say, "Damn it, you started something or other with my wife and now you're making her damned unhappy, and I'm going to horsewhip you."

He was especially mad because he had seen Neal out with Jean Nelson several times lately and what chance had one's wife with a professional beauty? It was unfair. If Nora must have her schoolgirl crushes—he was convinced they were no more than that—let her pick out a glamour man like Steve Estabrook; but Nora couldn't stand to have his name mentioned around the house, she flew into a long, positively neurotic description of Steve's faults.

Whatever Gene did say was so wrong Nora applied herself to her stinger in an unrelenting silence, and Gene was obliged to carry on a smiling wordless flirtation with two girls dining alone at the next table by the orchestra. One was pretty, and one was fat and in no time at all the orchestra leader had turned his expert eye on the pretty one, who blushed nicely and smiled so winningly that the pianist winked encouragingly at Manny the leader; the brasses winked at him, too, Manny was up to his tricks again. So now the whole orchestra made up to the pretty girl named Isabel, and Brent was only a jealously smiling bystander, while she tossed her head and made eyes at her fat girlfriend as a sample of what she could do. Brent, to punish her, stared raptly then at the youngest girl dancer on the floor but this was not rewarding as it turned out to be a girl named Mary Lou, seventeen, growing up fast to be a most vivacious, eager, and ugly old maid, dancing away with her cousin from Rollins College, her head butting his chin, her legs kicking out as all the girls at Miss Dodey's had learned to do. Mary was having such a perfectly peachy time that she was hardly aware of the present, her arms and legs flew about, her rangy neck, with the Duchess of Windsor knob of black hair, stretched hither and yon, she threw herself about with all the vigor of a born bad dancer, already she was telling the girls about it, what a perfect old lamb her cousin Mart really was, her bulging blue eyes would roll in ecstatic memory; she would walk—only the next week—through the school gardens after dinner, each arm around some younger and silently contemptuous girl, telling them what New York was wearing.

Brent gave her up and, after a tentative unsatisfactory glance at Nora's hostile face, stared at the beautiful blond singer in black lace, so beautiful she need not have had a voice at all, but apparently her good will was, like Nora's, only for outsiders for as soon as she finished her chorus before the mike, she came back to nag her elderly Jewish escort; she glowered at him just as Nora was glowering, she recoiled from his footy-footy efforts under the table but beamed radiantly when Manny nuzzled her in passing. But Manny's pleasant reception did not rouse envy in her boyfriend's heart, he merely rubbed his hands proudly and possessively—never mind the nuzzling, never mind the public flirtatiousness, just look whose diamond wristwatch she is wearing and who, he proudly asks the world, is the lucky fellow she just asked for a thousand bucks?

What a bunch of dopes we all are, thought Brent.

"Aren't you having any fun, Nora?" he blithely inquired. "It's too bad the Fellows couldn't join us, but we always have more fun just the two of us, don't we?"

"We do not," said Nora flatly.

"At least the waiters are glad to see us here," Gene said. "We don't have to stand around like immigrants at Ellis Island and wait for some celebrity like Neal to OK us before they'll give us a table. Of course, if you prefer those places we can go there next time."

"There won't be any next time," said Nora flatly and suddenly her fists clenched, and tears streamed down her face. "Can't you see we can't go on like this? Can't you see we haven't a thing in common anymore? Oh, Gene, don't be such a dope."

The champagne was ready, but Gene decided he would have to have a fleet of old-fashioneds before he could face it.

"We could take that house in Westport this summer, if you are still crazy to have it," he said inanely.

"Westport! You can say Westport to me!" cried Nora. "I suppose you think I want to settle down and be Younger-Married-Set till rigor mortis sets in."

"I *like* being Younger-Married-Set!" shouted Gene, so that a body of Elks at the next table thought he was a brother and blew their horns hilariously. "I like Westport. I'm going there this summer."

"*I'm* not. I'm going to Scandinavia like other people!" Nora sobbed into her napkin. "I hate houses and couples and the old bunch and anniversary dinners and each other's mothers a week every summer. I always did and I always shall! I like to live alone and eat alone and have my own friends, one at a time, and I like to have a place where I can cry all night without somebody asking what's the matter, and that's what I'm going to have!"

She dabbed her eyes, and Gene, after a reassuring smile at the two girl diners, suddenly bethought himself of the anniversary present and shoved the little box with the jeweled vanity case across the table.

"It's our anniversary," he explained to the waiter. "That's why she's crying."

Nora opened the box.

"Thanks," she said listlessly. "I can exchange it tomorrow."

The waiter had removed two untouched courses and now produced the squab, which both Brents faced with as much antagonism as if it were bread pudding. The champagne was poured.

"To your anniversary, madam," said the waiter, gaily, and Nora and Gene clicked glasses, then set them down eagerly to finish their cocktails.

"It's a farce, that's all our marriage has been," said Nora quietly. "We haven't a single thought in common."

Gene was getting mad.

"Can I help it if you want to be with people who don't invite us?" he demanded. "Is it my fault the Nelsons gave a dance tonight at Sherry's, and we aren't asked—oh, I know why you're upset, we may not have a thought in common, but I always know when something's eating you."

The orchestra was informed by the waiter of the little romantic celebration and played to them, *Put on Your Old Gray Bonnet,* and Nora sobbed into her handkerchief, for it was true, Jean Nelson was having a great party just so she could wear her new shell-pink naked chiffon and have Steve hanging over her, and if Gene wanted to think it was Neal, let him. Gene was like a country newspaper, things were all over before they got to him.

She sobbed quietly for she was very unhappy, her heart was breaking, no wonder cruel chips flew out hitting others.

The waiter finally took the squabs away, then the salad, and Gene said, "All right, then, get a divorce, I'll get along, don't you worry about me, there's plenty of other women," and he walked negligently over to the fat girl and pretty girl and asked them to dance, which they coldly refused to do, so he went up to the blond singer and tapped her on the shoulder.

"Rhumba?" he asked imperiously.

"Certainly not," she said, and the Persian-faced boyfriend scowled murderously. Whistling lightly, Gene walked busily across the floor to where Mary Lou was leaning raptly on her elbows gazing up at her cousin Mart.

"I'll take the kid for a turn, now," Gene said confidently to the cousin, at which Mary Lou screamed, though later she made a really wonderful story about it for the girls and how cousin Mart said haughtily, "Sir, the lady is with me."

By this time Gene was furious with Nora and was being regarded by his immediate neighbors as obviously a ripper, with the waiters closing menacingly around him, so to punish Nora for his own unpopularity he ordered a double old-fashioned. She was eating her ice for no reason at all and sipping champagne.

"You oughtn't to mix ice and fizz," said her husband.

"Babbitt!" she chokingly flung back. "All you think of is the right thing. And money! You and your Westport house! All your crowd thinks of is money, money, money—and show—the most cars, the most acres, the most stock in the biggest business!"

"What's the difference showing off the cars you've bought and the box-office hits you've had? What's the difference bragging about your acres or your fan mail—one's as bad as the other!" shouted Gene. "Showing off brains or swimming pool—both just plain luck, anyway!"

"You see we can never get along," Nora said passionately. "We simply have to split. I've grown, Gene. Can't you see I've grown past you?"

"All right! OK!" Gene declared. "We're through. That's fine. That's dandy. When do I move out? Tonight suits me. Waiter, check!"

He flung down the money and deliberately flagellated himself by not helping her on with her jacket. He followed her out of the room, but at the door she turned unexpectedly and ran back to the table.

"We'll take the wine with us!" she loftily informed the waiter.

"Opened—madam?"

She snatched it out of the pail and wrapped her chiffon handkerchief around the bottle. She directed a supercilious sneer toward the pretty girl and fat girl at the next table.

"I don't know what this place is thinking of allowing women of that sort here," she said very clearly and passed them with high scornful head, for she could have killed them for letting Gene down when he asked them to dance!

. . . exit laughlingly . . .

$\mathcal{M}$E OF ALL PEOPLE, thought Prudence; and
sometimes the idea frightened her, and sometimes it filled her
with a totally strange wild joy that was like nothing she had ever
known since the day she ran away for good from Silver City. She
wondered why this extravagant whim was so much more exciting than a command performance or the most fabulous of contracts. She found she had to tell everyone about it as if the words
would convince her if the idea didn't, and everyone—Nellie, the
bellboys, the astrologer Dolores—all, being so incredulous, permitted her once again to marshal her reasons. She called up the
Fellows. Anna merely said, "Oh, Prudence, you kill me. What a
great laugh you'll get out of a trip like that, won't you? But, seriously, wouldn't you have more fun going to Norway?"

That was what happened when reputed wits confessed romance. It turned out to be the funniest thing they ever did and

for once the laughter was annoying. Anna realized this and put an even worse construction on the venture.

"Dear, if you're so discouraged about a spot for fall perhaps Neal could do something for you," she said tenderly. "It wouldn't pay, perhaps, as well as the Vedado but it would be something to show you aren't out of the running. I do hope you've saved."

Saved! As if money were for saving in this town! As if there were ever any other way of showing you were worth a thousand dollars a week except by spending it! There was a long pause. What was getting into people, Prudence wondered, they acted as if she was a queen of the silents thrown out by sound and technicolor! Her kind of job was like politics, the only way you could show you still had a following was to keep at it, there was absolutely no believing that anyone ever left a good job of his own accord. Performers got out—this was common knowledge—because they knew they were through or because they were kicked out, no such thing as plain boredom or personal choice.

"Thanks," Prudence answered. "I'm really through with the racket, Anna. Ten years is enough. I want to find out what I'm like—inside, you know—and the only way is with a man I'm crazy about, someone I feel is really great, you know, instead of just a plain ham like me."

A mellow gurgle of appreciation from Anna.

"Oh, Prudence, you are a card! I wish I just knew what you were *really* up to. I only wish I had your sense of humor."

Prudence was baffled.

"I am serious, Anna."

"Oh, Prudence," laughed Anna. "What would we do without you? Do let us know how the crops are! I'll be seeing you on the *Kungsholm!*"

James Pinckney was more credulous but merely because an enterprise of his own had so stunned him he did not fully appreciate Prudence's news. Indeed, he was so nervous that he begged her to have the taxi drive once more slowly around the park before taking her on to dinner.

"At least you won't be having a good time, and I like to think someone won't," he said wanly smiling. "I'll be with Evalyn."

"In Bayreuth?"

"No, dear, I'll be in Spain. I can't give you the details, but Evalyn's summer plans have been so ruined the last two years by either Hitler or Mussolini that she simply swears to get even. Mussolini cut off her African trip two years ago, then this year she had so counted on Andalusia—well, when Mussolini sent troops to keep up the war Evalyn said we would just have to fight him to the finish."

Prudence was aghast.

"You don't mean you're enlisting?"

James shrugged. His long face looked pale and even spiritual.

"It hasn't been a very pleasant winter for me, Prudence. I honestly don't care what happens. Dol Lloyd's dying—we were just about to become good friends, too. It came over me that this was the thing to do—of course, Evalyn pushed me into it; I don't know why she thinks I'm the equal of Mussolini or Franco or Hitler, but there it is. It's a challenge. She's going along, and I'm terribly afraid she'll try to take a potshot at somebody, she's so sure the police would never lay a finger on a Philadelphia Vanderhoff."

He flicked his cigarette thoughtfully.

"It's awful to have that noble side come creeping out from behind your ulcers," he gloomily confessed. "I hardly know what to expect of myself next."

This was what happened when you were going to do the most sensational thing in your whole life—everyone else was doing something at that moment much more dramatic. It was a time for Van Deusen at least to listen, but Van had disappeared into God knows where these many months. Steve—even as she thought it—a voice came over the taxicab radio, a voice as soothing as a kiss on the brow, a perfect benediction of a voice, tender, benign, paternal:

"Butternut Biscuits are GOOD biscuits—pure—flaky—crisp. TRY them with soups and chowders—with hot CHOCOLATE they make the PERFECT Supper for the KIDDIES—ASK your grocer for them. Butternut—B-U-T-T-E-R-N-U-T—for Butternut Biscuits are GOOD biscuits; and GOOD Biscuits make HAPPY boys and GIRLS— This is Steve Estabrook and his Sweet Potatoes, way down in his Under-the-Sea Dance Hall. And now Stevie is going to pipe you a piping hot little melody called *Did You Mean It?*"

"What's Steve doing on Butternut Biscuits?" inquired Prudence in surprise. "What happened to Crandall Banana Flour?"

"Harvey Nelson kicked him out," James said. "But it worked out nicely for Brent is Butternut. Do you mind?" and he twirled the indicator around to a nasal, crisp editorial voice caught in a torrent of glittering generalities. "I want to get the news from Madrid."

"Goodness!" Prudence was impressed and even a little frightened at the sterner Pinckney. "Think of being bombed, James! Aren't you at all uneasy?"

James reflected, then shook his head.

"No," he said. "It doesn't scare me inside the way the thought of going back to Oklahoma does. And if I *should* actually get to fighting, it wouldn't be any worse than having to play football, I couldn't possibly be more scared. My insides are so conditioned to social and neurotic terrors that noise might straighten them all out. I don't suppose you ever knew it, Prudence, but I went twelve years to school in a little western village with every child in town running after me making fun of me for being good in music and drawing instead of carpentry and track, and after my grandmother left me her lace collection, they all called me 'Sis.' 'Sis' Pinckney, they'd yell, until I didn't dare play the piano anymore or weave. I was awfully good at weaving, too. No, war won't be so much worse."

"I see what you mean," admitted Prudence and was about to say more when James lifted his hand peremptorily for silence. The news was coming, and Prudence observed with curiosity that Pinckney's face assumed the rapt haunted expression of a face under the Beethoven Ninth.

... Silver City ...

*P*RUDENCE SAW THE Limited flash on its way to Chicago, and as the porter carried her bags to the Local, she had her first misgiving. What was it she wanted to prove—and was it to Jeff Abbott or herself this mysterious evidence must be given; what was it that drew her like a damned fool out of the life she had made for herself back to this sinister quiet? Years of confidence dropped off like broken stalks, things she had never realized she knew broke through with the first spasmodic rattle of the Local. She even remembered this very train, No. 11, no powerful instrument of space, either, but a county pet, recognizable by all citizens like the village postmaster or the town pump.

Thousands of miles from here, say in the Mongolian Desert, should this engine appear, someone would say "Why if it isn't old No. 11 from Shyrock County"; and there was no confusing it with No. 4, for instance, which never ran Saturdays or holidays, was more nervous and high-strung, shooting off to the South at Carway Junction; impatient with villages, it skipped Falmouth and Bakerville altogether, hung around Cincinnati with big-shot trains from Chicago and New York, and really lived for the Cincinnati run, though it must have looked as out of place as an old surrey there, its small-town air must have given it away, and certainly the powerful transcontinental brothers must have snubbed it as it snubbed No. 11. No, No. 4 was not the county's own, No. 11 was the real friend, the neighbor, the favorite uncle, No. 11 dressed up on summer Sundays to take people on excursions to Silver Lake; and no one cared when it broke down on the way home and got side-tracked, passengers just ate the rest of their picnic lunches, children sucked bananas and cracked eggshells over the floor, improvised quartets sang *"Shine On, Shine On, Harvest Moon,"* and *"My Wild Irish Rose, the Sooweetest Fallower That Ballowes."* No. 11 took the boys to college and the girls to business school, and now it was bringing back Local-Daughter-from-Scene-of-Eastern-Triumphs with no more complacency than it brought Daisy Purvis back from the W. & J. prom.

As it jolted into every station, Prudence's heart turned over, all the fears and insecurity of her youth returned. Jeff would not be there to meet her anymore than her father had given her the wrist-watch he promised, here was the land against which your own will was helpless, the land that dictated what you would be and what you would do, here was the land of little homes, wilted lettuce, apple pie, sugar on cucumbers, noodles, pot roast, bean soup, fried potatoes, rice pudding, pop, icebox cake, new mown grass, bonfires, chicken suppers. In a panic of being just one small scroll on an iron pattern Prudence stood up on the back platform, her hands clenched, wondering what in the world made people burn their bridges as she had just done so that she could not decently run back to New York until she had proved this thing, whatever it was.

In the coach she was conscious of her clothes being wrong, she should have worn all of her pearls and her diamond clips, against all these Best Dresses her French suit looked merely neat and elderly, she should have worn a pink or baby blue sport suit like these other women, and her hair should be scalloped like theirs till it hypnotized the passing eye with one, two, three, dip, one, two, three, dip. She should have put on rouge in a candid round circle and avoided lipstick and mascara as badges of wickedness, her powder should not be so foxily natural, it should have a frank egg tinge to show where artifice began and there was no deceit intended. She looked and immediately felt like a waitress against all of these ladies' frank enjoyment of their pretty things. She looked out and saw the water tower, the low waving cornfield beyond, the broken gate to Casino Woods, Basket-Parties-Welcome, the dance pavilion's walls thrown out already for the Lady Maccabees' Picnic; then the forest of baby larches wading in still water, their slim trunks shadowed in the pool and then the pool lost in the wheat field. There was the pink stucco gas station and WELCOME TO SILVER CITY and the rows of wheat fields edged by white fences along which ran the same old Burma Shave rhymes; there was the church, the Queen Flour Mills, the town pump, the schoolhouse, more fences, the new bridge, the Queen Flour Warehouses, the freight yard, the water tank, the smell of the flour, dry, milky, delicious that tinged the air all around. The same place and by now the same wretched girl who had left there, oh, the very same; here she was of her own choice back in the place she had labored twelve years to wipe out of her mind, shivering with the same terror of the Fixed Pattern.

"Silver City!"

Prudence's heart turned over. Frantically she wiped off her mascara and dabbed on rouge, mustn't say bad words, must be, must do, must *seem* like everyone; why, my God, she thought, it's got me before I'm there—here I am a home girl again, afraid of being myself because to be yourself is taboo.

Here it was every man for himself, drag out your own bags and scramble out as best you can. The little low station was the same as it was twelve years ago, even the baggageman was the same old man, and as the train pulled out, he waved to her, with a broad smile.

"Hi, Prue, back for good?"

Oh, God, I hope not, she thought, desperate as if his words had put a hex on her.

"Queenie know you're coming?"

"No," she said.

"I wondered. She went off on a trip last week. Mexico, or some place. Got a trailer now, you know."

The switchman went by, and she remembered him.

"Hello, Chuck."

"Why, hello there, 'Tracks,'" he said. "We never thought *you* would be back. Been in Pittsburgh all this time?"

"No, New York."

Chuck looked less impressed. The nearest city was always the biggest. You'd have thought they would have forgotten that Tracks episode, but villages never forgot.

"Well, welcome home," he said and helped the baggageman yank her trunks on to the cart.

"I guess everybody comes back to old Silver City all right."

Like saying, "Welcome to the grave," Prudence thought, trembling already with the fear his words put in her, like saying, "We've got you now, you got away once but not again, my fine friend." If she'd only got a round-trip ticket, she thought, something to hold on to in my pocket, something to remind her it was just a lark, an experiment. James, Anna, Neal hold on to me, for God's sake, she found herself praying—Steve, Jean—oh, anybody, don't let go the rope, don't let me slip down in this pit.

Then she saw an old open Ford drive up, and there was Jeff and the reason for everything.

"You never thought I'd come, did you?" she said. Yes, he was glad to see her; he could act as calm as he liked, there was no mistaking the sudden gleam in his eye, even if he didn't kiss her.

"I knew you'd come," he said. "I gave you a month to come to your senses."

He wheeled the car rapidly around the station.

"Where are we going?" she asked quite happily.

"Farm," he said. "You won't see anyone there, but I gather you don't want to. You're Mrs. Jeff Abbott now, if anyone does ask."

"I supposed I *would* have to say that," she admitted. "I don't have to *be* it right off, do I?"

"Up to you," he said casually.

They drove past the mills, past the tracks where he had first kissed her, and here they both laughed, wordlessly. There were the same stiff white frame houses scattered along this side country road, but there were changes since she had been here—trellised rose vines, rock gardens, box hedges all proclaimed the advent of the Garden Club.

"What does it make you feel like—all this again?" Jeff asked curiously.

"Like it always did," she said. "Like running away."

"You won't this time."

They drove in a weed-tangled yard, past an orchard of dead apple trees bent over like old women, gray with tent caterpillars, their gnarled branches flung up in perpetual dismay, and then came to the bare, unpainted house, uncurtained, walls veined with forgotten vines, windows bordered with damp shadows where the shutters had been ripped off.

"Home," said Jeff, jumping out. She ran after him into the house, as rugless, chairless, bare as she had feared. Nothing but a couple of kitchen chairs and a box in the living room, a heap of cigarette stubs in the fireplace and a coal bucket. The kitchen was better, an easy chair here by the stove, a corner cupboard and huge wooden table. And a bedroom off of this was furnished, if barrenly.

"I see a woman's touch is needed," Prudence found strength to say. "Aren't you going to kiss me?"

"As soon as you take off that lousy lipstick," he said, and she obediently wiped it off on the back of her hand.

. . . c'est mon homme . . .

*T*WENTY YEARS from now, thought Prudence a
dozen times that summer, with my face lifted and my hair—
oh, not dyed, merely restored to its natural hue, in a black lace
hat and musk perfume, drinking anisette at the wrong end of
the Riviera, I will tell people about this, and they'll die laughing. I will make it terribly funny, and people will bring their
pretty nieces from Hartford to meet me and hear about my
war with Nature. Twenty years? What do I mean *twenty?*
Make it fifteen and throw out the lace hat. In fifteen it would
be ice blue satin—by that time I will be matching my dresses to
my eyes as the only thing left of me that isn't faded and instead
of the nieces I'll have the nephews and I'll be so arch the very
violets will cower with shame and instead of the Riviera I'll be
in Hollywood at the Beverly Wilshire with two Dalmatians
and an Aunt Jemima personal maid and be pretending I'm

there on a visit instead of to sell my diamonds or find a niche in pictures.

And I'll tell about my return to the soil and about how I gave up the glamour of applause for my country lover; because New York stifled him, he had to be close to nature and simple things. I'll tell about the kind of simplicity he loved: a big house with no maids to interfere with his flow of thought, so all the simplicity had to be worked out by the little woman or else there was complicity instead. How he stayed in his study all day while she swept and tried her damnedest to fasten up curtains and to cook and count things for the laundry and have a vegetable garden like the simple peasants did and mend stoves and socks and pipes and pick berries and fry chicken because all those things show how honest you are, whereas trying to fix up your cracked fingernails or brush your hair is a sure sign of something phony.

And I'll tell about the healthy honest life he led before I came; about his bed falling on the floor because he was too lazy to fix it, so he slept there all tangled up in mosquito netting because his pleasure in the simple life didn't include fixing screens and how, even loving to eat, he never cooked himself anything but coffee and canned soup and cornflakes every meal.

And I'll tell how disgusted he got when I wanted to laugh or be ridiculous or sentimental, because if you're going to be simple, you have to be serious about it. And what a fool he made of me by praising my scrubbing and my gardening and my biscuits until I damn near broke my back trying to prove to him that I was nearly as good as the native matrons. And how he loved me to try to talk like the other women when we'd go to town, and how his eyes lit up when I spoke of huck towels or bullet beans or pan broil or any of the expressions that meant I was a regular normal wife. None of this chitchat out of *Town and Country* or *Variety*.

And I'll make it very funny how, with all my life in New York and pictures in the papers, I was still just "Tracks" to Silver City;

and with the Bly Flour Mills going to pieces there was not even a little local respect for money in the family; and so far as the town went, I'd left necking behind the Silver City freight house with Jeff Abbott to neck with gangsters behind the Grand Central Station and *I* came back home when I ran through the New York boys. So that it was Jeff, who was supposed to be making the sacrifice in taking me back, giving up a lovely bakery cashier named Bertha for a good-for-nothing like me.

And I'll tell about the foreman from my grandmother's mills, who came over every night to talk with Jeff, and the newspaper editor and how I was supposed either to ask their wives over to play contract while they argued intellectual politics or else sit and sew quietly and listen to my so-called husband talk about his soul and mind to strangers because it was too private a matter to discuss with his woman.

And I'll make it funny about how mad I got that what he loved in me was what was common to all women, particularly servants, and what was me—the part I had especially developed and made a career of—was something that made him scowl and bang doors. And if I laughed thinking of how fantastic this would look and sound to Pinckney or the Fellows or Steve or Jean, he wouldn't see anything funny in it. And no matter how bitter I got, how terrified that this would mow me down before I could handle it, I had only to see him hauling logs out to make his summer house, to watch his muscles as he scythed, ploughed my garden, or dug and I was a fool about him again, as if that strength was *for* me instead of against me.

But I won't be able to make it funny how perfect it was in his arms at night, how everything reduced itself to love that was made up partly of the fear of giving in to it and losing myself forever and partly of fear that it someday would stop. And I won't be able to make amusing the visits to the cemetery with graves marked out for him and me that his brother-in-law gave us for a present. And I won't be able to make it funny the waking up to a village with my grave in it and feeling that this real person he was after was already in that grave, had been there twelve years and the other half was now being killed because New York was its lungs. Some people aren't complete away from their city as a musician is nothing without his violin. So New York was my instrument, or I was its. A fish out of water is a dead fish, not a neurotic or discontented or irritable fish, but a dead fish.

No, there's nothing amusing about having to think carefully before you speak, so you don't say something so clever it insults the natives; and if no one seems to be amazed at the sheer housework you do—at making flowers and lima beans pop out of seeds—and if playing on the piano or accordion interferes with the master's mood, if the whole business of being the Little Woman doesn't seem funny to anyone—not even to Jeff, who thinks strings of twins and bouncing boys will come popping out next, then it becomes too terrifying to be funny; and even in twenty years in the lace hat and the blue lace dinner dress on a Mediterranean budget cruise with the old actresses, other fast old women, I won't be able to remember it without shivering and I'll forget the frantic desperate love I knew at nights because it wasn't any game, that love, it wasn't sport at all; it was the kind of love that lifted my great grandmother out of a Boston ballroom onto a covered wagon. The Indians got her, too; and when I tell the story, I will say just that; but they aren't going to get me.

. . . the rustic idyl . . .

*J*EFF LAY IN A hammock in the hot, still, choked
September afternoon and looked at the sky. It seemed to him the
first day he had seen the sky all summer, and it was very pretty,
with the hickory trees and the distant mills against it; if carefully
done would make an unusually bad oil painting.

"Prudence," he called. "Did you know we can see your grandmother's mills from here? I can almost see the National Guard
around them."

There was no answer, just the click of high heels on the bare
floor. It was odd how this click-clack had amused him at first, the
contrast of the forty-dollar slippers with the forty-dollar house.
Then the sound became an irritating static that came between
him and the music of his play, a reminder that something was in
discord. The sound crept into the play like dust into a machine,
clogged it, made him think of all the trivial nonsense—money,

luxuries, counterfeit content, that went with the forty-dollar shoes; the message that the heels tapped out in their own Morse was "Why am I here? When can I go? How long can this last?" Hearing it now, he was disturbed afresh, even though the play was done that day and for the first time he could see the sky, the grass, the cracks in the porch ceiling and he could hear the tanagers squawking over the cat's sudden appearance, see the red-winged blackbird dart toward the woods. In the bare, robbed apple trees beside the house he saw the thieving worms insolently defy his spray, swing from each other's legs to unseen trapezes, diabolically indigestible to the watching birds; now they were the orchard owners until highjacked by the beetles. All the length of the orchard he saw the bare trees, large white webbed packages in each forked branch, little surprises for next May, sardonic messages to the unwilling tree: *"Columbine will return."*

I must spray them again, thought Jeff, pleased at the prospect of the fine work program he was about to undertake, typewriter put aside. The heels tapped out "bed-making" upstairs, downstairs, "imagine *me* bed-making." Jeff shut his mind to it. A hot, breathless day, he realized, and pulled his shirt off idly, turned over in the hammock to cool his damp browned back, and now saw the great spider web spanning a whole corner of the porch, the web of steel bridges, spirals, beams all leading to the torture chambers where the capitalist spider—Jeff was already casting the insect world—invited the promising young bugs to take structural steel jobs. In no time at all—a scenario, thought Jeff, a sensation!—the ambitious little fellows have their legs and wings broken, without any life or unemployment insurance to help the bereaved families, although right now one ant family was gorging itself on a damaged cocoon just fluttered to the ground bound to a charred cedar bark. The fortunate creatures, having gnawed their way inside the ghostly vessel, now helped themselves to the sleeping barbecue and would never, never leave this

salvaged treasure, never, even though distant drums announce
the opening of a new lemon in the kitchen, and fresh pine shin-
gles drip nectar in the woodshed, even though a passing bee—a
widow on the make for any bug or flower, decided Jeff idly—
tries to break the news of their dear papa's demise in the steel
works on the porch. Beneath that suspended glittering steel web
lie the pile of vanquished dead, bumblebees, rival spiders, flies,
slugs, a dumfounded inchworm, a still whirling bluebottle fly
hanging himself, if he only knew it, with every move forward to
escape; and then the spider herself, high-stepping, arrogant, vil-
lainous—Queenie Bly, herself, thought Jeff—ran up a slanting
sunbeam to a rafter for a quiet chuckle and, never really idle,
gave a crafty thoughtful look around from this lighthouse for
further talent to corrupt, more homes to wreck.

"Prudence," called Jeff. "Did you ever stop to think your
grandmother looks like a spider?"

"No" a voice responded from a window, "I never stopped to
think."

The heels clacked away—to the front door again, crunch,
crunch over the new graveled path, clang of the mailbox.

"I told you there wasn't any mail," he shouted. Then he saw her
and not having really looked at her for weeks except as the eager
giver of comforts he was surprised that she was so fragile, her
shoulders were no wider than a child's, and her bare arms in the
sleeveless gray linen looked as undeveloped as a twelve year old's.

"I finished it," he shouted to her.

She came over toward him, her face with the unhealthy translu-
cent pallor of heavily cold-creamed skin, quite angry.

"If you were expecting to hear from Hyman, you'd look in the
mailbox a dozen times a day too!" she said. "What harm is there
in it? Why do you have to shout at me? I can look, too, can't I?"

That was the way it was. The closer they were together every
night the wider they split apart every day.

"We could go to the hotel for dinner," he offered. "Or we could get a bottle of wine and have the boys over to dinner."

Well, she had started it, she was so anxious to prove something. See, she could cook chicken and have his friends praise it just like Bertha from the bakery; she could bring beer and cigarettes from the icebox while the gentlemen talked big matters over the Little Woman's head and even laugh a little to herself until it got too serious that her labor should be no surprise but an expected service. It was funny at first to have him turn into such an old-fashioned man, rejecting the female overtures in conversation, deflecting it to bed or domestic duties while he talked recklessly of radical matters with his men friends. Her silence bothered him.

"What do you want to do?" he said.

"Talk," she said. "I want to talk about something that doesn't matter with people who don't mean what they say. I want to rest my kind heart for a thousand years while I play with loaded words and see who gets hit. I want to put my real soul back in the Safe Deposit forever before it cracks. I can have ten times more fun with the paste one. I want to have no feelings and to be cheap and superficial and pit my wits with a few pit-wits. All right, I'll make chicken."

Jeff rose out of the hammock. There wasn't one thing he liked about her when she talked that way. She was not even pretty. She stopped being pretty almost the minute she got off the train, for the town made her look pinched and artificial, drove her own worry outside, made her not as pretty even as the schoolteacher down the road or the butcher's two daughters or the happy wives. Bereft of her city fame she was only a restless woman whose language he neither spoke nor cared to learn.

"You might celebrate by getting in some wine," he offered.

"No," she said. "I wouldn't compliment this place by getting tight in it. This is a place to be sober and cut your throat in. I'll content myself with my recipes while you read your collected works to your men friends. They understand those things. I wouldn't."

"Prudence!" he blazed.

"Darling, I'm sorry." They flew into each other's arms, and after a while Prudence got out the Mrs. Caldwell's Cook Book, and the editor and the Mills foreman came over, and she heard Jeff read his play while she poured beer and she heard them praise it in awestruck voices but her own comment—as impressed as theirs—was not asked for. Nor did anyone suggest what should happen to her when Jeff talked about China, saying that with Hyman's option money he was going either there or to Spain; a man couldn't sit around on his fanny writing without getting first-hand knowledge of what was changing the world. Yes, she thought, he would just say good-bye and she would wait.

"There's only my work and you, there would never be anyone else," he had told her.

She went upstairs and read the letter from Jean Nelson again. That world was strange now, too. She was lost between her worlds; and if Jeff went away, there would be nothing left, not that real self he was so proud of rescuing, small, unhappy reality that it was, nor that cruel swaggering false self that at least had perfected a technique of living, a way of using a mask as a shield behind which she might go about her secret destiny.

"It couldn't possibly get one, it couldn't," she repeated and she knew then that she was almost lost.

. . . East Fifty-third street . . .

*A*MERICANS DRINK too fast," the wine salesman was saying to Steve Estabrook in the private party suite of the Fellows' hotel. "It's all wrong. The other night take this Italian friend of mine. Wine, you know. Very best Chianti, understand, it was all right. Well, sir, we kept pouring it down, pouring it down until, now seriously, I was stupefied. My friend says that's the way the Italians drink, drink till you fall asleep."

That's right, Steve said to himself, only try and do it, but a sponsor was a sponsor, and you had to listen, with recessions being what they were.

"Same thing here in America," pursued the wine man confidentially. "Take last night. I called on a couple of girls and another fellow at the Commodore Hotel. We had a Tom Collins, see. The Commodore's supposed to make the best Tom Collins in New York, I don't know what you think—anyway, gin, the finest club soda, lemon and orange, see. Well, we had one, we had two, three, four, you know how it is. Then they got too big for us, seemed like they slipped a taller glass on us so we switched to a bonded Scotch. Well, let me tell you, Estabrook, the result was we were all absolutely drunk, and the girls got sick. American girls, see. Well, one of them got to up-chucking—a splendid girl, too, teaches ballroom dancing, very fine teacher I understand though I don't dance myself—and we had to take her home. The other thought she might have a sip of Sibarita to settle her stomach, a fine $7.22 sherry Pedro Domecq and Company, and that put her right under, and that's the sort of thing that goes on all over the country. Americans don't know how to drink. Have another? Right. So you see, Estabrook, we've got to educate the radio public. Educational; entertainment—not like the Butternut program at all."

"Oh, no," said Steve, and then he saw Prudence come in, and Nora's eyes leaped across the room to him right away to see how he was taking it, so he stiffened his face, until the sponsor said, "Or am I boring you?"

Anna saved him by rushing up with a tray of drinks.

"Seventy-five cents each, Stevie, don't forget we're drinking for a cause now. I'll bring change when I get it. Isn't it wonderful James Pinckney is back and alive? Everyone is so thrilled. I'd hoped he'd serve on my committee, but he's terribly in demand, a changed man."

"I see Prudence is back, too," said Steve.

"From her Scandinavian cruise?" inquired Anna. "Or where did she go this year?"

Now he was bowing over Prudence's hand, an unwise tribute as it revealed a certain thinning of hair on his pate.

"Mrs. Hornickle, I believe," said Steve. "A little thinner but always dangerous to the eye."

Prudence curtseyed. Nora Brent watched unhappily from across the room, paid no attention to Van Deusen, a rejuvenated, suave, splendid Van Deusen too, richly tanned and wearing suede shoes, checked sport jacket, red tie, a living monument to California and a tribute to technicolor.

"Did you know Van has used his influence and gotten the Fifty-Six Club to give me a contract?" said Prudence. "Very small; of course, but very, very rich. Van is really being wonderful to me."

"I wonder if you'll be needing this key?" Steve asked casually. "I was going to ask if you wouldn't come in and feed my dog."

"I hate to see a dog starve," said Prudence. Peg out the old house of cards again, quick, quick, begin the old masquerade again. "What kind of a dog is it?"

"Any kind of dog," said Steve. "Any dog at all, Mrs. Hornickle."

Van, with a glance at an impressive wristwatch, came over. A respectful murmur went around, which he appeared to be far above—"there goes Van Deusen, a sensation in Hollywood, highest connections, scheduled for a triumphal season in New York and London."

"Must be going, I'm joining Franchot and Joan at 21, they'll be waiting," he said in the new resonant voice his Hollywood success had given him. "I'll see you later, Prudence, about your program, eh? I'd like to hear it, possibly suggest something. So you're marrying my little Mrs. Brent, eh, Steve? Remember she's used to a very fine husband. Gene is a perfect prince."

"I know," sighed Steve. "I wish you'd tell her that. God knows I've tried."

"I was just saying to Mr. Estabrook," the wine salesman was back, "that Americans don't know how to drink."

"Walk slowly toward the door and don't turn around till you've counted ten thousand," Steve breathed in her ear. "It's a game without any prizes, that's what I like about it, best fella lose and all that. I don't suppose you care about me enough to get me out of a little jam, Mrs. Hornickle. I've got to get the b'jesus out of here and quick. There's a good woman after me."

Prudence went on, edged out the door.

"People aren't the same," she said. "I don't like parties. Or else something's gone wrong with me. Nobody's funny anymore."

"Prudence," Steve said, "we're two such bastards, we simply have to stand by each other."

"I suppose you're right," she said and, standing behind him in the elevator saw the little bald spot on the top of his sleek head. Steve was slipping, she thought, a little phonier every year but at least he was gay, he did know how to play.

"Whatever mischief we got into this summer let's never do it again," he begged. "Did I tell you you never looked lovelier?"

It was a lie. Prudence's looks, he reflected with some surprise, were quite gone. She really looked as hard as nails, but then so did most women eventually.

A NOTE ON THE AUTHOR

DAWN POWELL was born in Mt. Gilead, Ohio, in 1896. In 1918 she moved to New York City where she lived and wrote until her death from cancer in 1965. She was the author of fifteen novels, numerous short stories, and a half dozen plays.

A NOTE ON THE BOOK

The text for this book was composed by Steerforth Press using a digital version of Granjon, a typeface designed by George W. Jones and first issued by Linotype in 1928. All Steerforth books are printed on acid free papers and this book was bound by BookCrafters of Chelsea, Michigan.

Also by Dawn Powell

ANGELS ON TOAST

THE BRIDE'S HOUSE

COME BACK TO SORRENTO

DANCE NIGHT

THE GOLDEN SPUR

THE LOCUSTS HAVE NO KING

MY HOME IS FAR AWAY

A TIME TO BE BORN

TURN, MAGIC WHEEL

THE WICKED PAVILION

THE DIARIES OF DAWN POWELL: 1931–1965

DAWN POWELL AT HER BEST
Including the novels DANCE NIGHT
and TURN, MAGIC WHEEL and selected stories